It was a rattlesnake, not a big one, but large enough to be deadly. It didn't move. A rattlesnake with its rattle raised, but silent. Its tongue was out, but didn't flicker.

Suddenly Marley's heart started again. Seen in more light it was less convincing; it was hollow and light, the plastic stiff.

He guessed there'd be something in every room, and there was. An unopened can of Drāno stood on top of his sugar canister. When he opened the medicine cabinet, a scroll rolled down with *BANG!* printed on it in red felt-tipped pen. A rubber tarantula lay on the pillow of the guest room bed.

There wasn't a trick or mocked-up threat in his study. The folder on Sarah had been brought from his file, laid on his desk; the lists and notes had been taken away. One sheet of paper was rolled into his machine, "STOP LOOKING FOR SARAH KLEINHAGEN" typed on it.

Blue Heron

Blue Heron

Philip Ross

TOR

A TOM DOHERTY ASSOCIATES BOOK

BLUE HERON

Copyright © 1985 by Philip Ross

First printing: November 1985

A TOR Book

Published by Tom Doherty Associates
49 West 24 Street
New York, N.Y. 10010

ISBN: 0-812-58794-4
CAN. ED.: 0-812-58795-2

Printed in the United States of America

CHAPTER 1

The scream and electrified guitar were indistinguishable, a single rising shriek of ecstatic agony. Human speech seemed briefly remembered, "*Oooooo! Doomee doomee doomee doomee!*" then lost in another howl. Drum and bass pounded palpable sound waves through the wall into the narrow hallway with the rhythm of a copulating dog. Marley had to beat on the door with the heel of his fist for nearly a minute.

Red, orange, magenta flashes reflecting from the enamel paint sidelighted the boy's face when finally he opened the door just enough to see. He wasn't a boy, but not a man yet either—face smooth, but with the tight eyes. His mouth opened, his voice was inaudible. Marley met him with the smile meant to reassure both of them of his good humor. He didn't try to raise his own voice above the music, but the young man recognized the word's shapes. He started to swing the door. Marley stopped it with his foot, shouldered, shoved in.

The first boy jumped away. The second rose from the pile of cushions in the corner. The girl didn't move. The sets of lights plugged into speakers at either side of the room pulsated, contouring, giving false size to her little naked breasts with their still undeveloped aureoles. The boys hadn't gotten her jeans off yet. Smoke with a sweet smell layered the light. But she was awake, saw Marley as she looked at him. She didn't try to cover herself.

The door boy took his friend's rising as an attack on Marley. Too many tokes, too many pulls at the Seagram's—he wasn't seeing clearly, not thinking at all. He hopped forward on his left foot, pivoted a kick at Marley's head with his right—just like at Richie Chen's Tuesday nights.

Marley took his charge like that of a playful puppy. As though romping, he rocked back, seized the boy's ankle, jerked, grabbed his shirtfront, and heaved the boy on past him across the room. He turned back on the other.

Older, smarter, soberer, the second shook his head, waved open palms at shoulder height, stepped to one side.

Marley moved to the stereo, pushed Off. Sudden silence was almost stunning. He went over to the girl, knelt beside her. "Melissa?"

She smiled slightly, vaguely, but looked at him.

He found her shirt. "Come on, Melissa. I'm going to take you home."

That seemed to trouble her. A little wrinkle came between her eyebrows. Marley slid his hand behind her shoulders, lifted so he could begin to slip the shirt on her. She focused on his face again, smiled again.

"Are you my father?"

*   *   *

"Who *are* you?" she asked as though there hadn't been a break, as though she hadn't slumped into sleep as soon as he put her into the car. Low sun flashed amber into Marley's eyes; when they passed clefts between the hills it blinded him momentarily in contrast to indigo shadows. Cool air may have awakened her. She sat up. Marley could see her in the mirror, her long dark hair tousled, tangled around her face. Puffy from sleep and hangover, it would be only baby-chubby and cute if she splashed it with cold water. Marley thought about where he might find some before he got her home.

"Where are you taking me?"

"Home."

"Whose?"

"Yours, Melissa."

"So who are you?"

"My name's James Marley."

"I suppose you're a private detective."

"No."

"What are you, then?"

"I'm somebody who's taking you home."

"Thanks. Thanks a bunch." She brushed at her hair, seemed to discover its disarray, carded it with fingertips while looking from side to side. "Where's my bag? You didn't go off and leave my bag!"

Marley lifted the embroidered canvas bag over the seat-back to her. She snatched it, pulled it open, then was aware of his eyes in the mirror. She took out a large-toothed comb, put the bag beside her. Marley noticed, though, that before beginning to comb and primp she assured herself that the small stuffed animal that might once have been a lamb was there.

"You don't look like a detective."

"Good."

"You're too skinny."

"I'm elegantly slender."

"And you have crinkles. See!" She watched him in the mirror. "Smile crinkles." She sat back, combed. "Are you a friend of my great-grandmother's?"

"I'm a friend of a friend."

"And she asked you to find me?"

"That's right."

"Is she paying you?"

"No."

"You're just doing this out of friendship? You know, you could have been dematerialized back there. Those guys are ultragonzos."

"Evidently not."

"You just surprised them. What if there'd been more of them?"

"Maybe it would have turned out differently."

"Aren't you pretty old to be doing things like this?"

"Don't let the gray hairs fool you, kid; I'm really only eighty-six."

"Yuk, yuk, yuk."

Marley switched on running lights. The sky glowed bright, pale green above, orange below, behind the hills; but all the road now was shadowed. Farther into the countryside it was winding, narrower.

She sat back, arms around herself, looking out of the right rear window, but not moving her eyes—not to watch anything they passed.

"Are you cold?" he asked.

"No."

"I get depressed at this time of day myself. It's a common psychological phenomenon. Hesperian depression."

"Hesperian? That's evening."

"Yes. All primates get it. Baboons. At sundown baboons go back to their caves and get together and eat fermented fruit; and they feel better."

"Is that true?"

"Honestly."

"Did you really come to get me just because you're somebody's friend? You're not being paid? Honestly?"

"No, Melissa. I'm being paid. Not by your grand—your great-grandmother. By her friend."

"You are a detective."

"I'm not. I just do odd jobs."

"So now I'm somebody's odd job."

Marley checked the mirror, but she wasn't looking at him. He shouldn't have said that. It was what he always said, so he hadn't anticipated it might hurt her.

The next curve brought them beside a little brook. Its blue luminescence shone like stained glass between black lead-lines—stalks of grass and rushes. Marley stopped. "There's a brook there."

She didn't respond.

"Would you like to wash your face?"

"Why? Oh, you mean I'm not all dewy-fresh like Gray's good little girl. Suppose I don't give a shit?"

He shrugged without turning. "Suit yourself. If you don't mind resembling the rear of a pig . . ."

"You're a laugh an hour, Mr. Marley." But she slid across and opened the rear door.

Marley got out too, stretched, arching his back, doing a push-up to and away from the car. Then he walked down to her.

"You didn't think about a towel, did you?" She seemed more resigned than bitter.

"Use the sleeve of your shirt. Let the air dry the rest. The cold will take the swelling down."

"Do I look that bad?"

"I hope you usually look better." He breathed deeply. "Good air."

"Smells like cowshit."

"I guess I like that better than what comes out of buses."

"The country sucks."

"Why?"

"Why do I say that? You want to know what I think makes me say that? Well, I'll tell you. I say that because the country sucks."

Marley shrugged. "I like the country. In the city I think you either lose yourself or you're self-conscious." He shrugged again. "I'm not trying to tell you what *you* should like."

"Why not? Everybody else does."

"At your age I imagine that's true." He chuckled. "Not just your age. My mother and father still tell me what I should do. But it is worse at your age. The worst thing about it is that sometimes they're right. But it's not my place"—he almost said *job,* but caught it—"to tell you things. And you can let *me* prefer country air, however bovine."

He breathed deeply again. While she thought he was looking away she turned her own head slightly in

the breeze as though checking for anything she might
have missed.

"Are you ready?" he asked.

"Yeah." But she didn't move. "What are you
going to tell Gray? My great-grandmother."

"Whatever she asks me, I guess."

"How you found me, what was going on?"

"When I met her she seemed very concerned about
you, Melissa. Truly. I won't tell her anything unless
she asks me, but if she asks, I think it will be
because she wants to know. Don't worry, the story—
the worst of it—isn't that bad."

"What do you mean?" She rolled back from her
haunches, sat on the grass looking up at him. Now
that the sun had set there seemed to be more light in
the sky than before. It showed clearly her baby-doll
lips, big brown eyes, enormous lashes. If she had her
hair cut, Marley thought, it would counter the effect,
make her look at least her age, if not older—fifteen
or even sixteen. "I mean . . ." He tried to find the
tone. It didn't matter; the job was done, but . . . He
could hurt her, and he didn't want to. "How much
do you remember? I thought you were awake. I
mean, they hadn't . . . Things hadn't gotten very far
by the time I got there."

"What do you mean?" Her expression said she
wasn't missing it, he was.

"I mean . . ."

She giggled at him. "You mean they hadn't gotten
into my pants yet."

"That's right."

"You really are too dodecahedral to be believed. I
mean, we went out for breakfast. We were just get-

ting started again. It's a good thing you aren't a detective. I mean, I got to the city yesterday afternoon. Come on, Sherlock, what would you deduce I was doing all the time until you busted in? I was fucking! I fucked both those guys all afternoon and night, and when they couldn't make it I fucked their friends.'' Head back, cool light full on her face, she looked up at him, mocking. But she was watching too: waiting for judgment.

Marley held himself very still, trying to decide. He knew at once not to rebuke her automatically, or ignore her, or make light of her. But he didn't know what to say.

"Are you shocked, Mr. Marley?"

"I guess so, Melissa. I'm always surprised that it still happens, but things do shock me sometimes.''

"It's the sexual revolution. Even someone your age must have heard of it. Don't you know everybody fucks now? It's fun.''

"Yes, it can be. It can be better than fun. Do you know that?''

"Tell me about it." She said it seriously, and for a moment he knew she was serious. Then she leaned back. "Show me.''

Marley bent and took hold of her arm above the elbow. He straightened, drawing her with him, pulling her to her feet.

"Ow-ow-ow! You're hurting me!''

"I'm sorry. I didn't mean to hurt you. Let's go home, Melissa.'' He kept his hand on her arm until he put her into the front passenger seat. He went around to his side, got in, put the key in the ignition. Then he realized she was weeping. He watched her for a moment, not sure what to do. He touched her hair lightly. She turned away, but he kept his arm out, fingers just touching her shoulder; and then she wheeled back around and clutched his arm and buried her face in the crook of his elbow and sobbed.

It was a "Great House:" white portico, old red brick, authentic Georgian. General Burgoyne had probably slept there.

Marley stood at the French door looking out at darkness, across the terrace to rowend fields and rolling hills beyond. He couldn't be sure whether he saw the different greens in grass and trees or only knew they should be different. The room was decorated in a woman's taste: couch in blue and ivory satiny stripes, wing chairs in forget-me-not brocade. Even the real flowers on the table and in the fireplace were blue and ivory. Pictures were good—Hudson River School, 1820's Primitives.

The elderly Asian butler had brought him there. Melissa had run directly up the curving central staircase without saying good-bye. She did look back for an instant, passing across the landing. Marley hadn't been able to read her expression—so quick and then away from him again.

He felt drained. Not merely from driving two hundred miles each way. An easy day's work, actually, he told himself; he just had hesperian depression. But that wasn't true. He hadn't been completely truthful with Melissa. Evening seemed a little sad sometimes, but he didn't let it depress him. Usually.

"Mr. Marley." The old woman stood just inside the doorway until he turned, then came to him, fingertips touching couch-back and end table for balance. She would never condescend to use a cane. She progressed the room's length, stopped before speaking again. "Thank you, Mr. Marley. I am . . . very . . . *very* grateful to you." There might have been artifice in that timing once, he thought; sixty, seventy years ago she might have calculated it—looking at a person so directly, pausing, concentrating her effects. Even if they had seemed artificial then, the effects must have stunned. She would have been beautiful. She had the aristocratic good bones: the high forehead, cheekbones, straight nose. Good bones last. Dimpled cheek and pouty mouth sag with the seasons; good bones are good to the grave. She was beautiful yet. White hair close-cut at the neck, but teased around the crown—up-to-date yet vaguely Victorian; thin fine strands, catching light, glowing. Her pale skin was powdered paler. All the glow and paleness contrasted with her dark dusty-purple dress; and the whole effect set off her eyes, dark eyebrows, dark irises. They had no folds around them. Fine wrinkles covered her face entirely, like tissue paper crushed and smoothed again, but her eye shape was sharp. It was stunning still to be looked at so steadily, focused upon so intently by so beautiful a woman. Disconcerting or flattering, however the man's self-image took it, she would own him merely for the looking at him.

Marley stood as he had turned, looked back. "Thank you, Mrs. Ten Broeck. I was glad I could be of service. To you, and Melissa."

"I couldn't have hoped you would find her so quickly."

"It's not hard to find someone who wants to be found."

She held her stare without change of expression, then nodded once as though acknowledging something she hadn't known she'd known. "Would you like a drink, Mr. Marley?"

"I would."

Her hand rose slightly, wrist turned. No more than was required to indicate the sideboard.

"May I get something for you?" he asked.

"A little brandy, if you would."

When he turned back from the bar she was enthroned in one wing chair. He wondered if she had difficulty sitting, did it when he couldn't see. He took the other chair, facing her. He drank, she sipped. He was tired. He was glad for her style, for the long pauses.

"You found Melissa with a boy."

"Yes."

"Yes." She did look away from him then. Her eyelids closed for a moment only, then opened again, confronting directly whatever she saw in the far corner of the room. "Just one?"

"No."

"Yes." She returned to him. "Do you believe in *psychiatry*, Mr. Marley?"

It struck him funny, but he kept his neutral face and voice. "I never thought of it as a faith."

"I believe in faces."

He wasn't sure whether the old mind staggered from lamp to lamp through fog, or simply knew and took the shortcuts.

"You have an open face, Mr. Marley. You look as

though you expect each next moment to bring good news.''

"Sometimes it does."

"What sort of work do you do for David Cheyney?"

"Odd jobs." But still she looked at him, waiting. "Whatever needs to be done that he doesn't already have someone hired to do. Everyone—sometimes— has something he can't or doesn't want to do for himself. Like finding Melissa. David has so many interests that the occasion arises frequently."

"But you don't work for him exclusively."

"No. He retains me; but I freelance as well."

"Your work often is dangerous."

"No."

"David said—I told him my fears as to the situation in which Melissa might be found. He said he had confidence in your ability to deal with it."

"It's not an ability I have to exercise often."

"I have taken Melissa to a psychiatrist. She has had twice-weekly visits for the past year. When she was yet a little girl I thought her merely precocious. Flirtatious. Then when her behavior was no longer amusing I thought I could correct it myself. At one time, when she was quite young, Melissa and I were very close." The eyes did not soften with memory, but they did seem to study something off past Marley's shoulder.

He sipped his drink. He became aware of the grandfather clock across the room, ticking.

"And you still expect good news?" She looked back to him. "How old *are* you?"

"Forty-eight."

"And you still expect good news. I am eighty-

seven. The psychiatrist, obviously and to my total
lack of surprise, has not helped Melissa. Nor have I.
Eighty-seven has no contact with fourteen, at least
not in this century.''

The clock ticked. Ice settled, tinkling against
Marley's cut-crystal glass.

"Would you like another drink, Mr. Marley?"

"No, thank you."

"Are you on duty?"

"Ah . . . no, but I'm tired, and I still have to
drive."

"I meant are you at liberty? Are you currently
working for David?"

He suspected it wasn't age, that the shifts were
meant to confuse, to throw off balance. "No, I'm not
currently working. I am at liberty."

"Would you work for me?"

"What would you like me to do?"

"Look in that envelope, if you would." She indicated with just the wrist turn.

He saw a manila envelope, 5×7, on the end table.

"There's a photograph inside. My grandson and
Melissa's mother."

It had evidently been snapped at a picnic. The
couple basked on a blanket on a lawn. There was a
wine jug, French bread, remains of Brie. By the look
of the people it must have been taken in the late
sixties or early seventies: field jacket, work shirt,
hair—the boy bearded, with fuzzy curls puffing above
and below a bandanna headband, the girl's long strands
caught behind one ear.

"Taken, I believe, on or about the occasion of
Melissa's conception."

Marley looked up at her, waited. She sipped her brandy, made no more comment. He looked back to the photo.

The boy was chubby. He wore round wire-rimmed glasses. He had Melissa's mouth, cheeks—or, rather, she had his. He looked cuddly. The woman was almost gaunt. Her high cheekbones suggested she could have come from the old woman's line, but she wasn't as pretty as Mrs. Ten Broeck must have been. She was lanky, her breasts but small rounds under a tight tank top; long-waisted, long-legged. Her knees apart, one up, her long full skirt draped between them. Both of the people were young; but he was a boy, she a woman. The boy looked at her in adoration. She looked at the person with the camera. She'd been startled—"Smile!"—had looked up quickly, and did smile; but her eyes were—not wary, exactly, but apprehending, assaying the unexpected. Marley had learned not to trust first impressions, but they occurred. He felt he knew the boy; he would like to know the woman.

That was all he was going to know from looking at the picture, so he looked back to Mrs. Ten Broeck.

"It was taken summer 1971. Brooks was still at Amherst—between his first and second years. She was at Smith. Her name is Sarah Kleinhagen. Her family were farmers somewhere in the West—Ohio, or . . . Illinois. Evidently reasonably successful, perhaps well off. Brooks, of course, comes from an old family of means; so it was obligatory—at that time— for him to espouse radical politics. He really was a dear boy, a sweet boy. His intensity was charming, and—I thought—directed to concerns of a more ad-

mirable order than those of his father when *he* was at
school. I refrained from irony when I wrote each
week sending the check for his allowance.''

Her eyes looked past Marley again. Whatever she
saw made her tip her head and let slide the heavy
book from which she had learned correctness of
carriage.

He would have waited, content; but he feared his
stomach would growl. ''What is it you'd like me to
do, Mrs. Ten Broeck?''

She sighed. Her smile faded. She straightened.
She still searched beyond though. ''To be wise. To
know the right thing before you've done the wrong.''
She focused on him again only after speaking.

He wasn't sure she'd heard the question. ''What
would you like me to do?''

''Find her.''

''Melissa's mother?''

''Did she discuss politics?''

''Who?''

''Melissa! Evidently not. Melissa has gathered to
herself all of the slogans used by the cultural revolu-
tionaries of her parents' generation as substitute for
thought; and she recites them as though they came
from incomprehensible but unquestionably divine rev-
elation. Her promiscuity, I believe, must be understood as a rite.''

''Why?''

''Look at her! Look . . . at . . . *her*!''

He looked again, and Sarah Kleinhagen looked
back.

''A girl needs someone to model herself upon. I
suppose every child does. At the least, a girl needs

someone close who can provide both affection and precept. I am too distant. It is inconceivable that Melissa could regard me as a person who is—or ever was—like herself, a person she might emulate. I can only waggle my finger and, it must seem, read strictures from a book of ancient etiquette. Melissa cannot become me, so she is trying to become her mother.''

''Is her mother like that?''

''Precisely! Since Melissa has never seen her mother, this character—this caricature, this behavior—is pure fantasy.''

''What is she like?''

''I met her twice only. Our contact was not cordial. I did not care for her, although that may in part have been inevitable in the circumstances. But it was established that she was not promiscuous. There could have been no question: The child was Brooks's. And however disagreeable I found her views, I sensed they were her own and undogmatic. Whatever our differences, I believe that woman would be as appalled as I at the ideal which Melissa has set for herself.''

''Do you have any idea where she is now?''

''No.''

''Your grandson? His parents?''

''Brooks is *not* . . . dead! When my husband died I knew it. When my son was killed I knew. When they came to tell me I said, 'Yes. Yes, I know.' Brooks is not dead. I will not permit any action to be taken to declare him dead.''

''He's . . . missing?''

''He was against the war. His first year at college—

what turmoil, what excitement, what passion it must have been. That woman. A group—a sort of secret society. They . . . they were accused—I know Brooks did nothing really wrong. He was too sweet. It was clear he could not expect a career even in one of the family businesses; anything he had he would give away. It is inconceivable he could do anything vicious. But he may have been involved by association—felt himself associated. When he can, he will return. I have no doubt. I have no doubt!''

A small round table of walnut veneer offered itself beside Marley's chair, but he didn't want to put his glass down on it. The ice had melted and condensation might leave a ring. He went to the sideboard, set the glass on a silver tray. When he turned back she was still staring at him, defying contradiction.

Fourteen years, he thought, twice the legal requirement for presuming death. But he didn't try to contradict her.

"Mrs. Ten Broeck, I really think you'd be better off with a professional detective agency. People who would have experience . . . who would know as a matter of routine where to look, what resources are available for tracing people. This is not the kind of thing I do regularly.''

"Exactly, nor do you look like that sort of person. I do not like detectives from agencies. I have thought about this carefully since meeting you yesterday. This is not a situation in which someone has run off or absconded. I do not believe that 'routine' procedures will be effective. I imagine that if Sarah Kleinhagen is, first, to be found, and then to be persuaded to accede to my request, that task will not be accomplished by someone identifiable as a 'professional detective.' I have David's opinion, now confirmed, that you are a person competent to deal discreetly with unusual situations, and that you achieve success. I ask *you* to help me, and Melissa.''

"You have no idea where Melissa's mother might be?''

"The conditions of the trust that I established for her were that she give Melissa to my adoption, and that neither of us should ever see or hear from her again, on penalty of termination of payments.''

"Fourteen years ago.''

"Yes.''

"You believe Melissa will change just from seeing her mother?''

"Possibly. If not at once, then in time. I am prepared to ask that woman to live with us. Melissa is the last of my line; and I love her very deeply.'' She held Marley's eyes with that stare. He was glad to be across the room from it. "Will you . . . Mr. Marley? Will you help us?''

He wouldn't let her will his assent. The clock ticked. Total darkness outside: He realized she'd be reflected in the glass doors—staring at him from behind too. He looked directly at her, not playing a game, but taking time to decide, as always.

"I'll try,'' he said, as if he had a choice.

CHAPTER 2

Marley had been on his way to the dining room, but he stopped as he passed the lounge entrance. A woman sat at a table by herself, turned three-quarters away from him, with a drink and a book. From the back she looked the type he liked: slender, elegantly dressed—not because her clothes were expensive, but because she could wear simple, tailored things with style. It seemed an unlikely place to meet an interesting woman, but you never know. He didn't frequent such places either; she might have had to stop there as he did because the hour was late, past suppertime, and the big sign in front assured an acceptable mediocrity. He decided to check her out.

Since she was reading, he assumed she hadn't come there expecting to be picked up. If he spoke to her she would look up, not pleased to be interrupted, ready to spurn an unwelcome advance. But he would not be standing too close, and would be presenting his open face, looking at her directly. He would say, "I'm James Marley. I like classical music, especially baroque, and good films, and good wine; and I dislike intensely our policy in Central America." If she were his type she would be amused and recognize the situation. She would introduce herself and let him join her.

He entered the lounge and moved among the tables toward the bar on a winding line that would bring him near her without being obvious. As he passed and looked down, though, he saw that the cover of her paperback revealed a flaxen-tressed woman in a flowing gown clutched by a swarthy, cutlassed man whose full-sleeved shirt was torn down the front. A castle loomed on a hill behind them. And the fingers holding the book had magenta nails.

Marley looped around and out again and continued on to the frozen scrod.

Aside from the food, he didn't mind staying there. Used to being by himself, he could lie on the bed with a book, oblivious. The book he'd brought was about the Mayans, well written, interesting.

On leaving Mrs. Ten Broeck, he'd decided at once to stop at Smith on his way home to Boston. With that plan made he hadn't thought about the search; and he hadn't wanted to think about Melissa. He read until drowsy. While undressing for sleep, though, he did glance again at the photo. Brooks Ten Broeck might have been sweet, and was certainly cute; but Marley wondered what about him could appeal to that girl. As he fell asleep, the further thought half-formed that if she had so much character then, what must she be like fourteen years later, fully a woman?

Two girls jogged past, "Harvard" and "Yale" undulating on their T-shirts. Marley looked after them, feeling both pleasure at seeing pretty girls and pain at

knowing that as time distanced his age from theirs it
was making him into a dirty old man.

In addition to enjoying the attractiveness of all the
young women, Marley was happy to be crossing a
campus simply to sense its excitement. He remembered when he was an undergraduate, when air like a
bite of chilled apple meant beginning, not end-of-
summer.

Although the fall term must have been under way
for a week or two, the registrar's office was crowded.
Late registrations, course changes, Marley assumed.
Rather than being annoyed at his interrupting her
routine, the pleasant woman with whom he spoke
seemed to enjoy it. Happy for a break or not, though,
she could not help him. Transcripts could be released
only at the former student's request. Addresses of
alumnae and their families were recorded in the alumnae office; but she knew they would not be given to a
stranger. She did think that they might be revealed to
another alumna. Marley was grateful for that information. He was sure he—or Mrs. Ten Broeck—could
find one. To start somewhere, he went to the publica-
tions office, where they did let him look through old
issues of the *Sophian* and the yearbooks of the time
Sarah was there. She appeared in the student newspaper
frequently as a spokesperson for some group or another, a writer of letters and opinions. From these
sources he was able to extract a number of names of
people whom Sarah must have known, including some
faculty who (the current bulletin informed him) were
still at Smith. He decided to try to see those first,
then to repeat this preliminary search at Amherst and
the University of Massachusetts.

*   *   *

"You have insight, and sensitivity. You have passion too; I know it's there, but it's locked inside you like an eaglet in its shell. Crack the shell, Jennifer. Break it, and soar!"

"I'll try."

"You'll do it, Jennifer. You'll do it." The man's hand held her upper arm. His thumb stroked twice, hard, across the top of her bicep.

Marley pretended to study notices on the hallway board. BERGMAN RETROSPECTIVE. RIDE TO BOSTON. TAKE BACK THE NIGHT. DECLARE SMITH NUCLEAR-FREE. He could see the girl at the threshold, turned back by the final exhortation. Starry-eyed: Only that cliché adequately expressed her look. And radiant: Her cheeks were flushed beyond high rouge-patches. He could see just the man's forearm and hand.

"I know you will. You're too good not to." The hand gave a final squeeze, then released, then touched with fingertips once more as it fell from sight.

"I will try. Robbie. Thank you." The girl smiled widely, quickly, with lips together, to the man, then again, but open, to herself as she turned out into the hall, away from Marley.

The man stepped forward to watch her walk away through the double doors at the hall's end. Marley couldn't tell if he focused on her springy step and head held high as she imagined soaring to come, or on the movement that gait gave her blue-jeaned bottom. The man turned back to his office when she'd gone, saw Marley. His eyebrows rose slightly, he half-nodded—another person acknowledged but not recognized.

"Professor Bascaglia?"

The man popped backward out again. "Yes?"

"Your secretary said you might be free now. Could I speak with you for a moment? My name's James Marley."

"What about?" His expression became guarded.

"One of your former students. It's a matter concerning her family." Marley was smiling, unportentous.

Bascaglia accepted it, smiled back. "Certainly. Come in."

The office was small. There were shelves, books, a desk. One wall was painted purple, three tomato-soup red. They were covered with high-contrast photos and posters—Hendrix, Jagger, Ginsberg, Joplin, Baez, Dylan. Both Dylans. Malcolm X. Che. Around them cluttered plastic-framed snapshots of students, friends—Lilliputian hordes surrounding the giants. Bascaglia smiled from some of them, sometimes bearded, mustachioed. Now he shaved cleanly, cut curly hair short, left the bald spot unconcealed. His desk was in front of the window. Two guest chairs faced it, another sat at the end. He moved his swivel chair back behind the desk from close to the end chair, where the girl must have been. He sat, indicating one across for Marley.

"How can I help you, Mr. Marley?" He gave Marley full attention, looking as though he did want to do something to help, whatever the problem.

Marley explained quickly. There seemed no reason not to tell in general terms. He left out specifics—Melissa's sexuality, Mrs. Ten Broeck's name.

Bascaglia knew Sarah had borne Brooks Ten

Broeck's child. "My God—the kid must be in her teens by now. My God . . ." He rubbed the bald spot. "No, I haven't seen her since then. Haven't seen any of them. They all split—vanished after . . . Well, you know about that." He watched Marley. Marley sensed he was probably an expert at watching, testing indirectly. "Like Hopkins's sprung rhythm, isn't it? Like the Michelangelo couplet in 'Prufrock,' isn't it?" Tests to see if his students knew, if they'd pretend they knew, how well they knew.

"No, I don't know about it, Professor. I'd be grateful—if you can't tell me where Sarah is, I'd be grateful for anything you can tell me about her." Marley showed no hesitation, twitch of mouth, shift of eye.

Bascaglia rocked back in the swivel chair. "She was wonderful—a wonder. Intelligence, insight, sensitivity . . ."

"Passion?" Marley said it neutrally, but Bascaglia caught it. His eyes had been habitually narrowed, as Marley's were open: Each had his own way of watching. He caught it, nodded, smiled.

"And passion. Not bottled up. You want them all to have those things. Everybody. Most don't. At first, when you're teaching, you think it's your fault. That's conceit. When you get older you understand there isn't a damn thing you can do most of the time. But sometimes you can help a little by making them try: Tell them they can, and they do. Sarah had it, though, all of it. And also . . . Sometimes I call it 'competence,' sometimes, 'weight.' There are people who *make it*. Do you know what I mean, Mr. Malloy?"

"Marley."

"Sorry. Marley. Do you know what I mean? Survivors. She was only—what?—eighteen when she came here, left after two years. Young. But from the first—a substantiality. She's one of the only two students I've ever taught who really is a poet. I mean, I think I helped her, but she was a poet without me."

"What happened to her? All of *them,* you said?"

"Blew up." He shook his head, looking away from Marley for the first time. "Overheated and blew up. Were you involved with the war, Mr. Marley?"

"Vietnam? Yes."

He was watching Marley again. "I don't think I'll ask in what way. *We* were against it. Well, of course, almost everyone was—in the colleges, in this area. Since the Northeast is the center both of enlightenment and of intellectual faddism, how could it be otherwise? We, at least, tried to do something beside circulate petitions."

"What?"

"It's a matter of record—some of the alumnae, trustees, politicians tried to have my ass for it—I wrote and advocated that when the government itself breaks its own laws and uses the law as an instrument of repression, then the people are not bound to obey the law when opposing that government. Beyond that, I take the Fifth." Bascaglia paused, as if waiting to see if Marley would produce a badge, as if he had waited for years, mentally rewriting his statement from the scaffold.

"What happened?"

"Nothing." For an instant Bascaglia's hand, resting over the edge of his desk, tightened. Then it relaxed. He shook his head, smiled. "I like to think—I thought then, and still like to think we did *some* good: made it harder for them, made the war cost a little more, let them know they couldn't just *rule* without opposition. But . . . we were an ant kicking the shins of an elephant. And when we realized that, that's when we blew apart. There were those of us who were too wise, or scrupulous, or chicken— opinions differ—to go further; and there were those who were determined to escalate. We went our ways. I to waste my idle hours directing house-to-house canvassing in Holyoke and Chicopee. Sarah out of it, to have Brooks's baby and disappear. Some of the others—it is alleged—set out to blow up SAC bombers at Westhover. Whoever tried it failed, but they did kill two MP's and wounded a third in the attempt."

There was no approval in the way he said the last, but no condemnation either. Bascaglia seemed to wait for the condemnation to come from Marley, defiantly.

"You have no idea where anyone is who might help me find Sarah?"

"Her family, I would suppose."

"I'm going to try them, of course. But as long as I was here I thought I'd see people who knew her. I thought you might be able to give me the names of—"

"No! I don't name names." Bascaglia suddenly became a snapping turtle, pulled down into the swivel chair, but ready to bite off any probing finger.

"Thank you, Professor." Marley got up. "I appreciate your giving me your time."

Bascaglia seemed angry from the memory of it all.

Perhaps he still expected the badge. "What *did* you do in the war, Mr. Marley?"

"Part of the time I worked for the American Friends Service Committee with the refugees."

There was a long pause. Sun highlighted red-turning ivy at the window behind Bascaglia's back; shadows splotched his desk.

"I'm sorry." Bascaglia seemed to seek a picture in the splotches. For the first time he avoided looking at Marley. Marley waited to see if there would be more. "I . . . I haven't told you the truth, Mr. Marley. Not the entire truth. I *don't* know where Sarah is. That is true. But I have heard from her and seen her. I do see her, maybe once a year. Sometimes I get a letter, sometimes she even calls me— but that's unusual. It's always from a pay phone, and I get the idea it's when she's away from wherever she normally is. The letters come from different places too. When we get together . . . She sets it up. She calls, using a false name, but of course I recognize her voice. We talk in a kind of code, and set a time and place.

"I don't ever ask her where she's living. I don't want to know. At one time the FBI was looking for her. They probably still are. She was not—I assure you—she was not guilty of any crime. But they wanted her to give evidence, to fink on her friends. Sarah's not that kind of person either. So I can't— truly can't—help you find her, nor would I if I could. What I will do, though, is this: The next time she calls me, or I see her, I will tell her what you've said. If she wants to contact *you*, then that's up to her. I have no idea when that might be, of course."

The confession and offer seemed to resolve all of Bascaglia's ethical tensions. He looked Marley in the eye again.

"Thank you, Professor. I understand your feelings, and I couldn't ask for more from you." Marley took a case from his breast pocket and extended a card. "Here. Here's my address and phone number, if you should be in touch with her."

Bascaglia took it, placed it carefully under the leather corner of his desk blotter.

Marley smiled, said "Thanks" again, and turned to leave.

"Mr. Marley . . . if you're going to go ahead and try to find Sarah, I'd suggest you don't. Those members of the group who did the Westhover thing—as it's alleged—they had reached a point of intensity, of desperation . . . of violence. That was a long time ago. They're probably all bank clerks by now—like we all are. But I suspect they would not like to be found. I guess . . . I understand the reason for trying to find Sarah; I'm sorry to hear her daughter has some problem, but I guess I'm trying to warn you that looking for Sarah could be dangerous."

"Thanks. I appreciate that too, Professor."

"And I apologize again for having misjudged you. Obviously, I didn't know you're a Friend."

"I'm not. And don't be sorry. That was the last part. Before that, I wasted gooks."

Marley worked for nearly an hour on the letter, saying enough but not too much, trying to get the tone right. He had decided without thinking much about it to write Sarah's parents rather than call. The subject of a never-seen granddaughter was bound to be emotional. It would be better to present it in a document that could be read in private and considered rather than with the immediacy of conversation.

He hoped the letter to her parents would be enough to locate the woman; but while he was at it, as insurance, he adapted the text and typed out copies to the people—eight of them—who seemed, on the basis of his research at Smith and the other colleges, to have been closest to her. As he had expected, Mrs. Ten Broeck had been able to get their addresses without difficulty. She was an alumna of Smith herself, her nephew Richard an alumnus of Amherst, someone of their acquaintance had called U Mass, and all calls had been returned within the hour. Such prominently wealthy daughters and sons of their schools were not required to wait for the mail. Writing the letters took all morning. Marley was glad he had resisted the urge to get into action when he'd gotten home the previous evening.

He made a sandwich for lunch, repacked the bag he always kept ready. It was 1:45 then, and he tried to decide what to do with the rest of the day. Until David Cheyney called with a new assignment, Marley had hoped to have time free. He'd planned to write. His hobby was history. As an undergraduate he'd written a paper on his own hometown in Vermont and enjoyed doing it. Over the years he'd worked out from there: West Dover, and Wardsboro, Newfane—eventually, all of the smaller towns around. Sometimes his papers were published by local historical societies, once in a while by *Vermont Life*. He thought, eventually, when he had enough, he'd rework them all into a book.

But having spent all morning on the letters, he didn't want to write anymore that day.

He tried to decide. He could go to a film. There was one at the Exeter he'd wanted to see. He could walk.

That would be good. He always liked movies, and going to one was the best thing to do when feeling lonely—which, strangely, he was. Usually after working, traveling, he was happy to be by himself, at home, simply writing or reading. But lately he'd been feeling as though he were rattling around in his life.

Maybe he would call someone for dinner. He thought at once of Phyllis, of course, but canceled that. There really wasn't any point. She'd accept if he called—if she wasn't busy—and they'd have a nice meal. She'd want to know what he was doing, and he'd be happy to hear about the school. And that would be all they'd have to say. They would look at each other a lot, and still feel close; and she'd probably sleep with him again if he asked her. But they knew their corners didn't fit to make one picture. And he couldn't sleep with her while wondering who she'd been with last week or might be with next. That wouldn't be fair, because they'd agreed they weren't going to Happily Ever After together. So she was free and so was he, but he didn't want to deal with it, fair or not.

He might call George and Gwen. They'd be glad to see him (they always were) and he to see them. They'd invite him for supper, and they'd all sit at the

table and talk till the wine ran out. Except that on a
school night, at short notice, the kids would eat with
them. Sweet kids, but all talkers, just as great as
George and Gwen.

Of course, there were many other friends he might
call; but somehow he really didn't want to see any of
them. What he really wanted to do was see the film
with an interesting and attractive woman—not one of
those he knew now, yet someone who in his imagination he would know very well—and come back with
her, talk about it and whatever else for an hour over a
good, simple supper, listen to music with her head on
his shoulder, then go to bed early.

Well, he would go to the film. Maybe he'd meet
someone there. He'd met Phyllis at a film; it might
happen again. Because he'd been studying the photograph that Mrs. Ten Broeck had given to him, trying
to develop from it an intuition about the character of
the woman that might guide him in finding her, it
neither surprised him nor seemed greatly significant
that the person he imagined meeting looked much
like Sarah Kleinhagen.

As the weather report had predicted, the next day
dawned high and clear. Marley was ready, up early
and off. His letters would be delivered tomorrow at
the earliest, so he saw no reason to wait around.

The day sang. As he crossed into New Hampshire
he lifted, as always, swelled into the sense of space,
of setting his own speed, of being able to swing his
arms without hitting anyone. That was illusion, he
knew. They'd bulldozed, suburbanized the southern
part of the state as much as Massachusetts. But the

idea of tall and green that came to him with the
Welcome sign became reality farther north as he
crossed the Merrimack at Concord and rolled on into
true countryside. He went up to Wonalancet, left his
car at the side of the road, ascended for three hours
and a half to the ledge of Whiteface. Small lakes,
scattered through the rolling meadow and woodland
below, were blue-white jewels set in deep green
velvet. Here and there a tree, or a branch of one, had
turned to autumn color, and the air was crisp with
fall's coming, but on that mid-September day most of
the foliage kept its late-summer look.

Traveling back to Boston in the evening traffic
wound up his spring again, but not as tightly as it had
been. Marley felt healthily fatigued, yet rested, too,
as always after hiking. And he wondered once again
if it would be practical for him to work from someplace in the country.

He wrote on Friday, worked the whole day. Cooked
supper in. Watched a TV movie he didn't like. Hung
around waiting for the Kleinhagens to call. They
didn't.   .

They didn't call on Saturday. They had to have
gotten his letter by then.

They didn't call Sunday.

On Monday the letter came. Letterhead stationery:
Walter D. Kleinhagen. Typed, carbon ribbon. Secretary's initials. *I regret I can give you no information
concerning Sarah Kleinhagen. Her whereabouts are
unknown to me. Sincerely.*

Marley was depressed; but then (he told himself) if

it could have been that easy, Mrs. Ten Broeck wouldn't have needed to hire him.

There were no responses to his letters to Sarah's friends. Perhaps some would still come. In the meantime he moved to the next group—people whose names had been associated with Sarah's but who hadn't seemed as close, and sent off letters to them.

That evening he got his first call, from a man with a smoothly modulated, confident, personnel-manager voice.

"I understand you're trying to locate Sarah Kleinhagen."

"That's right."

"Have you found her yet?"

"May I ask who's calling?"

"I'd rather not say."

Marley put good humor into his own voice. "I guess, then, I'd rather not say whether I've found her."

The caller chuckled back. "I guess that's okay. I don't know where Sarah is, but I've got one suggestion—if you haven't already tried her. It's really a long shot, though; I doubt it will do you any good. But if you'd like it, it's a girl named Christine Pedersen. She lives in Cincinnati. Would you like her number?"

"I appreciate any information."

"But you're not going to say whether you need it. Okay. I understand. Well, anyway . . ." He gave Marley a number.

"Thanks."

"Glad I can help, if I can. Hope you find her."

Marley placed the call to Christine Pedersen.

"Who?"

"Sarah Kleinhagen."

"Oh! Sarah. Sure. But, gee, I don't know where she is. I haven't seen Sarah for—God, it must be ten or fifteen years. No, like fifteen, fourteen, something. I really don't know. . . . We only roomed together in a house with a lot of other people for like a month. Then I got another place. I really hardly knew Sarah at all. Who did you say said to call me?"

Well, he'd been told it was a gamble. Marley pushed the phone away and began to try to think what line to take next, and then caught his breath and felt his ears heating.

He made himself wait two hours, then called her back.

"It's James Marley again. I called you a little while ago about Sarah Kleinhagen. I wondered . . . has anyone else called you?"

"Yeah. What is this? Some other guy called me about an hour ago. Look, I told you, I really don't know anything about Sarah Kleinhagen."

"I believe you, Miss Pedersen. Could you just tell me what the other person wanted?"

"He just asked if you'd called me. Now, look, I don't know what's going on, but—"

"It's all right, Miss Pedersen. I know you don't. And I'm sure no one will bother you anymore. It was just a mistake."

Marley, naturally, disliked acting stupid. He had not taken Professor Bascaglia's warning seriously. Evidently, he should have—would have to. Someone cared about where he was in his search, had found that he hadn't found Sarah, that he was desperate enough to take long-shot tips. He tried to feel better by believing his slip was a warning, and now he'd be wiser.

He brought himself back to dealing with what to do next. He had begun by focusing on Sarah, but, of course, there was another route. It was almost 10:00, but he chanced being impolite and called Mrs. Ten Broeck.

The butler answered, and Marley gave his name, but when Mrs. Ten Broeck came on she asked, "Who is it?"

"It's James Marley, Mrs. Ten Broeck."

"Marley?"

"Yes. James Marley. I . . . ah . . . I'm trying to find Melissa's mother, you remember, I—"

"Of course I remember. Have you found her?"

"Not yet. I—"

"Then why are you calling?"

"I wanted to keep you informed about my progress. I thought you'd like—"

"Have you *found* her?"

"No. I said I hadn't."

"Then you have no progress of which to inform me."

First Marley kept himself from hanging up, then tried without success to consider the dialogue comical. "I'm sorry to have disturbed you, Mrs. Ten Broeck. I did hope you might be able to help me."

"Please don't consider it, Mr. Marley."

It took him aback. But he was learning about her. "Thank you. I hoped you might help me by suggesting some friends of Brooks's and Sarah's with whom she might have kept in touch."

"I certainly know of none. I'm sure she was not introduced to any of Brooks's set here."

"Perhaps he might have mentioned someone. I've had no luck with her family. I'm trying to contact her old friends."

"Should I offer a reward?"

"I think that would be inadvisable. There mustn't be any sense of informing or of betraying her. I'm not asking where she is; I'm only asking that anyone who knows tells her Melissa needs her, and please to contact me."

"She has a message for you."

That gave Marley pause, and a surprising flash of excitement. Then he got the pronoun assigned. "Melissa?"

"She asks me to thank you for bringing her home. She says she felt you were truly concerned for her, and she is sorry she was not respectful to you. That is the gist. She asked for your address so that she might express herself more fully and formally, an act of social consciousness I have encouraged by not praising."

"That's very nice of her."

"She is a good child, despite . . . despite."

"I think so too."

"Anything can be forgiven one who is essentially good at heart."

Marley hoped she was right.

"Nonetheless," she continued, "I am watching her closely. I had to withdraw her from her school, of course. I have engaged a tutor temporarily, but unless you soon are successful, I see no alternative but to place her in some facility where she can be adequately supervised, at least.''

"I'm trying, Mrs. Ten Broeck. It will be a help if you can identify any friends.''

"I shall try. Perhaps . . . perhaps there might be something in Brooks's letters. He wrote each week—so faithfully. It was such a joy for me to receive them; he always related in great detail all of his activities, his thoughts and feelings. Well, not always, of course, a joy. I disapproved strongly of many of . . . But that is not the point, is it? Yes! Of course! He mentions many of his friends and associates, I'm sure. I shall make a list for you.''

"Could I— Would you mind if I looked through the letters myself? It might be more useful for me to see the names in context.''

"I suppose. I would not wish to give them out of my possession though. Could you come here?''

Back across the state again. Why hadn't he thought of this while he was out there the first time?

"Certainly. Tomorrow? Early afternoon?''

"Very good, Mr. Marley. I'm so glad to be of help. Don't hesitate to call at any time.''

"Of course, Mrs. Ten Broeck.''

Marley hung up, stared at the phone for a moment, and then did laugh.

CHAPTER 3

The hard part was *not* reading the letters. Brooks had typed them. Each subject or thought lodged in its own paragraph, while double-spacing distanced sections discussing widely disparate topics. Brooks had benefited from an excellent secondary education, no doubt, and he enjoyed the vocabulary and precocity of viewpoint of a young person raised in adult company. But beyond that, in logic of structure, or where corrections or interpolations were inserted by hand in characters as carefully formed as those of the machine, the pages testified to a neat and orderly mind. The hard part was to hold back from joining that mind on its Darien peak as it saw such brave new worlds. Marley disciplined himself to scan for proper names, then around those for context, and to read only when that involved Sarah or their group. Even so, Brooks's excitement was contagious. He was immature, naive, foolishly idealistic: "Despite the current evidences to the contrary among the power establishment of this country, I believe there is a basic goodness in all people. Society may corrupt it, but I believe the corruption is reversible, if not in this generation, then in the next." Yet he showed sensitivity and perception too: "Robbie Bascaglia . . . poetry professor at Smith . . . wildman: Walt Whitman, Dylan Thomas, and a hairy Italian bandit all rolled into one. . . . sitting on the floor, drinking cheap red wine from the bottle, telling us to let the Life Force flow through us freely, but checking out of the corners of his eyes to see how we're taking him. But a wonderful man. And he's right! If we . . ."

The grandfather clock ticked time by, yet seemed by that constancy to deny its passage. Marley sat at a secretary in the drawing room, his back to the French doors. From time to time he heard Mrs. Ten Broeck moving about the room, but she didn't interrupt him.

The parts of the letters that Marley read most closely—and again—concerned Sarah. He countered his sense of wasting time (it was the names of people who might help find her that he sought, after all) by telling himself that knowing about her might suggest another approach.

". . . girl named Sarah something. She's at Smith. She's only a sophomore, but seems much older. She has a way of looking straight at you when you're talking that's very disconcerting—as though she's checking to see whether what you say is what you're really thinking, which she knows without your saying it. I think it's actually just a trick, but it works.

". . . and then finally, after Bobby Atkins had finished his Malcolm X imitation, and Mal Grandgeorge had done his Lenin, and everybody had told everybody else how stupid his ideas were, Sarah Kleinhagen (as usual) cut through and suggested a way to do it that might actually work.

". . . got up my nerve and asked her to have dinner with me at Valentine. I don't know how she knew, but she had brought a present for me—a little book of verse by a man named Richard Eberhart, whom I hadn't heard of. . . . I played the 'Titan' (thank you so much, again) and she *listened* all the way through. She has that ability (like you, Gray) to be completely tranquil and yet intensely focused.''

References to Sarah became more frequent. ". . . went to the new Fellini film with Sarah. . . . Sarah pointed out (which I hadn't thought of) that . . . Spent the day with Sarah. . . .'' Her presence came into nearly every paragraph. Even when Brooks talked about course work, or events on campus, there was the sense of her—from actual discussions they had had, or from his awareness of what her reaction, her insight, would be.

Evidently Mrs. Ten Broeck had regarded the growing relationship with a disfavor of which she finally delivered herself. No reference to Sarah appeared in the next letter until the end.

"As you see, I have not mentioned Sarah, since doing so offends you. I will say only this: No, Gray, Sarah's ancestors did not come over with Peter Stuyvesant. On the other hand, her parents own several thousand acres of the best farmland in Illinois, and her father is the chairman and major stockholder of the local bank. They aren't exactly peasants. And what would it matter if they were! I'm sure they are people who have the integrity and decency that people have who are still in touch with nature! They must have, since Sarah does. She is a wonderful, beautiful human being! I love her, and I am going to

keep being with her! Please don't say any more about
her, or try to stop me, because I love you very much
too, and it would break my heart to have to defy you.
But I will!''

Mrs. Ten Broeck must have made a strategic with-
drawal. The next letter began, ''Thank you for agree-
ing not to make an issue about my relationship with
Sarah. I know you think it's just a crush, and I'll get
over it. Well, I won't. But I won't talk about her
anymore either.''

That he didn't disappointed Marley, even though
the letters grew ever more excited with outrage over
the escalation in Vietnam. Marley skimmed Brooks's
reports of his group's activities and protests, and of
their growing desperation. There were only one or
two new names mentioned as Brooks wrote so faithfully each Sunday evening throughout the autumn.
The last letter was dated December 4. What had
happened that Brooks no longer wrote? Or what had
he written after that date that Mrs. Ten Broeck would
not reveal?

''This is all of them?'' Marley asked.

''Yes.'' She came up beside him.

He was sure she would not satisfy his curiosity.
Perhaps at that time she had learned of Sarah's preg-
nancy. That would answer the question either way.

''Have you finished? Have you found anything of
use?'' she asked.

''Yes, I think so. I've got several names here that I
didn't have before. If I can trace them through their
colleges' alumni offices . . .

''I wish I had the time—and your permission—to
read all these carefully. They're wonderful letters.''

"Yes. Brooks is a wonderful boy."

"You must have been very close. For him to write so much. I don't think I wrote once a month when I was in school."

"He is a dear, dear boy. I raised him, you see. His father and mother were killed when he was only three."

"I see. But you haven't heard anything from him since"—Marley indicated the letters—"then."

"I will not hear of it! If Brooks does not choose to communicate, he has his good reasons!"

"Certainly, Mrs. Ten Broeck. I only meant—"

"I will not hear of it!"

Marley was getting used to the idea of tracks, and of jumping from one to another. "What time will Melissa be back?"

It worked. "By three, I should think."

He checked his watch. "I'd like to see her, but perhaps . . . I'd like to beat the traffic coming into Boston."

"She would like that very much, I'm sure."

"Well, I think—"

"But I must ask you not to tell her of your search."

"Why?"

"Melissa's emotional stability is extremely precarious just now. And so much of it does seem to be invested in her idea of her mother. This is the point of finding her, of course. But I think that until we have some assurance of your success it would be most inadvisable to raise her hopes."

"I see. Well, it doesn't seem I'm going to see her today anyway. Give her my best wishes, will you?"

*   *   *

But as Marley started to get into his car, another vehicle suddenly crunched around the gravel drive behind him.

"Hi! Mr. Marley! Hi!" Melissa leaned from the passenger window, waving.

Marley waited while she flung open the door, sprang out, and rushed toward him. After three steps, though, the woman in her restrained the girl. She caught herself, then came on slowly, shy.

"Hello, Melissa. How are you?"

"Okay."

"I got your letter this morning. Thank you."

She looked away, stuck her fists into the pockets of her dress.

Marley suddenly was aware the frock was a pinafore, and of his surprise that girls still wore them.

Melissa seemed to be studying the point of his left lapel. "I just wanted you to know that I was sorry, and that I appreciated—"

"Yes. And you said so very nicely. And now I don't think we have to talk about it anymore. Okay?"

The driver of the car joined them. A middle-aged woman, with hair in gray streaks, apple cheeks, bright eyes, and smile lines, but firm of jaw. She wore a maroon sweater set and a matching tweed skirt—a preppy mommy. Melissa used her arrival to break the moment.

"This is Mrs. Gaskill."

"James Marley. How do you do?"

"Mr. Marley. Isn't it a lovely day?" She looked upward at the peacock sky, inviting him to scan it with her, as though that were a greeting gift.

He accepted, and looked from vibrant zenith to pellucid horizon. "Yes."

"Mrs. Gaskill is my tutor. And my chastity belt."

Mrs. Gaskill both colored and smiled slightly, then suddenly, with a speed Marley would not have suspected from one so placid, struck out at the girl. Melissa, obviously expecting reaction, jumped away, giggling, just ahead of the jab.

"What you need is a belt in the mouth, flip lip." Then Mrs. Gaskill drew up, composed hands at waist, looked down her nose at Melissa. Like a participant in ritual, Melissa mimicked the posture, and the two of them intoned together, "Try to remember, my dear, you are a lady."

Marley grinned at them, greatly relieved at the thought that until he might find Sarah, Melissa was in good hands.

Keeping the dowager decorum and voice, Melissa turned to him. "Have you seen the grounds?"

"No, Modom. I have not had the o-poportunity of ava-lailing myself of that unparallelable-able pleasure."

Glee transformed lady to girl again. "Would you like to? Do you have some time?"

"Sure. That would be very nice."

"You don't have to come, Mrs. Gaskill. Mr. Marley's safe."

Mrs. Gaskill and Marley met eyes for an instant, and he nodded. She did too. "All right, Melissa. I'll be on the back terrace." She looked again at Marley, and he nodded again to show he understood Melissa must be delivered to her.

Melissa led along the flagstone path from the drive across the great house's front. Carefully contoured shrubs grew up to and between first-floor windows, and yellow chrysanthemums bordered the beds.

"The mums are very pretty," Marley said.

"Yes. They are pleasant, aren't they? We have daffodils in spring, and petunias there in summer." It was the grown-up lady speaking again. Marley imagined she'd apprenticed the tone from Mrs. Ten Broeck, hand in hand, leading guests on tours around the manse. The shifts from Melissa to Lady M amused him.

Melissa paused, saying, "I think the view quite nice from here," and allowed him time to admire it.

Marley responded appropriately. "Yes. The house doesn't seem to be so high when you're driving up, but it must be, to allow you to see that far."

"The farther range of hills is in Vermont."

"Is it? I used to live in Vermont. I grew up there."

Melissa again: "Really. Where?"

"Wilmington. It's about due east from here. It was a small town then. Rural. Now it's all built up. Skiing. Developments."

"Oh, that's too bad."

"Yes. I think it is."

"You really liked it before?"

"Yes."

"Gee. I'm sorry. I'm really sorry."

"Yeah. But there are a lot of other places that are still nice. You just have to get away from the skiing."

They rounded the corner of the house. The path wound between huge, shaped bushes—trees, really. Groundsmen must have had to use a cherrypicker to prune them. Behind, off to one side, spread tennis courts; beyond those rose a huge greenhouse. It reminded Marley of one at London's Kew Gardens. Though only a fraction of that one's size, it copied its design, and must have been three stories tall at its center dome.

"Wow! I guess you sure can grow your own flowers."

"We've got a whole tropical forest!" Aghast at the childish enthusiasm, Lady M tried to reassert control. "My great-grandfather was a botanist. As a hobby, of course. Gray keeps the place up in his memory. And I guess my grandfather and my father played there. And I did too. It was wonderful in the winter. It was always so warm in there. Gray and I used to play hide-and-seek. I had to count to three hundred for her. Or explorer-and-savage. I was the savage, and I crept through the bamboo, and I caught her. And I took her back to my village, and I was going to put her in a pot and eat her up for supper; but then she sang to me and made friends with me, and ended up civilizing me, so we went back to the house and had tea and cookies by the fire."

Melissa seemed to see it through the whitewashed panes. Then her pretty face went petulant. "Jesus, it must cost her a fortune to keep that place heated. You want to see inside?"

"Not today, thanks."

"The stables and garages are on beyond. But we don't have any horses now. You want to see them anyway?"

"No. Not today."

"Okay. Come on, I'll show you around to the other side. There's the swimming pool."

The empty pool lay almost directly behind the house, screened from the raised flagstone terrace by a low hedge. Marley and Melissa walked along the path between hedge and steps. Mrs. Gaskill had brought a book to the terrace. She sat reading, her back to them—discreetly, Marley felt.

"Mrs. Gaskill seems like a nice person."

"Yeah. She's okay. For a warden. You must have really impressed her. This is the first time she's let me out of her sight for two minutes in a week. I think she stands outside the door when I pee. And I think she saves hers up and only goes when she knows I'm asleep."

Marley refrained from replying. Melissa led on, head down and fists again in her pockets, until they were past the terrace. A stone bench stood at the entrance to a formal garden. Melissa turned and flopped down onto it, legs straight out.

"All right, I know. I brought this on myself."

"Did I say anything?"

"You don't have to say it. I know it by heart. 'I have only myself to blame.' "

Marley sat beside her. "I doubt that's entirely true."

Still, she wouldn't raise her head or look at him. "You don't think so? Well, what do you think is the root of this 'vile and immoral behavior'?"

"How would I know, Melissa? I'm not a shrink. I don't want to get into this. I just know there are things we do—forces inside us that make us do things—that we don't understand where they come from. We don't choose to do those things, and in that sense I don't think we can be blamed for them. They may be wrong, and we may feel bad about them; but that's not the same as being *guilty*. On the other hand, I think we can—we *have to*—learn to control those forces or impulses or whatever they are inside ourselves. As long as you're trying—as long as you *are* controlling them, I think you ought to feel okay about yourself."

Her hands still were jammed into her pockets, legs straight out. She seemed to be studying her feet. She waggled the left from side to side, then the right, then both together. "What are you doing here?"

"I'm doing something for Mrs. Ten Broeck."

"What?"

"I'm afraid I can't tell you. Professional confidentiality."

"Would you do something for me? I mean, I'd pay you."

"I'd be happy to do something for you, Melissa, if I can."

"I have some money of my own. I mean I can get it. I would pay you."

"Good. That's settled. Now, what would you like me to do?"

Finally she turned to him. "Find my parents."

After a moment Marley found he had to turn from her. "I see." He rocked his head up and down slightly, as though considering the request, actually thinking what the hell to say in response. Then he tried to make his question seem the normal one in context. "What do you know about them, Melissa?"

Hands out of pockets, palms clapped together and shaken, head up. "They were great! I mean, they were great people. They fought for what they be-

lieved. They were against the war in Vietnam, and
they were trying to bring power to the people, and
. . . They were freedom fighters.'' She glanced sideways, up at Marley, quickly, as though aware he
might think the title melodramatic. Clearly she did
not. "That's why they had to go into hiding. That's
why they had to leave me.''

"How do you know that?''

"That's what Gray told me—some of it. And my
father's friends. And things I've read myself and
figured out. But now she's trying to tell me it's not
true. About my mother. She's trying to tell me they're
not together, that my mother left my father. That she
. . . that she left me because she wanted to.''

"I'm sure that's not true.''

"I know it's not! They had to leave me for my
sake. Because . . . But they're still together! And
when I'm old enough they'll come back for me. And
then I'll help them, and fight beside them, and . . . I
know why she's doing it. Because she knows that.
She doesn't want me to leave her, 'cause then she'll
have nobody. So she puts me down. Every time I say
anything, or, like, have any idea of my own, she puts
me down. And she's trying to use my mother to put
me down. My mother and my father weren't married,
and— Why should they? What difference does it
make? I mean, maybe they would have, someday,
when they could. But what difference does it make,
for Christsake? But she says— Anytime I show I've
got any interest in sex, I mean even before the first
time I fucked—'' She caught herself, didn't want to
offend him. "I mean, before I had sex with anybody,
just the idea, and she would get all uptight. So now

she lies to me and tries to tell me my mother left us, and she was a 'bad woman,' and if I don't stop I'm going to be just like— And I told her, there isn't anybody in the world I'd rather be like than my mother! That frosted her knockers!''

"Do you think your mother really . . . really had sex with many men?''

"Well, I'm sure she wasn't a virgin queen! I'm sure nobody made her go around dressed like she was ten years old and didn't have tits. Sure, she must have. I mean, there's nothing wrong with it! All my friends at school, even if they don't do it, they're not made to feel . . . Just because they *think* about it. And my mother wouldn't let . . . I know, I mean, I know she loved my father very much, but . . . I don't know.''

A little breeze swept leaves across the terrace and over the hedge. They swirled above the empty swimming pool, some settling into it, some carried up again and wafted out to the lawn beyond. Marley followed the farthest flyer until Melissa seemed calm once more.

"Mrs. Ten Broeck has been saying bad things about your mother?''

"Yes. I mean, she did till I let her have it.''

"Ah. When was that?''

"A couple weeks ago, I guess. Why?''

"It doesn't matter. I'm sure she was wrong, and I'm sure she's sorry.''

"Fuck her!''

Marley made no flicker of rebuke, but Melissa flinched. "I'm sorry.'' She stared at the ground again.

"It's all right. She said a cruel, hurtful thing to you and you've got every right to be angry."

She ventured a sideways look at him. "You think so?"

"Yes."

"Well, I fucking well am! Fuck her! I hate her! Fuck her! Fuck her!" Melissa rocked back and forth in jerks of affirmation.

On the terrace Mrs. Gaskill raised her head, but didn't turn. Marley wasn't sure whether she had heard or was merely resting her neck. She went back to her book again.

"Do you think she heard me?"

"I don't know."

"I got to watch it. If I give Gray any more grief she's gonna ship me straight to Cape-Canaveral-on-the-Hudson."

"Where?"

"The cracker factory. Where they send all the space cadets. You know, kids with *problems*."

"Ah."

"You won't tell her what I said?"

"Of course not. I know, Melissa—from the talks I've had with her—I know she loves you and wants to help you. I'm sure she said something to hurt you only because . . . Out of anger at being hurt. Just like you just did. She's trying to help you. But I think she's running out of things she knows to do."

Melissa seemed both wanting and unwilling to believe. She mooted the issue. "Will you find my parents?"

Marley tried to think what he could say and be true

to his commitment to Mrs. Ten Broeck. "I'll look
into it. I'll see if it seems possible to find them—or
at least one of them, in case they're not together."
Melissa started to react, but he put up a hand. "I'm
not going to make any assumptions, Melissa. That's
not the way to do something like this. You have to
keep an open mind. And *you* have to keep an open
mind too. I'll tell you, Melissa, the one thing that
makes me hesitate to say I'll do this is fear that you'll
build too much on it. Fourteen years is a long time,
and a lot of things could have happened. And I don't
want to feel that if I have to come back and tell you
something you don't want to hear, I'm going to cut
the string on your kite."

For a moment she stared at him, her two hands
thrust down between her knees and clutched. Then
the horror in her face transmuted to a dullness. Marley
wasn't sure which look pained him more.

"I will try, Melissa." That brought brightness to
her eyes again, and tears. "But you can't put everything on that. Now, listen to me. It's a beautiful day;
look around and enjoy it. I think in Mrs. Gaskill you
may have a real friend. Your great-grandmother loves
you, even if she is giving you a hard time right now.
What you're going through now—it may be worse
than most in some ways, but it's like what every kid
goes through, and they all make it."

"No, they don't. Cindy Van Patten slit her wrists
last year. Don't bullshit me, Mr. Marley. Please."

Marley felt himself flushing, but held steady to her
look until sure she wouldn't think he couldn't. Then
he looked up at the high trees, their outer leaves just
yellowing, vivid against that sky.

"I didn't think I was, Melissa, though I can see it might sound like pretty superficial silver-lining stuff. What I meant . . . I've been through some bad times too, and I know the way you make it is by hanging on to anything you can—anything, everything, you can find in your life that's good—hanging on to that by your teeth if you have to. That's what I meant.

"I just pass that on as a tip, to help you. I think you will make it. If you're Sarah's kid—and Brooks's—then I think you'll make it. But I thought maybe I could pass on one of the tricks for doing it."

"Thanks." She rubbed at her eyes with the backs of her fists. "Every time I see you I end up crying."

"Here." He gave her a handkerchief. He wanted to put an arm around her shoulders, but didn't. He waited while she wiped.

"Thanks. But you will try to find them?"

"I will try."

"Oh, thank you! Thank you!" She flung her arms around him, hugging, then suddenly stiffened and drew back. "Oh. I'm sorry. I didn't mean . . ."

"I know. It's all right."

But self-consciousness engulfed her now, embarrassment. She wasn't sure yet how to express affection by degrees. Marley tried to cover for her. "I'll get right on it." He patted the back of her hand, feeling the gesture awkward but (he hoped) avuncular, to prove that some kinds of touches were permitted.

"You'll need to know about them. You'll need a picture, won't you? Come on, I'll get my album."

Marley had a picture; but then, he had come there for any detail he could find. "Okay, sure. Let's see what you have."

She sprang up, darting two steps ahead and then back to him, leading toward the house, like a puppy trying to drag him by her own enthusiasm.

"Mrs. Gaskill! Mr. Marley's going to find— He's going to *try* to find my parents!"

Mrs. Gaskill looked up from her book, smiling at seeing Melissa's joy, but perhaps also sensing Marley's reserve. "That's wonderful, Melissa."

"I'm going to get my album. I'll be right back." Melissa started to dash into the house, caught herself.

But Mrs. Gaskill nodded. "Good." She turned back to Marley, letting Melissa go in alone. "It would be very good for Melissa if she were with her parents. Do you think you will be able to find them?"

"I don't know. Actually, I have been looking for her mother. Mrs. Ten Broeck asked me to do that a week ago. I haven't had any luck so far. Mrs. Ten Broeck didn't want me to tell Melissa, but I didn't see how I could refuse to say I'd try."

"Yes."

"If she talks about it—try to keep her from building too much on it, will you?"

"Yes."

Marley sensed her brief replies affirmed a breadth of understanding. He liked her. She seemed to be that sort of calmly cheery, self-contained person whom everybody likes. She had a pleasantly attractive face: probably never really pretty, but good-looking enough. Getting on in middle age now— And then with that increasingly familiar shock, Marley recognized she was about his age.

"What are you reading?" he asked.

"Jane Eyre."

"Ah. You're reading it with Melissa?"

"No. We may. I may have her read it. I'm rereading some of the classics. My husband was in the English Department at Wellesley. I'm rereading some things to see what I think of them from my own perspective."

Marley caught the past tense. "What does your husband do now?"

"I'm a widow."

"Ah. I'm sorry."

"My husband and my son were killed in an automobile accident five years ago." She gave him the fact, not as though it didn't matter, but not disclosing the extent of her grief.

"I'm sorry." Marley respected her tone, and went on. "So, you're in the tutor business."

"Yes. Education is the only trade I'd ever been exposed to. I had a good education myself, up through college—and an excruciatingly proper background, but no advanced degrees. So, I couldn't teach formally without going back to school. And I enjoy working with young people individually."

"If they're like Melissa, I can understand that."

"Yes. They aren't all. But most of the ones I've worked with are really very good."

"You travel around from manor to manor? It sounds sort of eighteenth-century."

"Yes. It's interesting. If they put me too far below the salt I don't stay. I still have an apartment in Wellesley."

"Do you? I have one in Boston."

"It's a very nice city, isn't it? I thought of moving in from Wellesley. There are so many associations there, of course. But I have friends. And you can't run away from things, can you? You just have to pick up and go on.''

''Yes.''

''Here!'' Every attempt at maturity abandoned, Melissa ran out to them as she had run in. She put on the table, in front of Marley, a green leather, gold-leafed photo album. She opened it for him as if it were the Scripture. ''There they are! That's them: my father and mother! When they were in college.''

There they were, again, as always. Melissa looked at the two of them as Brooks looked at Sarah, as a dream embodied; and Sarah looked out at reality.

''This is the only picture I have of my mother.''

Melissa's tone made Marley vow to himself that if Sarah lived, he would find her. She turned the page. ''Here are father's baby pictures. They probably won't help you much.'' Yet she lingered. ''Wasn't he cute?'' she asked before turning to the next.

Every stage of Brooks's life was pictured; and Melissa knew what story went with each. ''He won a prize for composition. . . . He loved animals. . . . He could play the flute just beautifully. Isn't he handsome!''

Home for the holiday, hirsute but trim, in jacket and tie, he stood in front of the Christmas tree, arm around Mrs. Ten Broeck's waist—the last picture, that last Christmas. He smiled for the camera, for the occasion, but his eyes looked anguished.

''He's a very nice-looking man, Melissa.''

''Do you think you can find him?''

''I don't know. I'll try,'' Marley lied.

*   *   *

Gray clay spun smooth and wet under the woman's fingers. She kept her eyes on Marley, sure by touch alone of the shape her vase was taking. Obviously, she couldn't stop in the middle of throwing the thing, but could deal with a customer while her hands were busy. "Hi," she called over the rumble.

"Hello," he said. "My name is James Marley. I wrote you a letter about a week ago. I'm trying to locate Sarah Kleinhagen. You didn't answer, but I was passing through the area, and thought I might as well stop by."

"I didn't answer because I don't know where she is. Would you like to buy a pot?"

He scanned the shelves across the front and one side of the shop. She had her wheel at the other side, where she could run it and the shop at once. From a back room her kiln preserved in the place an artificial summertime. Marley began to sweat in his tweed jacket; she kept cool working in a cotton T-shirt. Her breasts showed through it. But, of course, he thought, she was of that generation that equated bralessness with integrity.

"They're very nice. I'm not asking anyone to tell me where she is, only to pass the word to her that her daughter needs her."

"You said that. What kind of a pot were you looking for?"

"Her daughter really needs her very badly. I've just seen her. I was over at Brooks Ten Broeck's home—Mrs. Ten Broeck's—and thought I'd stop here on the way back to Boston. Brooks mentions you often in his letters. You must have been very close to

Sarah. This one's very nice. I like the looseness of the design in the glaze. It's almost Japanese.''

"I studied for three years in Japan. Fellowship. If I could help you, I surely would." She looked like a person who smiled easily, but after her first greeting had chosen not to do so. When she loosened her coarse hair (if she ever did) it probably framed and softened; pulled tight and braided, it made her face more than plain: severe.

"Professor Bascaglia says that sometimes Sarah comes by to visit him. I thought perhaps she might come over here too."

"The ones on the bottom shelf, in the corner, are Japanesey too. Actually, I've been trying to work away from doing that too literally. Just keep the spirit.''

Marley examined the Japanesey ones, and then some mugs above them. He tried to sense how to get on a better side of her. "I'm really not connected with the police,'' he said. "I don't care—I don't want to know anything about what anybody did back then. I would like to know something about what Sarah was like, just so that I can come up with ideas about how to get this message to her. Can you tell me about her?'' She seemed intent on getting the rim right. "What pot would you like me to buy?''

"You don't have to buy a pot unless you like it. That's very insulting.''

Marley regarded her for a moment, turned, and left the shop, the bell on the door jingling behind him. Before it could stop he shook it again, coming back in.

"Hello, there!'' he said, smiling broadly. "I'm

James Marley. Could you tell me something about Sarah Kleinhagen? I might even buy a pot, too, while I'm here. If I see something I like. If that wouldn't offend you.''

It took her a beat to decide. Then the humor he thought he had seen in her face came back. "Hi. I'm Francey Straub. What would you like to know?''

"What Sarah was like. What her interests were. Why . . .'' He thought, finally, he might ask it. "Why did she fall in love with Brooks Ten Broeck?''

"I can think of about ten million reasons! Bite my tongue! Well, I mean, when a man is intelligent, charming, politically and socially concerned, sensitive, and not *bad*-looking, a person shouldn't hold against him he's rich, should they?''

"I thought Sarah—all of you—were against capitalism and wealth.''

"Not all of us. I mean, Sarah was socially committed—straight arrow. But she didn't have anything against money. She liked a lot of the things you can get with money. She just thought everybody ought to have an equal chance to get some.''

"A leveler-up.''

"Yeah. We used to have some pretty heavy sessions about that with some of the other guys.''

"But you don't mean it was just Brooks's money?''

"Oh, no. Brooks . . . He and Sarah . . . I mean, you got to remember how it was then. I mean, we were into the Revolution, except it was the Weather*men* at first? You know, some of the guys thought *they* were supposed to *man* the barricades and make the speeches, and the women were supposed to run the mimeographs and be available for screws. Well, Sarah wasn't about to let herself be screwed by anybody—in any sense. She could write better speeches, and give them better, and she was a lot smarter than most of them. So, you know, they respected her and resented her too. She was kind of a virgin queen: All the guys had the hots for her. Well, you must have seen pictures of her: those cheekbones—and she had a kind of low, Lauren Bacall voice. I used to try to talk the way she did, and we'd get lower and lower until we could hardly hear each other. And I know she was no prude. But they didn't want her on her terms, and she wouldn't have them on theirs.

"Then, the next year, along came Brooks. He was smart. Brooks was really brilliant, sensitive. . . . What did I say? Charming, et cetera, et cetera. *And* rich. And he *adored* her. Well, come on! Why shouldn't she fall in love with him? I mean, so he was more like an Einstein teddy bear than Tom Selleck. So you close your eyes."

She took a wire, looped it around the base of the vase, and deftly cut it away from the wheel.

Marley said, "I've read his letters. I know he was really infatuated with her."

Swinging on her high stool, she put the piece on a shelf behind her, then dug more clay from a plastic trash container and plopped it down on the wheel. "In love, in love. I mean, Brooks was very super extremely idealistic. Well, he could afford to be. I mean, I guess everything he ever wanted Mrs. Ten Broeck got for him. I don't mean he was bratty-spoiled. God! Just the opposite. He never whined or threw a tantrum. It was sort of that he expected if you ask, please, very nicely, you can have it. So he thought the world was just a peachy place. And when he found it wasn't, he was very upset about that, and he thought something ought to be done about it right away. And there was Sarah, who was there ahead of him and knew exactly what to do—and was gorgeous and sexy besides, and who liked him. What's the matter with her kid?''

''She's coming into adolescence, and she needs some help.''

''Oh, that. Who doesn't?''

''Badly.'' It was the first time Marley had said anything at all about Melissa's trouble. But Francey seemed to be the kind of person who (when she decided she would tell) told all; and he caught her openness. ''What were Sarah's interests, hobbies?''

''Poetry. That was really going to be, you know, her vocation. Going out for a walk or a picnic in the country—it was a lot less built up around the valley then. And then, of course, the Movement. I mean, that's what most of us were working on most of the time, except for a little while with the books now and then to keep from flunking.''

She pummeled the clay, then started the wheel again. Marley watched as she formed the lump into a uniform mass with the flat of her palm.

''Is there anything else you can tell me?''

''Such as what?''

''I don't know. Do you see her?''

She regarded him for another moment. ''Sometimes.''

''Okay. If you do, if you have any way, pass the message. Will you?''

''Sure.''

"You do make nice pots."

"Yeah, I know."

"It must be nice. . . . If 'the Movement' didn't change the world, at least you ended up making nice pots."

"What do you mean? What do you mean! We made them end the war, didn't we? Every time they want to send in the Marines now, the country says, 'No more Vietnams!' And who's Jim Crow? And you just try not giving equal pay for equal work, or . . . or dumping your toxic waste. Okay, they try; but they get sued and they lose. What do you mean, we didn't change the world?"

"I'm sorry. I've just heard some people who were involved say—"

"Assholes! What do they expect for only twenty years work?" She looked down suddenly at her wheel. "Shit! I can't argue and throw at the same time." She stopped it turning, beat the clay down into a lump again.

"I think I would like to buy a pot," Marley said.

"Mr. Marley?" The woman's voice sounded bright, good-humored, yet firm and businesslike. Marley instantly assumed he'd won a prize, and all he had to do to collect was to—

"Yes?"

"This is Catherine Gorman O'Keefe. I received a letter from you concerning Sarah Kleinhagen."

"Oh, yes."

"I think I may be able to help you."

"That's very good news."

"I prefer not to discuss this over the phone. Could we get together?"

"Certainly. Where? When?"

"I live in Somerville. Just off Davis Square. Would you like to come by? This evening maybe?"

They agreed on 7:30, and she gave him directions. She said "See you then" with an enthusiasm suggesting she'd be counting the minutes.

Marley checked his notes to see who she was. Catherine Gorman: not a person he'd really hoped for help from. Not mentioned in Brooks's letters. Her name had appeared as one of six, including Sarah's, on a letter to the *Sophian*. He'd taken her name and sent his own letter to her because he was trying anyone.

He found the house easily in an old blue-collar neighborhood now being whitened. Three-story houses stood shoulder to shoulder on both sides of the street. One had a bathtub Madonna in front, another a plastic gnome. The address he'd been given displayed itself in bright brass numerals on a house as old as the others, but with new windows, new paint, new bushes on either side of a new brick stoop. The sidewalk in front was new brick, too, with spaces left for saplings still supported by stakes and wires. It all made him think of a cleaning lady who'd won the lottery. He went up on the porch and rang the bell, and Catherine Gorman O'Keefe came to meet him— not so soon as to suggest that she'd been by the door, but quickly enough that she'd been waiting for him.

"Mrs. O'Keefe? James Marley."

"Catherine. Yes, hello!" She offered her hand, and gave him a firm, dry squeeze and a wide, warm smile. A pin-striped skirt (she wasn't wearing the jacket at home) and tailored blouse, but a floppy soft blue bow at her throat: a professional person, properly dressed, but who wasn't attempting to hide that she was a woman. "Please come in."

A man stood framed by the arch to the left, greeting smile already in place, so Marley got only a glance at the hall: white walls, dark newel elaborately turned, framed photo of something in mist over an antique chest with yellow flowers on it.

"This is my husband, Mickey."

"James Marley."

"Hi, Jim. It's a real pleasure to meet you!" His handshake was firmer, drier, held longer than hers, his smile even brighter. Perhaps it seemed brighter because it was bigger: face broad, jaw strong, chin cleft. A full, dark mustache set off his really good teeth. Blue eyes. Marley expected the back of his hand to be tattooed.

"James. If you don't mind. I've never felt like I was a Jim."

"Sure thing, James. Come on in." He released Marley's hand, and with his own extended the hospitality of his living room. Leather and chrome. Bright cushions. An "electronic entertainment center"—racks of records and tapes, big screen, brushed-steel components, controls enough to fly to the moon. "Get you a drink? Coffee, something?"

"Thanks, no. I just finished dinner before coming over. Lovely place you have here."

"Thanks! Yeah, these old houses have so much more scale, graciousness. And they built them to last."

"Quite a change in the neighborhood. I haven't been up this way—beyond Harvard Square—in several years."

"Tremendous. Extending the T into Davis Square upscaled the whole area. It was going down to used furniture and second-hand-clothes stores; now it's antiques and boutiques. Fantastic opportunities—new-wave enterprises, far-sighted real estate investment." His eyes lifted from Marley's to those sights and came back, as though to suggest they weren't too far, and Marley might see them, too, if he looked.

Catherine came up beside her husband, put her hand on his arm, but spoke to Marley. "As you may suspect, James, Mickey is in development."

"A good thing to be in, I imagine."

Mickey grinned like a boy who knows where the pies are cooling. "Well, I won't give you the promotion now, James; but if ever you should be interested . . ."

"Thanks. I will keep it in mind. However, right now I'm interested . . ."

"Sure. Sit down. Please."

Marley sat on one end of the couch. Catherine sat on the other, and her husband took what was clearly his chair, a large leather one that swiveled and tipped. He didn't make use of those amenities though. While Marley did sit back in his place, the others perched.

"So, Catherine, you said you could help me find Sarah Kleinhagen."

"I hope so, James. But first, I'd like to know more about why you want to find her. Your letter said her daughter needed her, but that's not very specific."

"It's about as specific as I can be, except to say

the need *is* urgent.'' Marley saw this information registered, but if it provoked an emotional response in either of them, that response was not sympathy or compassion.

Mickey asked, "Do we take it there is some sort of health problem?"

"I really have to respect the confidence and privacy of the girl, Melissa, and of her guardian. Again, I can tell you there is a certain problem, it is serious, and that finding Sarah will help to solve it."

Catherine asked, "Ah, the girl's guardian . . . I know that Sarah had a child by Brooks Ten Broeck. Is the guardian a member of the Ten Broeck family?"

"Why do you ask?"

Mickey answered. "Because . . . obviously, we— Catherine wants to help in any way she can, but we were wondering is the girl's guardian offering any sort of . . . consideration for this information?"

"Consideration?"

"Consideration." Mickey looked levelly at Marley. "Let's be direct about it. Payment."

"I could put the matter to her."

Catherine was as steady. "I hope you won't think us too mercenary, James . . .''

Marley sensed with certainty that she didn't care what he thought.

". . . but the Ten Broecks are very rich people, and *they* didn't get that way by giving things away."

"What sort of consideration did you have in mind?"

"In exchange for a down payment I would give you this information. Assuming that it enabled you to achieve your objective, then I would expect an additional amount.''

"What kind of figure are you thinking about?" Marley looked back and forth at each of them, but they didn't look at each other. Evidently they had worked it out before he came.

Mickey spoke for them again. "I think we ought to let the guardian suggest a figure. If, as you say, the problem is serious, then I would assume the figure would reflect that; and we'd be able to judge whether this information is important."

"Exactly what information do you have? Do you know where Sarah is?"

They'd anticipated that question, of course, and it was Catherine's to answer. "I think our point is that we're not prepared to give any information—answer any questions—until we understand the basis on which we're working here."

"I see. However, it's hardly possible for any offer to be made until I can advise Melissa's guardian of what she would be offering on—what its worth might be."

They did glance at each other then. Catherine returned to the prepared position. "I believe I can be of help in finding Sarah."

"You were two classes behind her, weren't you? She was a junior when you started at Smith. She left in the middle of that year because she was pregnant. That means you overlapped by only a few months."

"We kept in touch. She lived in a house with some other people over in Amherst—near the U Mass. We kept in touch. And after she left." She looked at Marley with an unswerving, determined directness that convinced him she was lying.

"So you feel you knew her fairly well."

"I feel that, yes."

"What was she like? As you knew her?" Marley asked with apparently genuine curiosity, as though wanting to know about Sarah were his only objective.

Catherine seemed to assume, though, that the point of the question was to check her credentials. Marley wasn't sure how much of her pause was given to considering whether to answer, and how much to what.

"Joan of Arc. I guess that's what she seemed like. I guess that's how she thought of herself. She was widely known—some might say notorious—in the whole college area, not only at Smith, but Amherst, the University. She was quite imposing. You know she's very tall, and she had the look we were all trying to have then: long, straight hair, hardly any bosom. You know, skinny and intense."

Marley thought he detected both deprecation and wistfulness. Catherine was short, her hair was sand-colored and kinky, and—though she must diet and work out, and had herself under control—she tended toward pudge.

"She was rather intimidating; but of course that was the time when we all were being brothers and sisters and nonelitist, so of course . . . She had a great knack for not coming across as at all superior while letting you know she was. Well, maybe she was. She was one of those people, you know, who got A's and never seemed to have to study, and couldn't understand that some of the rest of us did.

"I don't claim that I was extremely close to Sarah, but I did know her."

"You weren't involved in the raid on Westhover, were you?"

"I certainly was not! I had nothing to do with that group. I wrote some letters—signed some letters, with other people; and I helped Professor Bascaglia in Holyoke. But I had nothing to do with any illegal activities. Nothing whatsoever."

"I see. May I ask what you do now?"

"I'm an attorney."

"Really?"

"Yes."

"Did you know the FBI may still be looking for Sarah?"

"They are?"

"I'm told they may be. If you know where she is, you ought to tell them. As a matter of fact, I think they'd be put out if you knew and didn't tell them. Especially as you're an officer of the court."

"Are you threatening my wife?" Mickey spoke calmly, just getting the facts on the table as a businessman who believed in directness.

"I hope not."

"It wouldn't be in your interest if the FBI got Sarah, would it? Then she wouldn't be able to help her daughter."

"Oh, yes. She's not wanted except for questioning. There's no charge. Still, I would think that anyone who knew where she is and didn't tell might be considered obstructing." Marley seemed to offer only an opinion on the deal they were discussing. "You'd probably know the law better than I, Catherine."

Catherine and Mickey conferred again in a glance. They had made a mistake, Marley appreciated, in sitting so near and opposed to him. They'd meant to be two against one, but that forced them to turn heads and show him when they weren't sure.

Mickey tried the save. "I don't think Catherine said she knew where Sarah is. I think she said she believed she could help you find her."

"How is she going to help me find her if she doesn't know where Sarah is?"

"I believe I might know some people who might know. I have a high level of confidence that I might be of help. But I don't think—legally—that's at all the same as saying I'm withholding any sort of information in a way that could be construed as obstructing justice."

"I'm sure you're right, Catherine."

There was a moment of silence while they waited for the next move. Then Marley smiled at them, slapped his hands down on the tops of his thighs, and rose. "Well. I certainly do appreciate your offer of help. It's nice to know somebody cares. We'll consider your offer, and if we want to take you up, I'll get back to you. Lovely house. You've done a lot to it, I can tell."

Mickey was up at once. "Thanks. It's really been fun fixing it up. I grew up on the next block, and it's a great satisfaction to me to see the neighborhood come up again."

Catherine got herself up too, got on her don't-worry, we're-going-to-win-this-case face. "Thanks so much for stopping by, James. I do hope you'll let me help."

"Thank you, Catherine. I certainly will think about what you've said."

"Good. By the way, James, if I may ask, are you an attorney yourself, or a private detective? What is your interest in this matter?"

"No, I'm not a detective or attorney. This isn't my usual line of work. I'm just doing this for Mrs. Ten Broeck because she needed some help."

"I see. But, if you don't mind my asking, you are being compensated?"

Marley kept right on smiling. "Yes, I am."

"I would have thought so. And rightly so too."

They all kept right on smiling, but Marley managed to get away without shaking hands again. As he walked out to the street he fantasized about coming back in the middle of the night and heaving a bomb onto their porch.

Marley poured a slug of Scotch. Taking a sip helped, but some of the bad taste remained. He started to carry the drink to the living room, but paused, then swerved to his bedroom instead. He'd hung up his jacket when he came in, put pens and notebook on the dresser. He opened the notebook to the rear, where he kept his tally pages. He studied the entries. He decided the actual out-of-pocket expenses were fair. He crossed out the record of his time.

He went back to the kitchen, put some ice in his glass, sat down in the living room with the Mayans. He was near the end of the book, and they were about to vanish. That would happen abruptly (he knew how the story came out) and then there would be the chapter of guesses why. Although interested, he didn't get to it that evening. He kept looking through the printing on the pages and thinking "Joan of Arc. . . ."

CHAPTER 4

Marley smelled trouble, literally, instantly. He froze, left hand still on the knob of the hall-closet door. An odor that was not the smell of his apartment, faint but definite, tinged the air. It was not simply a smell like garlic, or curry, or the scent of flowers bought on impulse on his way home the day before, an aroma not normal, but frequently there, and therefore accepted. This was foreign; it didn't belong. It was perfume, heavier than a woman's perfume—after-shave, men's perfume.

He had noticed no tampering at his door. He had a good lock. Someone might have broken in at the back though. Someone had gotten in somehow. Was he there now?

Marley stood absolutely still. His heartbeat shot up, but he kept breathing carefully, quietly, and listened. For a minute. For two.

He wore a raincoat and jacket. They'd encumber him if he had to fight. But he wouldn't want to be caught while taking them off. He thought about that. And whether to go back outside quickly, and what he'd do then—call for police? What would he tell

them? Or whether to make more noise in the hall and
give the intruder time to go out through the back
again. Or whether he should try to catch whoever it
was, and that that was probably a stupid idea, but he
wanted to know who it was. Someone being there
made him angry.

Marley thought all that together without directing
his mind to any of it. He focused attention on being
still and listening and trying to feel if someone lurked
there now. The hairs on the back of his neck were
up.

Cars went by on the street below, their single
passages rushing up and hushing into the constant
distant din from Boylston Street and all around. His
refrigerator hummed, two rooms away. Overhead,
through muffling wood and plaster, through the
Cosentinos' cushy carpet, he barely heard their stereo
speakers woofing syncopated bass notes.

Another three minutes. Rock-and-roll in a car outside. A heehaw siren on Storrow Drive. Marley reached
the point of hearing a high-pitched tone he suspected
was his own bloodstream. But he heard nothing he
thought he shouldn't. Perhaps whoever it was was
gone.

The sounds he heard were always there. It was
never silent in the city. And never dark. Unless he
drew the blinds and curtains, light from the street
was always enough to read a book with dilated eyes.

His were not. He'd turned the hall light on when
he came in, and been standing there for a full two
minutes now. If he was going to go on in, he should
either turn it off and wait, or turn others on as he

went. He decided that light would give him an advantage over anyone who'd been waiting without it.

He decided to leave the coat and jacket on.

He moved slowly. Like the Cosentinos, Marley was considerate of people below: his wall-to-wall was thick and padded. He made no noise.

He crept up to the living room entrance. He set himself, then came around fast, sweeping his hand up to hit the switch.

Blue-white light flashed, striking his eyes like a sheet of heated steel. The impact blinded him, shocked him with fear, staggered him backward. Wheeling around, back against hall wall, he flung his arms in front of his face to ward whatever attack might come through the red void whirling before him.

He cowered, defenseless; but nothing hit him. Gradually the red shape darkened, blackened, shrank, was only in his eyes when he blinked. Nothing hit him; no one was there. Nothing moved in the dark living room; he heard no sound. In another minute he went back in, turned on a lamp—looking away as he did. The lamp that was controlled from the wall switch had been moved out into the room, its shade taken off, a photo flash put in. Nothing else had been disturbed.

Marley went on to the dining room. Again averting his eyes, he put on the light over the table. No flash. The dimmer brought soft light up slowly. The entire set of his Czech crystal goblets had been carried from the cabinet and placed on the table by someone who understood their delicacy. Downlight filled the glasses to glowing and sparkled around their thin rims. They were set in a careful circle under the light, its many tiny bulbs reflected, multiplied, over the curves of their graceful bowls: a miniature galaxy, glittering, around a hammer brought from the back-hall toolrack.

The tremor in Marley's fingertips moved up his arms and set his hands shaking—not because of fear any longer: It was anger rising to rage. He clenched his fists to quell it.

He was sure now no one was there. Still, he moved with caution. Even so, he nearly stepped on the snake.

It coiled on the floor just inside his bedroom doorway, wedge-shaped head raised, drawn back in that tight flat *S*, tensed to strike. Shocked by an icy jolt of horror, Marley stood transfixed, staring as though to learn by heart the diamond design flowing down its back. He had reached for the light switch, seen it, frozen. It was lit from behind him, from the hall, with the light and doorway shadow slant across it, half its body wound in darkness. Its tiny eye was fixed, and glinted.

Marley stood like stone, his mind as frantic as his muscles were still. He knew he couldn't move faster than it could—to hit or kick it, or jump away. He mustn't try, mustn't move. If he didn't move, it might not strike. It must be as terrified as he. If he didn't move, it might retreat. His arm still outstretched toward the switch, growing stiff and heavy, wanting to waver, Marley held himself immobile, staring at the snake, willing it to loosen its coil, to flow through its own loops and slither.

It didn't move.

It was a rattlesnake, not a big one, but large enough to be deadly.

It didn't move.

A rattlesnake with its rattle raised, but silent. Its tongue was out, but didn't flicker.

Suddenly Marley's heart started again. He could feel every squeeze as it pumped, felt the surge in every vein. He could breathe, and took huge lungfuls. Shudder after shudder ran down his back. He forced his arm to lift, to turn on the light. Still thrilled by terror, he made himself lean over and pick the thing up. Seen in more light it was less convincing; it was hollow and light, the plastic stiff. Yet he had to summon all his will to touch it.

He guessed there'd be something in every room, and there was. An unopened can of Drāno stood on top of his sugar canister. When he opened the medicine cabinet, a scroll rolled down with *BANG!* printed on it in red felt-tipped pen. A rubber tarantula lay on the pillow of the guest room bed.

There wasn't a trick or mocked-up threat in his study. The folder on Sarah had been brought from his file, laid on his desk; the lists and notes had been taken away. One sheet of paper was rolled into his machine, "STOP LOOKING FOR SARAH KLEINHAGEN" typed on it.

Marley sat in his regular chair in his living room, the place where he might feel most secure. He sat, though, still wearing his outdoor coat, and his hands still shook. By concentrating he could control the quiver enough to get the glass of Scotch to his mouth. Gradually the Dutch courage helped him tame the

terror, and he breathed deeply, set his smile, and got
his wrath recaged.

Marley was angry, very angry, but that was all
right. He smothered the fury: the outrage at his home
being violated, the fear and impotence turned into
bloodlust. He fisted his anger into the tight, hard
kind. It focused and sharpened.

He thought about the person who'd done these
things. He hated that person, and respected him too.
The man had broken and entered, taken some papers;
but hadn't committed one serious crime. Nothing of
value stolen, nothing damaged, no one injured. Yet
he had threatened everything in Marley's existence.
He had shown he could come and go in Marley's
home—in his life—at will. He'd shown he could see
what Marley admired, found precious, that his sensi-
bility, so acute, would know what to smash, how to
do it to cause the most exquisite pain. He'd shown he
could maim or kill, not merely by those devices
displayed, but by an infinity of others equally arcane.
By that he'd shown that no moment of Marley's life
would be secure: No door could be opened, no shoe
put on. Marley could never brush his teeth free from
fear. And the overkill: Any one of the tricks would
have made the man's point. And the humor.

Marley sipped Scotch, hated that man, thought
about what to do. Marley wasn't heroic. There had
been times when the odds were too great and he'd cut
and run. But this time . . . He couldn't abandon
Melissa, and . . . And this time he was really angry.

He finished half the Scotch he'd poured, then took
off his raincoat, jacket, and tie and hung them away.
He put the bulb back in the living room lamp, the

glasses back in the cabinet (one at a time, as he always handled them) the hammer and Drāno in the back hall. He tossed the creepy-crawlies into the trash. It all had to be done, and doing it gave him a sense of restoring order, of taking control again.

When he had that sense he returned to his chair and his drink and began to think out what to do. He assumed, first, that the person—or persons—who'd threatened him were the ones Professor Bascaglia had warned of. He could probably get their names; but what was the point? Unless the professor knew where they lived, and could be made to tell, Marley wouldn't know where to find them. However (point two), he didn't have to find them. They'd found him. They must be nearby.

He tried to put the anger aside. What he should do was call the FBI. They would be interested, take action (as the Boston police might not) because they already wanted whoever had threatened him. They would give him protection, and might capture Whoever. Such capture wouldn't bring Marley the savage joy of personal physical vengeance; but getting them without seeking that should afford him greater satisfaction.

But if he brought in the FBI, there'd be no getting rid of them. They'd want to know about his search for Sarah. They'd intervene, interfere. What little hope he had that one of Sarah's friends might help would vanish totally. How would Bascaglia react if he knew Marley was directly in touch with the FBI? He was the person so far who offered the best chance of contact with her. And even if they'd lie back, let him go on, and just report, how could he go on? It was one thing to try to find Sarah, try to persuade her to come out of hiding, let her make a choice and deal with the Feds if she had to. How could he knowingly, secretly, lead them to her?

He couldn't; so he couldn't call the FBI. But he had to protect himself; he had to neutralize Whoever if he was going to go on with his search. How? He tried to analyze the facts.

He'd been out for supper. After spending all day inside he hadn't wanted to cook, had wanted to get some air. He'd walked over to Boylston, gone to a trattoria there. He hadn't been away more than an hour and a half.

The enemy must have seen him go, and followed him, in order to know how long he'd be away. To know now if he'd been sufficiently frightened and given up, they'd have to keep watching him.

For a few moments he fantasized trapping them. He saw himself getting around behind them, like Steve McQueen in *Bullitt*. But it would be foolhardy to try that alone. The way to do it would be to have help, to set up an ambush. He thought about that. He could get help. By being connected with David Cheyney he could get most anything. He could call Harvey Curtis, head of security at Dynatech. He could rent a couple of Harvey's men. The pictures flashed in his mind: leading his enemies into some dead end, or even just closing in, crowding them shoulder to shoulder out on the street.

And then what? Kill them? Obviously, that couldn't be thought of. Turn them in? There he was, back at the FBI.

Whatever his anger, his fantasies, he didn't really

want to catch them, not now, at least. He simply had
to neutralize them and get on with his work. He
could buy some protection: one man to stay in the
condo, a bodyguard to go around with him. They'd
have to be paid for; he wasn't working for David.
Well, Mrs. Ten Broeck could afford it.

He wondered how much it might be. Two men, for
how many days? Maybe, when his enemies saw him
protected, they'd give it up. The trouble was, his
defense would be passive. That was the value of the
FBI: They would go after whoever was threatening,
which would either catch them or scare them off.

Suddenly Marley smiled to himself. It felt so good
to be a genius.

He came out of the condo at 8:30 the next morning. He paused on the front steps and looked back
and forth as though he were trying to cover his
checking by checking the weather. The sky at that
moment was clear, but so intense as to worry any
mistruster of things too good.

Marley went toward the Gardens. He paused at
Arlington, waited through Walk until it flashed Don't,
then dashed. The red was on before he reached the
other side, holding traffic at the mouth of Marlborough. It seemed a clever ploy. But one man got out
of the car that had drifted down the block behind
him. He waited at the crossing for the next light,
easily keeping Marley in sight as he went into the
Public Gardens.

It was too early in the day for strolling tourists.
Most people passing through the Gardens were moving briskly to work. Marley matched their pace, some-

times skipping a step or lengthening his stride to keep among momentary congestions. The stratagem hid him instant by instant; but without alleys for him to spring to for cover, the man who followed could lie well back, equally hidden, without any fear of being shaken.

Chill air foretold that fall would come to Boston too, but none of the leaves had started to turn. There still would be days for the office girls to sun at lunchtime.

Marley reached Beacon but didn't cross. He did cross Charles, then took the first path back into the Common. Continuing his blending-into-the crowd device, he worked the long diagonal over to Park and Tremont. Pausing, he scanned all around, then suddenly turned and lemminged with the mob down the stairs of the Park Street station. If he hadn't paused to check, if he'd gone around the crowd at the entrance and then slipped in with it, he might have escaped undetected. As it was, the follower saw him descend and broke into a run to catch up.

Park Street was an ideal place to throw off pursuit. It was the hub of all of the underground lines. Marley used it in a most clever way: At the bottom of the stairs he drew to one side, pausing a moment, then forced his way through the cascade and into the counterstream of commuters arriving—up the escalator, back out of the station. He kept his head down while riding up.

But his timing seemed off. The man who was tailing him was on the stairs as Marley passed (looking away) but not too far to fight his way up again.

Back on the surface Marley appeared to feel secure. He set off on Tremont Street, moving quickly, making use of groups of people, but not deviating from the direct route to Government Center.

He found the directory, located the office of the FBI. The man whom he hadn't managed to shake let him go up alone.

It was over an hour later when Marley came down. Another man was with him, a stocky man, short-cropped hair now silver, wearing a three-piece suit, but looking as though when younger he'd probably posed for Marine Corps posters.

Almost as soon as they reached the street a car drew up for them. It took them back near Marley's apartment, but let him out around the corner two blocks away. He walked on home while the car pulled up by a fire hydrant. Shortly afterward another car with two well-dressed men in it came down Marlborough and parked in the No Stopping zone at the Berkley Street corner. In ten minutes more an AAA Acme pest-control van double-parked outside Marley's condo, and two men wearing coveralls carried black cases inside. One of the men was the silver-haired man, entirely unconvincing as a trapper of termites.

"All set, Mr. Curtis."

"Good. Thanks a lot, Tommy. Okay, James. Now, you've got fifteen seconds from the time you first start to open the door coming in. That ought to be plenty. But don't loiter. Once that thing goes off . . . More than about five seconds can damage your hearing permanently. You just flip this switch down." Curtis pointed to the toggle on the panel's face. "To arm it again, you have to hold this button down while you flip the switch up to On. The red light, here, will come on.''

"Right.''

"If we wanted to take some more time, we could hide it better; but even if they guess we've got something like this in here, I don't think they'll find it in time." He closed the antique washstand door.

"I doubt they'll even try. I really do appreciate this, Harvey.''

"My pleasure.''

"I never expected you to involve yourself in this personally.''

"It's kind of fun. Breaks up the week.''

"And I said a couple of men.''

"Well, if you're going to do a thing . . .''

"You'll send me a bill.''

"I'll send you a bill.''

"I mean it, Harvey.''

"Okay, I'll send you a bill. I'll just deduct what I owe you, and then you can owe me. Okay?''

"Thanks, Harvey.''

"My pleasure. How long do you want to keep them going, outside?''

"Just till tomorrow morning. I'm going out of town for a day—at least. Maybe one of your men could follow me to Logan. If I think I still need anything after I get back, I'll call you.''

"Don't you think we'd better keep at least one team around while you're gone? The Feds would.''

"I'm guessing they're already long gone.''

"Well, just to be sure. . . .''

*   *   *

In addition to feeling safe again, Marley went warm inside and suffered lump-in-throat whenever he looked from the window and saw his guards ostentatiously unobtrusive at either flank.

But the point of it all was to make it possible to go on looking for Sarah. He would have to justify the effort by being effective.

Simply sending letters to the names he'd found wasn't working. He could hope that the message might finally reach Sarah, and she might then call him. In the meantime, he would have to do something more. He had no new leads, so he'd have to do better by old ones.

It still seemed that Sarah's parents should be the best bet. He shouldn't have taken so flat a no for an answer. He had decided to see them. Face to face he might be able to persuade them to tell if they knew. At least, if he met them, he might judge if they were lying, and then he could try to work on that.

He went through all of his notes again to see if anyone else seemed worth a more intensive effort. (The notes taken from his file were the typed-up copies that he made for the sake of Being Well Organized. And the act of typing them helped him think them through. He did that again, copying out of the little notebook he kept always with him, replacing the ones Whoever had taken.)

Bascaglia, of course, should be tried again. He had lied at first about having seen Sarah. He might be lying yet. Marley called him.

"It's James Marley, Professor. I'm trying to find Sarah Kleinhagen, you remember?"

"Of course, Mr. Marley. Any luck?"

"Not yet. That's why I'm calling. I've taken your lead, Professor. I'm not asking anyone to tell me where Sarah is (if they know). But I am making another plea that if they do they ask her to contact me. The matter is urgent. If she'll contact me— She can do it in any way, meet me at a time and place of her own choosing, anything. No one need ever know where she's been, or what she's been doing, or who got my message to her. That's not important. But it is important—really important, for her daughter's sake—that I talk with her."

"I understand, Mr. Marley. I'd be happy to do whatever I can, but I really don't know what else I can do."

"If you might think some more about who might know— Or anyone who might know anyone. Again, I'm not asking you to tell me. Just contact them and have them pass the word."

"No one comes to mind, but I will think about it."

"Thank you, Professor. I'm trying anything."

"Yes. By the way, what sort of response did you get from her family? If you don't mind my asking."

"A two-line letter. Her father says he doesn't know where she is."

"I'm sure that's true. Sarah and her family had a falling-out."

"Did they? Well. I'm going to try them again anyway. I'm going to fly out there tomorrow to see them."

"I doubt it will do you any good."

"You never know. Even if they don't know where

she is, they can tell me things about her—personal things—that might give me ideas or leads.''

"I wish you luck with them. The parting must have been pretty bitter. I know Sarah is still bitter about it. Sometime I'd be interested to hear what they tell you.''

"Well, thank you, Professor.'' Marley considered telling him about the threats his former colleagues had made, but decided not to. It was probably better not to let anyone else know about that shadow over the search.

Whoever had taken Marley's typed notes had removed Sarah's picture too. But he hadn't gone all through Marley's files, and so had missed the other folder with the copies. Marley took out one to put into the restored dossier. He paused, then, and instead pinned it up to the corkboard over the desk. He studied her face, and found himself returning the smile she'd had for the camera.

CHAPTER 5

A dark speck shimmered at the horizon, then rose, materializing as a sharp-sided shaft. Gables faceted against flat white sky. It resolved into a grain elevator floating over level fields, its base erased by heat haze.

The air baked in the early October Indian summer. Marley had the dashboard vents open, his jacket off. He could have used the air-conditioning—the car he'd rented at O'Hare had it. He didn't like air-conditioning. He tried opening side windows, but at seventy miles an hour the wind roared and buffeted. Traffic was moderate, but all of it moved that fast and faster. The Highway Patrol didn't seem to care. One parked on a cross-track between north and south lanes, visible from two or three miles away on that road so straight and flat. Nobody slowed.

The grain elevator was sided with corrugated metal, not dark at all close up. Still, it made Marley think of a fairy-tale tower. Just past it he found the turnoff, the cluster of tall old trees, the frame houses with long front porches. Did people sit there summer nights, listening to crickets, distant barking, screen-door slams?

Or had the highway down the state—it couldn't take a curve because Illinois planners know only straight lines—driven folks to television? A steepleless church meant Jehovah's Witnesses to Marley, but the sign said Evangelical Lutheran. The gas station and garage (the only store in town) sold cigarettes, beer, sandwiches. Gasoline cost more than on the interstate, but the station hung on because of the services.

"Yes, sir! Check your oil?" Marley realized he was in the land of the big smile, a land where a boy just past high school could pump gas for a year or two but still expect to better himself. Marley smiled back. He'd been born in Vermont, but he'd traveled.

Kleinhagen place? Couldn't be missed. Left fork out of town, two sections over, turn right, go three. Big mailbox. Can't miss it.

Marley thought, you can't miss any place in that part of Illinois if you know north and can count: checkerboard fields, grid of roads—one each direction every mile, north and south, east and west. It would be a labyrinth, though, if you lost your place: no landmarks, no differences, just corn, the road, the ditches beside the road, the walls of tan corn. And flat: Drop a dime on edge, don't chase it—it'll roll all the way to Indiana.

Marley couldn't miss the Kleinhagen place—the mailbox, the gravel road dividing the corn. He didn't see the house, though, until nearly at the end of the drive. The field ended fifty yards from it. Fill had been brought in, a mound made to give the house some little prominence, a view over fields from the picture window. But the house was a low ranch, probably built in the mid-fifties, redwood-sided. A catalpa tree and some locusts shaded it. Flagstones curved down from front door to drive. Marley ignored them, continued to the back, to the family entrance by the attached garage.

A baby-blue Eldorado was berthed outside. The initials *GCK* in white script above the door handle personalized it. A maroon Mercedes stood at a disdainful distance. A Pontiac Trans Am had been slung in beyond, abandoned at an angle. The cars suggested more people than Marley had expected. He hadn't called. He hadn't wanted to be cut off or told not to come. He'd chanced no one being home, having to wait or come back, but had hoped by arriving in the late morning to find Sarah's mother alone.

He turned off the ignition, waited, not knowing the custom in Illinois. In the country, in Vermont, unless you knew the folks, you waited in the car until they came to the door. It wasn't just etiquette—there might be dogs who might not take to strangers.

A woman appeared at the aluminum screen door. She waited behind it, but smiled. Everybody had been smiling since he got on the plane at Logan. Marley doubted it could last. He got out and smiled back.

She opened the screen door. He knew he didn't look like a salesman to her. His suit was eastern cut, expensive-looking. He had a nice face, mature. He was smiling, but not too intensely.

"Mrs. Kleinhagen?"

"That's right."

He approached. "My name is James Marley. Forgive me for not calling before I came out. I just took

a chance on your being here." He said the last as
though it explained not calling. "I've come down
from Chicago." He came right up to her. "Actually,
I've come from Boston to see you." He wasn't too
forceful, not pushing, but he hoped she'd step back
and let him into the house.

She didn't. "What about?" She was pleasant, curious, but steadfast.

"Your daughter."

She didn't shut the door against him, only drew
her outstretched hand to herself, and the screen swung
back between them. "No. What. . . . No."

"You know your daughter has a daughter?" he
asked gently, in case she didn't.

She gave only a nod. Yes, she did know. Only the
fact. Nothing else about her only grandchild. Glare
on aluminum screening veiled her, but not enough.
Pain and grief weren't masked.

"Melissa," he said.

"Yes. Melissa. I know. Sarah always said if she
had a little girl she would call her Melissa. It was my
mother's . . ." Pain ate deeper, spreading. Her eyes
started to fill with it. She wouldn't weep, drew herself up. "We don't talk about Sarah. I'm sorry."

"Melissa needs her."

"I'm sorry. It's better not to."

"Melissa *needs* her. Your granddaughter. She's
having serious trouble, and she needs her mother."

"It's better not—"

"She's a young girl—a young woman; she feels
completely alone. She needs help. *She needs her
mother*."

"We don't talk. . . . It's better. . . ."

He wouldn't leave. He'd brought Melissa's need all that way, carried it heavy on him. The strain of that weight showed on his face. He faced her with it through the metal mesh. There was screen between them, but not the inner door shut yet. Sun beat hot on his back, sweat ran down inside his shirt.

Tears were running down her face. "We don't . . . You've seen her?"

"Yes."

"We put the past behind us. We don't talk about . . ." She shook her head slowly, not letting the pictures form, saying no, trying not to—failing. "What's she like?"

"She's pretty. Still a little babyish-looking. Lots of dark brown hair, curly, down over her shoulders. I brought a picture."

She had no more will to hold her hand back. Palm up, surrendering, she pushed open the screen.

"And these are some from the Kleinhagen family reunion in 1965. Oh, that was a wonderful one, that year! Most of the Kleinhagens moved on to Iowa, but they all still come back to Walt's father's place—actually it was his grandfather's, of course—every—"

The picture showed a dozen children old enough at least to hold a slice of watermelon, young enough to let themselves be taken silly—slices bit down the center, held to chin to frame the faces. Sarah was with them, but past the age, doing it for old times' sake, grinning with the rest, without the glee.

Marley looked at all the albums. "If you can't tell me where she is, I'd appreciate anything you can tell me about her." He'd come to the right place. He heard about, he saw, the thin little girl with Tonied curls—dark hair curly, down over her shoulders—assert herself, be plain in plain pigtails she could braid herself. He saw her on her pony, saw her on her horse. "Oh, he was *mean*. Walt never should have bought that horse for her. He bit. Everybody knew he bit. The first day Walt gave him to Sarah he bit her. But she hauled back and swung her arm full around and slapped that horse—smack!—on the side of his face, and do you know he never bit her again!" Fourteen years. The albums weren't dusty although brought from a closet somewhere. She must look at them, but "they didn't talk about Sarah." Now she had fourteen years' worth of talking.

Marley looked and listened, and watched Sarah's mother. He hadn't formed an expectation of her. He tried never to do that. Usually wrong if he did, he found it more interesting to be surprised. She was a farm wife, but not "American Gothic." Wearing a cream-colored skirt and vest, maroon frilly blouse, she was bridge-partying after lunch. Her hair glowed auburn—only she and her hairdresser knew for sure, but Marley had a strong suspicion. Thickening, but she still had her figure. She would be ten years or more older than he. Two books from the best-seller list lay on the table by her chair, public library copies. Both were serious literature, one with explicit sex.

She wasn't American Gothic, but still Mother. "And this is the picture they printed in the *Bloomington Pantagraph* when Sarah won the poetry contest her junior year in high school. They printed the poem, too, if you'd like to read it."

"I would."

THE COWS

Crossing the meadow, east to west,
All of the cows, together.
They pause to rest, and then decide
That side's not best,
And all drift off to try the south, together.

Telepathy? Not command.
All of the cows, together,
Just understand and move away.
To say it's planned
Implies more sense than they all have together.

They don't discuss,
Seems each knows
(All of the cows, together)
Whether she goes or stays a while.
Like styles in clothes or politics
We take up all together.

"Did you like it?"
"Yes."
"That was just her. Just exactly her. The way
she'd take the most ordinary thing and see something
behind it. But kind of offbeat too."
"Yes. I see." Marley saw behind Mrs. Kleinhagen
too. Through the picture window he saw the dust, the
dust-covered pickup, wind out of the cornfield and
around the drive.
"I'm sure Sarah was a wonderful girl. Melissa's
wonderful too. But she's in trouble. She's only fourteen, and she's ruining her life." He hadn't intended

to push, but his intuition said he had to reach her alone.

"What kind of—"

"Only her mother—only Sarah can save her. Melissa's life is going to be destroyed unless I find Sarah." He was putting it on strong. He felt he had to. He picked up Melissa's picture again, held it in front of her, over the table between them, over the albums, over little Sarah. "Melissa's a sweet little girl, but she's getting all twisted and hurt. You can't let that happen to her. You've got to try to save her. She needs her mother." He pressed, whetting the blunted grief. She might not know, but he had to make her tell if she did. He hadn't time to do it gently. "A girl needs her mother."

Pain began to break her. She might have told if she knew, but sudden panic blanked the pain: She heard the truck doors slam. She froze, then frantically grabbed at the albums to put them into the compact box that fit out of sight under her grandmother's wedding dress that her mother had worn, that she had worn, that Sarah should have worn. But there wasn't enough time. She realized it, froze again.

Marley's luck ran out: Walter Kleinhagen didn't smile. He had seen the stranger's car, was prepared to be hospitable. His face was ready to smile as he came through the kitchen. Then he saw fear on her face, saw the scraps of Sarah's life under her hands. His jaw clenched, and his lips tightened.

Marley recognized a man used to seeing things and understanding quickly. Although he wore jeans, checked western-cut shirt, and cowboy hat, he had a banker's haircut, banker's rimless glasses, banker's eyes behind them.

A young man loomed behind him. He had longer hair, no hat, his mother's nose, his father's eyes.

"Who is this, Glenda?" Kleinhagen spoke in a soft voice. He seldom had to raise it to get people's attention.

Marley stood, answered. "James Marley." He didn't put out his hand, knowing it would be ignored.

"What do you want here?"

"I'm trying to find your daughter. Sarah."

"You won't find her here."

"I was hoping you might be able—"

"We're not. I wrote to you. Did you call before you came out here?" He was watching his wife.

"No."

Kleinhagen took that in mitigation for her, shifted back to Marley. "You could have saved yourself the trip. You're not police."

"No. I represent the guardian of Sarah's daughter. She's—"

Walter Kleinhagen's hand swept once, slicing the flow of sound waves. "I don't care who you are or who you represent. We have nothing to say to you."

"Walt. . . . Sarah's daughter, Melissa, she's in trouble, and—"

"No, Glenda. No." It was a firm command by a man used to commanding. But he spoke to her and looked at her gently.

Marley tried, deciding he had nothing to lose. He held up Melissa's picture. "Your granddaughter, Mr. Kleinhagen. Your granddaughter's sick, and—"

"Take that thing away, God damn you! I don't

want to see that picture! I don't want to hear about
that girl!'' He shouted, and then had to justify it to
himself more than to Marley. His voice was controlled again, low again, but tight now.

"Our daughter broke our hearts. We gave her
everything. Not spoiling her, not *everything* that way.
We gave her love; she never doubted for that. We
gave her a home, a real home, a happy home. She
had everything she needed. More. She had her pony
and her horse, but she had to take care of them. We
gave her a sense of responsibility too. We gave her
values. And she went away—she was set she had to
go east to school, that was the best, so that was
where we sent her—and it was like we had never
done anything, never done anything right. Everything
we did was wrong, everything we believed was wrong.

"And then she got herself pregnant. *And she gave
her baby away for money*. And now you come here
with a picture of that child, and expect us . . .

"People don't die of a broken heart, not unless
they let themselves. We just said—we had to say—
'our daughter's dead to us.' We loved her, but she's
dead; and you can't dwell on the past. The only thing
you can do is to put it out of your mind and go on.
I've told you, Glenda. I've told you to burn those
things. It only hurts your heart to look at them. Every
time you—'' He wheeled back on Marley. "Who the
hell are you to come here and rake up the past! You
bring a picture— Who is that girl? Have we ever
seen her? Have we ever heard from her? Why do you
bring her here now to torment us, to torment my
wife! Don't you see what this does to her! Don't tell
me you didn't see. If you asked about Sarah, if you

saw Glenda with these pictures, then you had to see— What the hell kind of rotten person—'' He gritted his teeth, got control again. ''Get out of here. Just get the hell out of here and leave our dead buried!''

Marley should have noticed the car, bright red against tan-yellow corn, parked a hundred yards beyond the Kleinhagens' drive. He did see it, only to register no motion as he scanned left and right before turning out onto the road. But he didn't really notice, didn't wonder why it was there, not moving. Anger, shame, encapsulated him in heat greater than from his sun-baked car insulating him from awareness outside his guilt. ''What kind of person?'' ''Had to.'' ''Couldn't he see how it hurt her? What kind of—'' ''Had to. For Melissa.'' ''No other way? What kind of person?''

He turned left automatically. Looking inside himself, not in the rearview, he didn't see the Chevy pull out. He stopped at the stop sign, didn't see the Chevy coming up behind, fast. He looked left and right, crossed the intersection, picked up speed—20, 30. The Chevy was up to 40 at the intersection, didn't stop, to 50 and accelerating, coming up on him. Marley didn't see it until it reached his left rear window. He snapped his head, then tromped brake, twisted wheel right, reacting to the car passing so fast, so close, not in the first instant to the shotgun aimed at him.

Standing on the brake pushed him back; his car slowing suddenly threw off the gunman's aim. Shot grazed and shattered the windshield, missed Marley. Shock swerved him toward the ditch. The car scraped, tilted, tipped over, 45 degrees. He held the wheel, kept himself from falling totally, but was thrown half down into the righthand seat. He pulled himself up again. The windshield was shattered, crazed. He couldn't see out where he was, hauled himself farther to look through the blasted-out hole.

The Chevy was halted fifty yards down, a screen of dust hanging behind it. Heads came out of windows, trying to see him.

Marley's righthand door was jammed down against the ditch side. He pushed, trying to open the door on the driver's side, had to move it upward. It was heavy. He put his feet against the transmission tunnel, braced, shoved. He looked out as though through a hatch. Dust was drifting. He could see the men in the other car seeing him. He lifted the door, but it wouldn't hold at the open catch. Marley pushed himself up, got a foot inside the steering-wheel rim, lifted himself, squeezing out. Dust was thinning. Heads pulled back inside the Chevy. The driver gunned the engine, shifted to reverse, gunned again. Rubber burned. The engine screamed.

Marley's legs were out, free of the door. He dropped it, dropped to ground. The Chevy came hurtling at him, weaving, howling, the shotgun coming out of the window on the passenger side. Marley ducked around behind his car, low. He leaped across the ditch at the wall of corn, hands thrust forward, sweeping stalks aside. There were two, three, four stalks in each hill, enough space between hills to push, squeeze through. He took three bounds to his right, along the row, hit the dirt. The blast and shred of pellets

shattered corn over him. Rows had been cultivated,
stalks hilled. He was low enough, protected enough.

He heard them getting out of the Chevy, chanced
they wouldn't be trained to move with gun ready to
fire. He arched onto toes, sprinted from there. Six
steps, then he threw himself left into the next aisle,
breaking stalks, falling on them. Blasts—one-two—
came at him, but wide, high. There was a pause. He
guessed the gun could be a double-barrel, not a
pump—two shots very quickly, then a pause. With a
double-barrel there would have to be some pause
even for a skilled fast-loader. Of course, it could be a
pump fired twice only. Marley gambled. He sprinted,
smashed left, fell again.

"He moved again!"

"Don't shoot. Save it."

"What're we going to do?"

"Go after him."

Marley heard cornstalks snapping as the opening
where he first went through was widened.

"Hey! What if he's got a gun?"

"Why should he?"

"But what if—"

"Shoot first!"

Marley went up onto knees again, low enough to
see under leaves that laced row to row. It was like
looking down a long tan tunnel. He crept along it,
knuckle and toe, in the direction he had been head-
ing. He could hear his pursuers two rows over and
behind, pushing leaves aside. He came to a wider
break between two hills, eased left again, putting
another row between.

"Can't see a fucking thing!"

"Look under them."

They were bound to think of it eventually. They couldn't see him though. He was three rows over. They could see through that many directly to the side, not at an angle.

"I'm sure I heard him go this way."

"Shut up."

One grunt, one officer.

Marley felt he was roasting. Leaves were too thin to screen the sun's sharp rays, yet seemed a tangle thick enough to blanket down dense heat from dry earth's radiation. He still had on his jacket and tie. He loosened the tie, but was afraid of noise if he tried to take the jacket off, afraid his light-colored shirt would show. Contrast between sunlight glare and zebra shadows hurt his eyes.

"What the fuck are we doing!"

"Shut up!"

"We can't sit here all fucking day! Somebody's going to come!"

"Okay, go on!"

Leaves were brushed, shoved aside, swept back, pushed again by the second man. Marley used the sound to cover slipping through one more row.

"What's that?" Still whispered.

"What?"

"Didja hear?"

"No. See anything?"

"Where?"

"There."

"No."

"Listen!"

"What?"

"Shhhh!"

"Nothing."

"He can't be in this row. Go over one."

Stalks were forced apart. "Shit!" Some cracked, snapping over.

"He's not here."

"Go on to the next one."

That put them only two rows away, and more nearly parallel to him. Marley sprang forward, dashed three bounding strides, threw himself flat. Blast! Blast! Leaves were torn, stalks shattered just over his head pressed cheek-against-ground. He was up, running again, arms crossed in front of his face. Leaves slashed them. Head down, driving legs as hard as he could, he ran, counting steps—one, two, three, four—That's all! He threw himself forward to the ground again, found himself flat, out under open sky. He'd reached the end of the row—what he'd run for—before realizing he was there. He'd thrown himself out of the corn onto the tractor turnaround. He scrabbled up to his knees, looked both ways. He saw only empty road—nothing to nowhere, an illustration of vanishing points in a book on perspective, a picture crying for something in the foreground. Marley could have cried for something in the foreground.

The men were running, crashing, up the rows behind him. Marley sprang to his feet, sprinted away along the shoulder, his jacket flapping, arms and legs pumping frantically.

"Yeah! There!"

Marley cut left into the corn again, ducked to a crouch, kept running. The gunman, far enough away, excited, misjudging, fired over and behind. Marley dashed ahead, cut through two rows, ran on again, cut, ran. He was close to panic, wanting to run on and in, deeper and deeper into the field. He fought it, halted, held his breath. Then made himself take great breaths, then hold them. He listened.

No crashing followed him. Silence. Then a cricket chirruped nearby.

"Marley? Mr. Marley?" The officer's voice called to him. "I don't know exactly where you are, but I know you didn't get far enough not to hear me. So you better listen. You're going to get away this time. There's no way we're going to find you in this whole fucking field, so you lucked out. So you get off with another warning. Stop trying to find Sarah Kleinhagen. Now, I told you once; but you were too stupid to take the message. Get it now. You see the FBI can't be with you all the time. Learn, Marley. You give it up, and so will we. You keep trying to find her, we'll snuff you. No shit, now, you dig? Okay."

Marley heard their voices receding. In two minutes he heard the car start. He heard it for a long, long time, the sound getting smaller and smaller like the telephone poles toward that vanishing point. Sweat soaked his shirt even after he removed his jacket and tie and unbuttoned it. Sweat ran into his eyes, and he wiped at them, and they stung. But he stayed where he was for a long, long time, and then crept through the corn quite slowly to be sure. He was frightened, and then—after he was sure he was safe—he had to deal with getting out of there. It was only later that he had time to get angry.

CHAPTER 6

"Mr. Marley? I'm Clifton Letterman, Special Agent, FBI." He extended his badge. "May I talk to you for a few minutes?" He had a sharp face; high, narrow nosebridge; deepset eyes; tight, wiry reddish hair; no hat—the new FBI. He was shorter than Marley, younger. Marley was beginning to realize most people he met now were younger.

Marley nodded, stepped back into the room. Letterman followed, glancing once left to right to check it—no more needed: See one Holiday Inn room, you've seen them all.

"I hear you had an exciting afternoon."

"Well, I now know life in corn country doesn't have to be as dull as they say."

"I wonder if you could tell me anything more about what happened."

"More than I told the State Police? No."

"You didn't see the men who attacked you?"

"Not to identify."

"Any impression?"

"Just what I said: youngish to middle-aged by their voices. Good diction, but 'fucking' everything.

108

Thirties, probably, and been to college. I'd know the voice of the one who was the chief.''

"Trying to stop you from finding Sarah Klein-hagen.''

"So they said.''

"Why *are* you trying to find Sarah Kleinhagen?''

Marley had told it all to the State Police, but he didn't mind telling it again.

"Why does the daughter need Sarah?''

"Why do you want to know?''

"That's confidential.''

"So is why her daughter needs her.''

Marley smiled, Letterman didn't—different expressions, both carved in stone. Then Letterman smiled too, but with only one side of his mouth. "Okay if we sit down?''

"Please do.''

Two chairs, tweedy-looking plastic, flanked a wood-grainy-looking table facing the TV, so the men had to sit a little sideways to look at each other. Marley appeared expectant, as usual, and let Letterman begin.

"What do you know about Sarah Kleinhagen's political activities while she was at Smith?''

"Are you asking me, or getting ready to tell me?'' He was smiling again, as though joshing an old friend. "I know she was in an antiwar group that went extremist, that's all.''

Letterman knew he wasn't an old friend, but the geniality engaged him. "You know about the West-hover thing?''

"Only that it happened. I'm sure you know more than I do.''

"Probably. We think we know who did it, or some of them. We think Sarah might know for sure."

"I heard she'd left the group to have her baby."

"True. Or, at least, there's no doubt where she was when it happened. She's not a target. But she might be a material witness."

"Which is why someone didn't want me to find her. You haven't found her either."

"No."

"Well, it isn't likely I will if *you* can't, is it?"

"I don't know. We haven't really tried hard. We *have* tried to find the ones we think did it. We'd concluded they were out of the country, until we heard about you today."

"You heard quickly."

"Age of information. Kleinhagen name's flagged. So, we'll start looking again. Lots to work with now—probably a stolen car. When we find it, fingerprints, who knows what? Shotgun shell casings, footprints in the field. You've been a big help to us already."

Marley grinned. "You think I can help some more."

"If you find Sarah, any leads at all, let us know."

That was what Marley had expected, and feared. He deflected. "I should be asking you."

"I don't know; I get the impression we're not going to expend resources looking for her until we have some progress on the others. So you'll be out in front for a while anyway. That is, assuming you haven't been scared off. I do assume you haven't been scared off. Naturally, I read the printout on you."

Marley still looked pleasant, but this time it was Letterman who made a point of smiling.

"That's why I wanted to ask you something else: We'd appreciate it if you'd just go on looking for Sarah and leave those guys to us."

Marley's nod might have been agreement, or merely acknowledgment he'd heard. Behind that blandness he felt unambiguous relief. They weren't going to follow him closely while he looked for Sarah. To keep it that way, he would say nothing about the previous threat.

"We don't want a repeat of the Tucson thing."

Marley lost his smile.

Letterman continued. "*We'd* like to have them alive, and *you* might not get off again if you caught them in some state that doesn't still have the frontier ethic."

"That was a long time ago."

"Yeah. There haven't been questions about excessive violence in connection with anybody you've killed recently."

Marley took a moment before replying. "That's right. Neither of them."

"Clearly self-defense, no charge brought. No actual physical contact, much less beating to death with bare hands."

Marley took a slow, deep breath. "It was a long time ago."

Letterman watched him. "Good," he said. "You seem to keep yourself pretty cool now. Try to stay that way, okay?"

"I do."

A cold, crisp fall night—the Illinois Indian-summer warm front had tracked south of Massachusetts, a high-pressure ridge coming behind. Old-timers would say the full moon changed the weather. Marley read his watch by its light, decided he had cooled himself long enough. It was three A.M.: optimal knock-in-the-night time.

He closed the car door silently. Frost glowed on fallen leaves. His shadow seemed sunken in them, an irregular entity eating into light as it crossed toward the house. It was a fine old house: traditional, proper, small, with a steep roof, center door, shutter-flanked windows, white clapboards. Only the roof and windows on the second floor were visible over an eight-foot hedge. It was private, discreet. Upstairs lights had been out for two hours.

The gate swung in without squeaking. Marley passed under a topiary arch, went up to the paneled door. He didn't knock—neither with brass tap nor fist-heel pounding—but leaned on the bell button to get the same effect. Thirty seconds, nearly a minute passed before a light came on, shining through panes over the door. Then clumping sounded down the stairs, heavy from haste, heavier from anger. The door jerked open. "What the hell—"

"Good evening, Professor." Marley shoved the door hard against him, forcing in, one hand pushing Bascaglia's chest, bare, hairy, showing through a hurriedly wrapped robe. A protesting shout was squelched as Bascaglia recognized Marley. Marley shoved again, rocking the shorter man back a step. He closed the door behind him. "Let's talk, Professor. About your trying to kill me, and whether I'm going to kill you." He spoke with a mean voice, but softly. Bascaglia was shorter, but stocky, muscular.

Maybe he could fight. Marley tried never to fight. It couldn't happen again if he didn't fight.

"What are you talking about! What are you doing? What do you mean, *kill* me!" He seemed outraged, incredulous. He must have feigned attitudes for years to keep his students from guessing his mind, to shake them, make them think. He was good at it, even at three A.M., shocked out of sleeping soundly. He worked well on instinct.

Marley crowded in on him again, keeping a lion-tamer's distance: close enough to intimidate, not enough to force a strike. "Won't work, Professor. Who knew I was going to Sarah's family yesterday? Who knows the people who don't want her found?"

"I didn't try to kill you!"

"You did!"

"I did not!"

"You knew they'd try to kill me!"

"I did not!"

"You warned me!"

"I didn't *know*!" He realized as soon as he said it. Marley stopped, held the distance, held the stare, let it sink in. Out of that instinct Bascaglia tried diversion, halfheartedly, knowing he was caught. "I warned you. I did warn you."

"That justifies your putting them on me?"

Bascaglia's lips parted, closed again. He probably had a rationalization that placated his conscience, but realized quickly it wouldn't placate Marley.

The floor above them squeaked. Marley stepped back, looked up. A girl leaned over the banister beside the stairwell. She had jeans on, but her ankles were bare. Her shirt was buttoned once, clutched together below. Her hair was mussed, tossed strands incandescent from light above.

"Robbie? What's going on?"

Marley shifted back to Bascaglia. "Send her away."

Bascaglia wavered. He feared being alone with Marley, then realized an opportunity. "You'll have to go, Susan. I'm sorry, something's . . . It's all right."

Susan also was unsure, but embarrassed, relieved to be freed from whatever it was. She went quickly back to finish dressing.

"Unlocking her shell so the eaglet of passion can soar?"

"None of your goddamn business! She's over the age of consent." He blushed though.

Marley didn't care, but kept the pressure. "What is this, Professor? One of the burdens of a dedicated teacher, or a professional fringe benefit? She is a student, isn't she? Does she get an A?"

"I told you it is none of your business."

"Everything about you is my business. You've made yourself my business."

"What do you want from me?"

"I'll tell you. As soon as she's gone."

Footsteps sounded along the hall. Susan came downstairs looking at Bascaglia, trying not to look at Marley, trying not to *not* look at him. She was blond. Her fair skin was flushed.

"I'm sorry, Susan." Bascaglia handled it. He still was shaken, but began to feel himself bringing the crisis under control. "I'm very sorry, but something has come up—an emergency. This is Mr. Marley."

"Hi." She acknowledged Marley softly with a reluctant glance, then looked back to Robbie.

"Mr. James Marley." Bascaglia persisted. "Mr. Marley, this is my friend, Susan." He was skillful, suave, as though helping her, making her presence respectable and ordinary. But making her look at Marley again.

"How do you do, Susan? I'm sorry to inconvenience you."

"That's all right." She looked at him, then in hope toward her coat hanging on a peg by the door.

"I'll call you tomorrow, Susan. By noon. If I don't reach you by noon, call me. Okay?"

"Okay."

He helped her with her coat. "You can get home all right, can't you?"

"Sure."

He put an arm across her shoulders. "I'll see you tomorrow." He opened the door.

Marley moved up, smiling, but in position so Bascaglia couldn't dash through too.

He hadn't planned to try. He had his hand still on her back, guiding her out. "Good night, Susan." He watched until she was through the hedge, but didn't try anything.

"All right, Marley. Now I think you'd better leave too."

"Be serious, Professor."

"I am. If you injure me, Susan has seen you. She knows your name. Your card—your address—is still in my office. Susan knows you came here uninvited. You are an intruder in my house. I suggest that you leave at once, or I'll call the police." He was pleased

with himself: not the ineffectual intellectual, he could
handle a dangerous situation.

"Don't call the police. Call the FBI. Special Agent
Letterman, in Chicago. I've got his number with me.
He's interested in the men who tried to kill me,
thinks they were involved in the Westhover thing.
He'd be happy to hear from you. I could even call
him myself for you, unless you'd rather talk with
me."

It knocked Bascaglia's wind out, but he covered,
head bobbing, nodding to himself, his thick lower lip
pushed up, frowning. "Okay if I get dressed?"

"Okay if I make sure that's all you do?"

"I didn't think they would try to harm you. Truly I
didn't. I did call to warn them— After you talked to
me the first time, I called to tell them you were
looking for her. I didn't know they had come after
you, threatened you. Truly, I did not. And I did call
again to let them know you were going to Illinois.
But the message I left—they weren't there, I got their
box—was that I didn't think you'd get anything from
her family. I thought they should be warned. I thought,
at most, they'd check to see if you were getting
anywhere, then split if they had to. I truly never
thought . . ." He must have realized that words alone
couldn't convince. He had spent his life studying,
teaching words, knew their limits. Heels of hands
together, tense palms veed outward, his fingers radi-
ated sincerity beyond words. He still seemed afraid
of what Marley might do.

No lamp had been lit in the living room. Moonlight slanted through west-facing windows. The men

could see each other well, but in the dark. Bascaglia sat on the front edge of his Eames chair.

Marley pulled a Shaker straight-back over in confrontation. He didn't expect trouble, but didn't want to have to rise from a deep seat if any came.

"You know where they are. You know they're wanted for murder."

"Who the hell are you to say *murder*! 'Wasted gooks,' you did! We've got a memorial now, in Washington, to the Vietnam vets. Weren't they murderers? *I* don't call them that, not the poor average sons of bitches just doing what they were told was their duty, serving their fucking country. They thought it was in a good cause. But if we can forgive those 'gook-wasters'—if you can forgive *yourself*—it's vile hypocrisy to go on accusing and hunting a few people who fought and killed on the other side. Fighting against that fucking war was a good cause too. That was a truly good cause, and the whole country knows it now!"

"Okay, Professor, but that was a long time ago. The war's over. They weren't fighting it when they tried to hit me in that cornfield."

"They saw it as part of the same . . . Okay, you're right. I'm *sorry*. What can I say? I don't condone it. But I understand. To them it's self-defense. If what they were trying to do fourteen years ago was right—*and it was,* take that as axiomatic—and someone is still trying to hunt them down—"

"I wasn't hunting *them*!"

Bascaglia thrust forward, finger jabbing. "*You* see that, of course. But from *their* point of view—"

As though driven back, Marley suddenly relaxed

against the chair and smiled. "Is it still like this in college?" he asked. "Do you still sit around with quarts of beer and argue all night?"

Bascaglia uncocked his finger and holstered it against his palm. "Sometimes. Yeah, the kids do." He let himself sit back too. "I get sleepy earlier than I used to. And I've heard all the arguments. Especially my own. Sometimes, though."

"I'm glad to hear it. I mean, about the students."

"Yes. They keep coming, thinking there's something to be argued about and settled and then they'll know." He shook his head. "But that's not what you came to do. What are you here for, Marley? You aren't going to kill me."

"No."

"At first I thought you were."

"Good."

"What are you going to do?"

"I'm going to find Sarah Kleinhagen if I can. I'm going to try."

"I don't know where she is. Truly, I do not."

"Do they?"

"Who? Oh. No. I'm sure they don't. I'm positive."

The tone made Marley look more sharply, and Bascaglia avoided him.

"Why? Why!" But Bascaglia would not respond. "You mean if they knew, they'd try to kill her too."

"They don't know where she is. Nobody knows."

"She does know about them. That's what the FBI thinks. She could be a material witness. It's true, isn't it?"

"I am not going to say anything about the allegations concerning—"

"Don't say! Don't say anything that's going to compromise your principles, Robbie. I sure as hell wouldn't want a man to compromise his principles. Just tell me whether these guys would try to kill Sarah Kleinhagen."

Bascaglia hesitated, deliberating between loyalties. "They might," he said. "Don't try to find her. Please."

"I have to."

"Why?"

"I'm being paid to," Marley said abruptly. "Now, listen to me, Professor. There are several ways I might proceed from here. My first inclination is to *make* you tell me how to find those guys, and then go after them myself. That is not the most intelligent thing for me to do, but I am powerfully moved that way. What I *should* do is give you to Letterman, let him get it out of you, wait for the FBI to take your friends for me. But that would take time; and for my own reasons I'd prefer to keep the FBI out of this, at least until I find her. And except for my annoyance with your friends, except as they constitute a continuing threat, I don't really care about them. I wouldn't know about them. . . . The FBI thought they were out of the country. They're in more danger now than if they'd just kept low and let me find Sarah. Tell them that. Tell them to cut their losses. Sarah's no threat to them unless they're caught. They're more likely to be caught if they surface again. And if *I* catch them . . ."

Marley's emphasis was slight. The levelness of his threat impressed Bascaglia more than theatrics might have.

"I'll tell them. I promise. I promise you—if I can do anything about it—I promise you they won't come after you again. I think I still have some influence. At least, I have some power; I can threaten. . . . I'll stop them."

Bascaglia tipped his head back against the chair. He closed his eyes and sighed. "Christ," he said, "Christ," eyes still tight shut. "How did we get here?" He looked toward the windows. Silhouetted mullions were highlighted like bars. "We thought we were bringing the Revolution. We really thought that, that it was going to be different. Better. The 'greening.' It was happening—civil rights, the blacks, then the women's movement beginning—the war focusing it all, exposing the contradictions. By the end, even the hard hats were coming around."

"Tell me about Sarah."

"That's it. She was it. Face scrubbed, Honor Society pin. Straight from the cover of *The Saturday Evening Post*. Wholesome. Open. Kindhearted. Truly caring. I don't think her family ever let her know there was any party besides Republican. She wasn't shallow—I don't mean that—but simple, in the sense of direct, and . . . decent. Just fundamentally good. Everything our mythology tells us Americans are. And she came here, and she heard and saw what was going on, and understood, and she was outraged. Morally outraged. And that's why we believed. I mean, we believed already, of course. If we led the way, the country would change. The people were okay. But she proved we were right.

"She and Brooks.

"She was decency, righteousness; he was the milk

and honey of human kindness. Sweet. That's the first thing everybody said about Brooks. She was outraged, he was hurt. I mean, it hurt him, it pained him personally that this country was— You know that picture—God—the one of the Vietnamese girl running toward the camera with her back on fire? The first time Brooks saw that he cried. I mean, *that picture* . . . The rest of us swore, or broke something, went out—Brooks sat down on the floor and cried.

"You know, they accused us of a lot of things: being anarchists—against any authority, the kids just spoiled, rebelling against their parents, taking it out on the country, ego trips. . . . Maybe for some of us they were right, partly right, sometimes. But Sarah and Brooks—they were the proof, they were our touchstones. If you took something to Sarah, something you felt or wanted to do, and she said it was all right, then it was all right." Bascaglia looked away from Marley to the window again, through it, beyond the mullions. " 'Trust green.' "

"What?"

"One of Sarah's verses. I haven't thought of it for . . . Something . . . *the green is true* . . . something . . . *root shatters rock, shoot racks stone. The green will* . . . We called her the Voice of the Earth. Always the farm girl, always put what she wanted to say in nature metaphors. That one is similar to one of Thomas's, of course. She intended that, but she used it differently. It was political. I can't remember how the rest of it . . . I guess that's Freudian. She was telling us *we* were the life force, *we* would prevail."

Abruptly he leaned forward. "Look, Marley, I've

got a nine o'clock class. I really don't think there's anything more I can—"

"I need help!" Marley took a breath, took a moment. "I'm not the Inquisition, Professor. I'd just like to have some help. Nobody is answering the letters I sent. But maybe there are other people whose names I haven't gotten. And there are some names I couldn't get addresses for. Your friends who tried to kill me must have been two of them, but there are a couple more. If you can help me, don't make me keep slogging along the hard way. Don't you think you've made it hard enough for me already?"

"I didn't mean to. I'm sorry." The anger went out of him and he slumped back again. "I'm a decent man, Marley. Despite what you may think. I don't knowingly harm anyone. I . . . Yeah, I screw the girls, some of them. Not the ones who might be hurt by it. Usually, the only trouble they have is when the novelty wears off and they have to figure how to let *me* down. They get a 'life experience' out of it, and I get an illusion of continued potency. That's one of the few illusions I have left. Things didn't turn out. About the only thing I have left that I hope is not illusion is my loyalty to what we believed and tried to do, to those people. I'm sorry to cause you trouble. I'm sorry I nearly got you killed. But I will not identify anyone to help you."

The patch of moonlight on the floor had crept close to Bascaglia. Reflected upward, it revealed his face clearly. Marley could see fear there, but determination as well.

"I'm not really asking you to help *me*. I'm asking you to help Sarah's daughter."

"Send her here and I'll teach her poetry if that'll do her any good. That's all I've found I can do for anybody."

Rage made Marley's vision seem to swim, and his lungs filled involuntarily for attack. He gripped the tops of his thighs, held the breath, set his smile until the instant passed.

But Bascaglia had seen. "Don't judge me! After what you've done— What you're— Now! You find Sarah, bring her out— You could be bringing her out to be killed! You don't know! Don't try to put it on me. Take that on yourself if you want, and then judge yourself!"

Marley made good time back to Boston. In the hour before dawn he met few cars on the Pike, a half-dozen trucks, until he reached the suburbs, where there always was traffic, he'd found. Anywhere, in any town, even out in the country, some one person might be late from a date that had blossomed to unexpected bliss, or someone might set off to make a long trip all in one day, or one could be coming to deliver the milk or the morning paper, or one going home from hospital duty. Around the city, with so many people, there were all of those all at once; a thousand of them drove through the night, and there was never any silent hour.

It took Marley less than ninety minutes to get across the state, and only the next-to-last twenty were hard, from fatigue. At first he was still too keyed to be tired, still angry at Bascaglia—less now because of the cornfield attack, more because of the man's indifference to Melissa's need. And he did worry about the threat to Sarah. He hoped his warning would be effective, but resolved to be cautious in going on.

The lack of sleep hit him when he got back home. He was hungry, too, but filled himself with some deli potato salad he had had in the fridge—ate it standing, leaning against the kitchen counter—and a glass of milk, then pulled the shades and went to bed.

Tired as he was, his body rhythms wouldn't let him sleep in the day, and he was up again at eleven. He fried some ham and eggs and got to work, trying to think what other approaches might lead him to Sarah.

Sarah looked at Marley steadily. No matter where he went in the room her eyes were always directed at him from the photograph he had pinned over his desk. When he got up to pace, think it through, she watched. Her look disconcerted him. It was the look Brooks Ten Broeck had written about—when she knew what you were really thinking, when she was deciding whether what you'd brought her was all right.

He took the picture down, got out his big magnifying glass. On the fine-grained film her face was still a face, not blurs of light and dark, even though now almost life-size. He couldn't see all of it at once through the glass. He studied her pleasant smile. She wore no lipstick. He moved over the high cheeks, the smooth, shiny, well-scrubbed skin. He thought, the pioneer woman. Those eyes again: he held the lens over them and felt he and she were evaluating each other through it.

He sat, laid the glass aside. The face that launched

a thousand protests. He could believe it. How could she turn that face away from her own child? From her own family?

How could a man with his face order fire down on a village?

He looked away from that, back to the desk, and—almost startled by the owl eye there—jerked the glass away from Brooks Ten Broeck's face. Taking up the photo, he folded it carefully first to one side, then the other, and made a smooth tear down the center. It would be easier to carry just her half.

CHAPTER 7

Marley shook water from his raincoat as he unlocked his mailbox. He disliked rain in the city. He disliked autumn rain in the city in particular. Gray autumn days at home brought a sense of comfortable drawing-in, of the earth preparing to rest. In the city they brought mildew and the promise of slush.

He ought to go out again, see a film, have a good dinner, use the city for what it was worth—try to get *some* value out of the day. Nothing else he'd done in it had been worthwhile. He'd spent it at the library, scanning contemporary poetry. That would have been disheartening, he had decided, even aside from his failure to find anything by Sarah in what he'd read.

He had been hoping that Sarah would still be writing poetry, that she would be published, that he would find the right publication, and recognize her eyes behind any pseudonymic mask.

He retrieved the bills, circulars, and appeals for money from his box and, up in his apartment, dropped them onto his desk. It was only 4:30, but he decided, given the day, that it was late enough to have a drink. He poured a shot of Scotch, sipped it uniced, masochistically enjoying its burn. No calls had been recorded on his answering machine. With a growing sense of martyrdom he returned to do his duty by the mail. In addition to the ones he'd seen, there were three envelopes caught inside a tabloid circular. He had become so sure that the whole day was junk that he had the letter out before he saw:

Mr. Marley: You may find the person you are looking for by . . .

Rain slackened as Marley drove north. By Manchester it was only mist; by Concord he had dry highway under gray sky. Low cloud extended to Canada, the radio said, but brightness increased. Marley felt that it did anyway.

He and Sarah were neighbors. Although his apartment was in Boston, Vermont was his home. And Sarah was to be found next door in New Hampshire—a few hills and a narrow river away. That had amazed and pleased him.

Eagerness to meet her at last pressed his foot on the accelerator. Watching speed, keeping himself from tailgating in heavy traffic, took all the control he could manage.

Low clouds in Franconia Notch hid the Great Stone Face, but he had enough sense of mountains walling either side to awe him. Despite lines of tour buses, crowds of sightseers, he felt small and isolated, as though he were passing by sufferance of powers unseen in the mist above.

He crept with traffic through the Notch, down into the valley, and off the interstate into the village. He paused to check the written directions, but need-

lessly, as he had them by heart. He found the state
route, drove slowly to lose the extra time he'd made
driving fast, until he came to the side road, and then
to the foot trail leading from it. He parked and got
out. Despite the grayness of the day the foliage was
brilliant: beech leaves yellow, maples red and orange.
Underfoot, their wet mosaic muffled his steps. The
trail rose slightly, turning. In fifty yards he could
no longer see back to the road. He walked on. That
was the last of his instructions.

The wood had been cut over, was growing back.
Thick-trunked seed trees stood here and there, but
saplings and underbrush filled in between. He could
see for varying distances into them. Away to his
right, something moved.

He thought something had moved. He stopped,
looking. He wasn't sure. Everything was still again.

Something did move! It was at an angle to his
path, then again at his periphery, but definitely a
dark shape. He stopped once more.

Suddenly fear and a sense of incredible stupidity
swept through him. He had not doubted—he had
known the letter was from Sarah herself. How had he
known? How had he known it wasn't sent by the men
who would kill to keep him from finding her? In the
absence of any further threat from them throughout
the past week, he'd assumed that his feint toward the
FBI, or Bascaglia's influence, had neutralized them.
He'd been careful; he was positive he wasn't being
followed, but there had seemed no longer to be a
need.

He stood still, facing where the movement had
been, his mind racing. A quick dash into the under-

brush to his left? There had been two men before. If it were them again, a good ambush would put one on each side. Should he look left to check? Would that show he suspected, precipitate attack? Should he wheel and sprint for the road?

He didn't know. He no longer *knew* it was Sarah. But he didn't know it was them either.

He breathed deeply, managed to swallow, tried to get control, to slow his heartbeat. If it was Sarah, he would have to keep walking to meet her.

He moved slowly, watching only by shifting his eyes. He'd prowled before through undergrowth, alert for attack. If ambushers were nervous, if they moved, you might see them in time. If they stayed back, still, you probably wouldn't. He'd been lucky before. He saw nothing to the left. On the right the shape shadowed him. But it was coming nearer. He realized there must be another path, closing at an angle toward his. He and the person, the shape now distinguishable in flashes between screening foliage, walked in the same direction, but were converging.

His path passed a pine trunk four feet thick, and suddenly bent around it into a wide space where several trails joined. He stopped.

She had reached the place first, stood waiting at the end of her path, still partially hidden by a spray of beech leaves. He stood, afraid if he moved abruptly she might dart back and vanish like a deer.

He took a deep breath, then walked slowly to her. He smiled.

"Miss Kleinhagen, I presume."

He was glad he had gotten used to her looking at him from the photo. Even so prepared, the intensity of her eyes surprised him. He hadn't expected to see them levelly—she was as tall as he.

She looked away for an instant, smiling faintly. "I haven't used that name for a very long time. Call me Sarah."

Hairs on the back of Marley's neck had risen, not so much from her voice as from having known what it would sound like. She spoke deliberately, below medium pitch, quietly, but with a confident strength. He used the same tone.

"I'm James Marley."

"Yes." She didn't offer her hand, but nodded slightly and repeated his name. "James." She looked at him in silence for a while, but he had no sense she was waiting for him to begin. She was studying him, and he understood, and waited. "What do you have to tell me?" she asked finally.

He gave her the three sentences that explained what he did, why he was working for Mrs. Ten Broeck.

He gave her Melissa's picture.

She looked at it for several moments. He could not read any emotion in her expression. She put it into her pocket, turned back to him. "Why does Melissa need me?"

"A little over two weeks ago I was asked to find her. She hadn't come home after visiting a friend." He had decided instantly to tell the story, not give a name to Melissa's need. Sarah looked at him steadily, but as Marley went on he saw her expression change. He saw how much she looked like her father, then how her face became her mother's at the screen door. He spoke as gently as he could, but he

knew she would have to hear it all, and to decide for
herself. He told it, including Melissa's own words.
Then he gave the background.

"Apparently something like it had happened before. The local police had found her in a lovers' lane
with a car full of high school boys. Before that—that
Mrs. Ten Broeck knows of—she had tried to seduce
the gardener's helper and one of her teachers. Mrs.
Ten Broeck has had her to a psychiatrist, but it hasn't
helped."

Sarah set her jaw as anger joined the shock and
pain in her face. She jammed her fists into her jacket
pockets, and stalked past Marley into the clearing.
She whirled back on him. "One of the reasons Mrs.
Ten Broeck wanted custody of Melissa was because I
was an 'immoral woman' and I wouldn't be able to
bring her up decently! What am *I* supposed to do
now?"

"She thinks if you come back you can be an
example for Melissa. You can—"

"You mean a horrible example? An object lesson?"

"I think Mrs. Ten Broeck realizes she may have
been wrong. I believe she's—"

"I know what she is. Don't try to apologize for
her to me!"

Marley waited, breaking the pace so she wouldn't
cut him off again. "I was hired to find you. That's
all I have to do for Mrs. Ten Broeck. For Melissa's
sake, I would like to persuade you to go back there.
Right now she's a sweet kid with a bad problem, and
she knows it's a problem, but she can't help it. In
two years she'll be just anybody's slut unless they've
locked her away and lobotomized her. If they don't

do that, I think she'll kill herself one way or another before she's twenty. If there's anything I can do to prevent that, I have to. Don't you?''

She continued to face him for a long time after the anger went out of her and let her shoulders slump. Then she turned again and began walking slowly away. When she came by the great pine she veered to it and turned and leaned with her back against it. She took out Melissa's picture, stared down at it. After another moment Marley crossed. He stood within the reach of lower branches, but not confronting her. She was weeping. She did not look up at him. He had a long time to study her.

Fourteen years older than in the photograph. He should have expected change, but had been surprised by it. She was still thin, but no longer gaunt. A little fullness had come into her face, and to her figure revealed by a high-necked pullover and corduroy jeans. She cut her hair shorter, shoulder-length, and turned it under, controlling it with a scarf instead of a bandanna. No gray hair showed, and he realized she wore makeup: a little color on the lips and cheekbones, eyelids lined, brows and lashes darkened. That's what had made the look seem even more intense.

Perhaps she felt him assessing her. She took a handkerchief from her pocket, wiped her eyes. She looked up and turned her own examination on him. ''Do you know Mrs. Ten Broeck well?''

''No. I met her only two or three weeks ago.''

''Did you think she's a sweet old lady?''

''No. No, that was never my impression.''

A little smile tightened Sarah's lips, left them as

quickly. "I think she's capable of anything. Including bringing me back—though she despises me—if she thinks it will help *her* great-granddaughter. And including dismissing me again if it doesn't work. Or if it does, and she thinks she doesn't need me anymore. I can't accept that. I gave up my daughter once. I can't do it again."

"Why did you give her up, Sarah?" It wasn't part of this business, it might anger her, alienate her. He had no right to ask. He wanted to know.

She accepted his questioning her. He could believe she even admired him for caring. He could read her nod that way.

"At first Brooks and I were going to live together and raise Melissa ourselves. Of course. We just agreed to let Mrs. Ten Broeck take care of me when it was time for her to be born. I wasn't very well just then, and Brooks was so afraid. So . . . For Melissa's sake. It was after she was born that I had to decide.

"Everything was coming apart then. Everything I had expected to do with my life. Everything I believed in—politically, socially—hadn't worked; it was blowing up. Brooks was dead. It was all—"

"Brooks was dead?"

"Of course." She stared at him for a moment. "You mean she still insists . . . !" She shook her head. "When she makes up her mind . . . Brooks is dead. He . . . he died the night Melissa was born."

"How? How do you know?"

"He— It doesn't matter. I know. The point is . . . What do you know . . . you must have heard something . . . about our group. About the Westhover . . ."

"Yes. I have heard a little."

"Well, then, you see. That's what it had come
to—all the things we wanted to do, everything we
believed: peace, nonviolence, 'we shall overcome'—
just by the moral truth. And that we had ourselves
come, some of us . . . Even— I didn't know what I
believed anymore, what I could believe. Maybe Mrs.
Ten Broeck, her world, was right. I got over thinking
that after a while, that her values were right. But I
guess I've never been able to be so confident again
that ours would lead to something better. And even if
I didn't like her, despite everything we disagreed
about, I couldn't say she was all wrong, that she
would hurt Melissa. She had brought Brooks up, and
there was nobody in the world kinder and more
idealistic than he was.

"And what were my alternatives? Even if I could
have taken Melissa back home to Illinois, I'd have
been the Kleinhagen girl who went east and got
herself into trouble, which is just what she deserved
for always thinking she knew better than anybody
else what was right. That's what my parents wanted.
They would have forgiven everything. And they would
have brought up Melissa with as much love as they
did me. But with more care. They would have made
sure she never was infected with any of the ideas that
turned me out wrong despite all they did for me. And
because they would be such saints about it—they
really would—and because of who my father is, it
wouldn't matter nearly as much to people that Melissa was a bastard.

"But I couldn't have done that, even if I'd been
willing. The police, the FBI . . . I knew some things
about the Westhover raid. There's no point in not

telling you. I knew who was involved. But I would never tell. They were wrong, but I would never . . . I hoped to avoid that, but my father— So, I couldn't stay at home anyway. I would have to be in hiding. As I have been.''

She shifted, putting her shoulder against the rough black trunk, so that she more nearly faced Marley.

"So, I could have taken Melissa off someplace and brought her up myself. Some city, where it's easy to get to the welfare office, or, if you work, where there are daycare centers for your kid to grow up in between visits to your apartment.''

She continued to look directly at Marley for a moment, letting him know she understood that's what he would think she should have done.

"That's what I had planned actually. But Mrs. Ten Broeck convinced me it would be a cruel and selfish thing to do to a child who would otherwise be brought up with the best of everything. And every time I've thought of trying to get Melissa back—and I have thought about it—I've stopped myself by asking what I could give her, and what I'd be taking away.''

She dropped her eyes and tilted her head until it rested against the tree.

"I understand," Marley said. "Why—why haven't you been back to see your parents? You could have seen them secretly if you had to do that. Why don't you write to them, or—''

"I did. You've talked to them? Of course, you must have done that first.''

"I went there.''

"You did. What did they tell you? Did they tell you they threw me out? My father threw me out? I went home. I told them about Melissa. My mother cried, and my father nearly had a stroke, he was so angry. But he would have forgiven me. They would have forgiven me. Except that I didn't ask them to forgive me. I was very, very unhappy; but I didn't think I'd done anything I had to ask them to forgive me for. And they've never forgiven me for that. I asked my father for help—legal help, so I wouldn't have to . . . But he said it was my duty. He's very big on duty. And if I wouldn't, I was an accessory, a criminal. And he wouldn't harbor— I tried calling my mother once, but he was home, and he told her to hang up, and she did. I wrote—often, for a while, then once a year. I couldn't give an address, but I asked them, if they wanted to see me, to put an ad in the *Chicago Tribune* on a certain day. And I'd be in Boston and get the paper. I always told them I was sorry for what had happened, but I never asked for forgiveness; and they never placed the ad."

She had pushed away from the tree. She faced him directly.

"So, what do you think? You had to know. It's worried you, hasn't it, how a person could do such terrible things."

"No. I've known people who've done much worse. I wondered how *you* could do them."

"Now you know."

"Yes. I understand." He smiled, shrugged.

She put her hands back into her jacket pockets, smiled back, shrugged too—imitating him.

"What are you going to do now?" he asked.

"If Mrs. Ten Broeck believes I can help Melissa, then let her do one of two things. Either send her here—give up custody, and let me bring her up—it doesn't seem, after all, I could do any worse. Or, let her agree to recognize me as Melissa's mother and treat me as Brooks's widow. No—she won't accept that. As Brooks's wife.''

"Were you married?"

"No. Of course not. We were above marrying and giving in marriage. We were going to respect each other as male and female human beings. That category doesn't merit much respect from Mrs. Ten Broeck, so I have to put this to her in categories she knows. If I come to her house, it will be as Brooks's wife, not as the governess of his daughter.''

"What if she won't accept either choice? What about Melissa?"

"Oh, no. No, no, no. I've done that, I've been there. I learned fourteen years ago it's a hard world. You don't change it, you don't make things right just by rushing in with a warm and pure heart. I *will* help Melissa if I can. I'll try to do it on my own, without any help from that woman if I have to. If she won't accept either choice, then let it be on her.''

Marley nodded. "All right. I'll tell her. I'll call her and tell her.''

"It has to be in writing. I'm sorry. I don't trust her. I had to sign a written agreement, and it covered everything—demands I might make that I would never have thought of making. Anyone who is that careful, that untrusting, cannot be trusted.''

"I'll tell her.''

"And another thing. She will have to do what I asked my father, see that I will have legal assistance. That I will never have to give any evidence.''

"If you have evidence, I would think you'll have to give it."

"Not if you have the right lawyers. Not if you have enough money behind you. Not in the courts in this country."

"I don't know. I'll tell her. And I guess I'll have to tell her that you'll need protection as well."

"Why?"

"Two of the people who—'it is alleged'—were involved in the Westhover raid tried to kill me back in Illinois, just down the road from your house."

"My God!"

"Yes. And, to be honest with you, Sarah, Robbie Bascaglia thinks they might try to kill you too."

"Why!"

"Evidently, because you could identify them."

"I would never. . . . That's the point. That's why I changed my name, why I cut myself off from all my past. I wouldn't give any information against my friends. I can't believe that they'd hurt *me*! I can't believe that Mal, that they'd . . . They weren't like that!"

"Somebody's like it. Somebody killed some MP's at Westhover. Somebody tried to kill me."

Marley spoke calmly but must have convinced her. She looked back and forth, trying to see into the underbrush as he had done.

"They know you're looking for me?"

"Yes. But they don't know I've found you. Does this change anything?"

"I don't . . . Robbie said they would kill me? When did you see him?"

"Five days ago."

"I'll call him. I can't believe . . . Yes, it changes!
I have a life here. It's not much, but it's all— If I
have to run off and hide and change my name again—
Damn her! God damn her! You call her and tell her
all right, she's found me. And if she's put me in
danger, she owes me protection. Tell her she owes it
to me for Brooks's memory, if nothing else."

"I will. Can I call from somewhere back in town?"

"There's a pay phone in the village. You don't
think you could have been followed?"

"No. Not this time."

She looked around again, then caught herself. She
smiled at him. "Good. But if you don't mind, James.
I'll walk back to the road with you."

He almost offered his arm, but instead bent his
head in a sort of bow. "My pleasure, Sarah."

Marley's return to the window of her car startled
Sarah. She had been staring down at Melissa's photo.
Her eyes were wet.

"She agrees," Marley reported.

Fresh tears started, and Sarah wiped at them
brusquely with the heels of her hands. "It took a
while."

"Conversations with Mrs. Ten Broeck seem to.
Not because she disagreed though. I don't think she
liked it, but I think it was about what she expected."

"She'll put it all in writing?"

"Yes. It'll take a few days. She said she'd call her
lawyer at once. But with the weekend, we won't
have it before Monday, or even Tuesday."

"You're having her send it to you."

"Had to. I don't know what name you're using."

"Cameron. My mother's maiden name. You could have asked."

"I thought it was better this way. It's a nice name."

"Where?"

"Here."

"You'll stay, then."

"I thought I might as well. No point in driving back to Boston and up again on . . . Yes. I planned to stay."

"Everyone should stay in Franconia sometime. Have you been here before?"

"No."

"It's beautiful. Franconia Ridge, Kinsman Ridge, right there at the end of town." She gestured along Main Street toward the solid bank of clouds into which the lower slopes disappeared.

He nodded in mock appreciation. "Magnificent. Breathtaking."

"Especially when the leaves are turning. Everyone should see it. Everyone tries to. You do have a reservation?"

"I didn't know. There's a motel, or the inn we passed, or the farm that had rooms?"

"You can try. But if you don't have a reservation on foliage weekends, you'll probably end up sleeping in your car."

Neither of them smiled, but they seemed to need only every other line to understand each other.

"Ah . . ."

"Yes," she said. "On the couch. I don't want to involve any of my friends, and I would like to have company. Unless you were just trying to frighten me for the purpose.''

''Only on the couch.''

''How did you know I wasn't married now, or living with someone?''

His face went quite blank. Those possibilities had never occurred to him.

As they shopped for groceries, Marley tried to answer all Sarah's questions about Melissa.

''Well, she's twelve going on twenty-four—every two seconds. You know what I mean.'' He didn't know much, really; so he said the little he did know, and described her, and told of his two meetings with her again and again. But Sarah seemed not to tire of hearing it, nor of her own repeated cycle of joy and anger, outrage and sorrow. They left Marley's car in the market parking lot so that he could ride with her and go over it once more.

Marley flung the Scout door open and jumped out to have an unobstructed view. The dirt track had ended in a turnaround. From it a path led down a three-foot bank, then rose through thirty yards of white-and-purple-aster-spattered hillside to an A-frame cabin beside a waterfall. With twisted roots, ever-greens grasped boulders up the stream, climbing in a solid, dark green swath through lacy yellow and scarlet hardwood crowns. A deck looked over the steep stream gully. He peered around trunks on his side, trying to anticipate the view. He could see only that no lower foliage blocked it.

He heard her open the car's rear door, went to help

carry groceries. "Sarah, it's unbelievable! No one would know from the road you're back here."

"The isolation isn't so splendid in winter. Especially when you have to carry everything over from here by yourself."

"You have it plowed?"

"Only to here. I have to slog the rest."

The idea of that effort didn't daunt him. He was delighted with the location, even euphoric when they got inside.

The cabin was essentially a single space: living room at the front, high windows all across it; kitchen area at the back; a bathroom partitioned off at one back corner. Up a steep open stair like a ship's ladder lay a loft, unwalled to the front. Looking up, he could see the side of a platform bed. Pine-paneled roof formed the cabin's walls. All was sparsely furnished—foam pad on a base, and cushions, for a couch; two wooden rockers, very old but not good enough to be antiques. Wood stove. Coffee table made from a slab of wood on blocks. She had a cassette player, several racks of tapes, and a small TV on one of the open plywood cabinets that ran along each side.

The cabinets were piled with books, magazines, newspapers, letters, greeting cards stood up, scarves, gloves, a straw hat, a knitted hat, small rocks, odd bits of wood, dried flowers in ceramic pots and jars, and propped-up prints of flora and fauna. Clutter spilled over onto the couch and the floor beside it. At the window a small table supported a typewriter and further heaps of books and papers.

Marley emptied the bags onto a counter while

Sarah put things away. Every surface in the kitchen
shone. He decided that Sarah was fastidious, but not
neat. In his apartment every object knew and kept its
place, leaving dust between them undisturbed except
for Mrs. Colangelo's visits. Evidently where Sarah
and he were not alike, they were complementary.

"It was just a shell when I bought it. Insulated,
but an awful fiberboard paneling. No plumbing—an
outhouse. Really!"

"How did you learn to do it all?"

"I got some books, and some tools, and I did it."
She smiled. "That was good, James. Most men ask
who I got to do it for me. I had some help with the
plumbing and electrical system."

"I like wiring. It's very logical."

"Yes. That wasn't hard. I just had it checked for
safety. The interesting part was planning the system.
I couldn't afford to have service brought in—it's half
a mile to the road, and they were charging fifteen
dollars a foot. I use a Pelton wheel in the brook, up
above the fall, when it's running, and a generator in
the winter. It comes in as 240, and I break it down
inside the house."

"Could I see?"

"Really?"

"Really."

"I'll show you the interconnect first. It's in the
cellar." To the left of the loft ladder a hatch ring was
set into the floor. Sarah lifted the trapdoor. Another
ladder led downward.

Marley followed. Filled with admiration for her
self-reliance, he focused on that rather than on the

tools, hardware, coils of wire, plumbing fixtures, and scraps of wood disarrayed over workbench and floor.

They went out and looked at the water wheel, and the gasoline generator in its shed behind the house.

When they returned he paused on the deck. Looking out, he could see over trees below the house to a hillside across the valley.

"That's west, isn't it? You must get the sunsets."

"Yes. They can be quite lovely."

"The whole thing's lovely. Not a sense of another person anywhere around."

"No, here we feature trees."

"Well," he said, "I've lived with people, and I've lived with trees. On the whole, I prefer trees."

"I've felt that way too, James. But they're not much for conversation. Believe me, I've tried."

"Are you lonely?"

"Yes. Oh, I have friends. I work. I'm out a lot. But . . . These leaves will fall, and then we'll have the quiet waiting of November. And then snow. And that will go away, even though it always seems it won't. And mud time, and spring. Variety and continuity. I love it. But it's a bass figure. I don't have any counterpoint."

"Let me try to do something about that. Let me take you out to dinner tonight."

CHAPTER 8

A good dinner: good food, candles on the tables, wine of a quality he hadn't expected at a country inn. Marley had gotten the last unreserved table. Because of the crowd, service was slow, but neither he nor Sarah cared.

She told him about the area, bits of its history, its social structure, politics, anecdotes about its people, further descriptions of its seasons and their activities. He questioned, and they meandered among the things she told him; but mostly, she told. He delighted in hearing all those things she'd waited so long among the trees to tell. Every word of Brooks's admiration for her intelligence and insight seemed confirmed.

By her perception, by the way she looked directly at him as they spoke, Marley understood why Bascaglia and the others had brought their plans and themselves to her for judgment. He began to feel he'd like to tell about himself.

To his surprise, he found she knew some things already.

"It must be interesting, working for David Cheyney.

Do you negotiate the sale of small countries for him, or what?''

She asked the question after a lull. She might only have been making conversation politely, conscious of having talked so much about herself. But Marley sensed she wanted to surprise him with her knowledge. He went on guard.

"It is interesting. No, I don't. But sometimes . . . Say that the negotiations aren't going well, sometimes I can find out why. Suggest a new approach."

"Is that how you got that man away from those kidnappers in Italy?"

"Essentially. Okay, Sarah, how do you know?"

"James, do you really think I'd let you know where I was without knowing anything about you? I have a friend in Boston—he's with one of the big law firms. He knows me only from here. I asked him to find out something about you. It's pretty scary when you think about it. Big Brother is here, just like we said. If you have the right connections, you can find out about anybody."

"What did you find out about me?" Marley smoothed the sudden tension out of his voice, tried to sound curious and flattered.

"That you work for Cheyney. But despite that, that you have a reputation for integrity. What you did in Vietnam."

"Oh?"

"It's nice to know someone who tried to help those people. I'd like you to tell me about it."

"I will. But not here, not now." He knew she was misinterpreting his reticence, and he let her; but that was not the same as lying, so he could do it without avoiding her.

"Do you get to travel much? I mean, abroad," she asked.

"Yes. Fairly frequently."

"God, I envy you. That's something I've always wanted. Only I never could— Even if I'd gotten the money, I could never get a passport."

"Well, now you can."

"Yes. Oh, yes!" She clenched her fists and with arms tensed pounded them softly on the table, unable totally to suppress the thrill, no matter how decorous the dining room. "Tell me about it. London—have you been to London? And Paris?"

"Yes."

"Which?"

"Both."

"Tell me. Rome? Yes, of course you have. Tell me."

"About what? Which one?"

"All of them! Everywhere!"

He told her about sunlight and shadow sharp on the Spanish Steps in the morning, people rippling over them in the liquid summer night; about Wren churches, their seventeenth-century piety secure amid swirling scarlet omnibuses. He told, trying not to act too much the man of the world, and couldn't help but bask in her seeing that he was.

Despite the delight he knew they both felt at meeting each other, it was awkward when they returned to her cabin. In other circumstances she might have invited him in for a drink to prolong their contact, but neither would have expected him to stay the night.

"Would you like a drink? Some coffee?"

"No, thanks. I've had plenty. I'm fine. I imagine you're tired." He was tired, but he could have talked and listened to her all night. And looked at her. She had heightened her color, made herself more feminine in frilly blouse and skirt.

"I am, a little. I didn't sleep well last night."

"Neither did I."

"Well."

"Well."

It struck them simultaneously, and they grinned together. And they continued to feel their closeness even after she'd retired up to the loft and he'd bedded down on the couch.

He awoke and dressed first. Later, after they'd finished making breakfast together, and were drinking more coffee, she saw the folder in the couch and knew that he'd found some of her poetry.

"Did you like it?"

"Very much."

"Which?"

"All of them. The one about the Mormons."

"Beech Hill."

"Yes." He found it. "Is this true?" He read the first line. *"The first Mormons settled on Beech Hill . . ."*

"Yes. Some of them, at least. They came here after being run out of New York State. Before they went west."

He read more:

"The stones of their foundation are still in place,
   more or less: a home-guard of whiskered veterans
   of the war with chaos.
Slumped and stooping they may be,
and generations of trashy saplings have grown
   behind,
but never mind,
   stones know their duty, they hold the line.

"I like that. I've seen those walls running back in
woods myself. Where is this place?"

"Only a few miles down the road. Would you like
to see it?"
delighted at the prospect.

Although fog yet lay thick and white over the
mountaintops, sky glowed blue above them. The day
would be fine. They packed a picnic lunch and set
off.

Sunlight showed the hillsides splendid, variegated,
every hue of yellow, orange, and red, every tree
distinct, separate flowers in a garden bank. Con-
trasting spears of dark green spruce set off their
brilliance.

Marley and Sarah drove in her Scout to a dirt side
road, then parked and walked on. They were facing
east, and light came through the leaves as though
burning in them. The road ended at a brook that
raced and splashed, carrying leaves that settled on it
flashing between moss-covered stones and away. Crossing carefully on the stones, they made their way to a
path that took them uphill into denser woods.

Less remained of the settlement site than Marley
had hoped, but there were walls and cellar holes
enough for him to form a picture of its layout.
He prowled through them, hoping to find some ar-
tifact under leafmold. After a while Sarah lost
interest. One particularly crimson leaf lying against
a patch of chartreuse moss caught her eye. She
picked it up, then found a bright yellow one to put
with it. Then there was a strikingly mottled red-
orange and green, and then a maple shaded delicately
from tip to base.

"What are you doing?"

"Look at this one. And these. And look at this!"

"Wow!" He joined in, seeking the brightest colors, the strongest contrasts. They showed each other
their treasures as they found them, each delighting to
discover and reveal a new glory to the other. Soon
each had both hands full.

"Now what are we going to do with them?"

She shrugged.

"If you dip them in paraffin you can keep them for
a while," he said.

"They still fade."

"Everything does, eventually."

"I know." Suddenly the joy was going out of her.

"Come here." Marley indicated a step away where
a clear shaft of sunlight struck between trees. Sarah
moved there with him. He smiled, then flung both
handfuls of leaves up above them. She threw hers,
too, and they laughed together, watching the little
tongues of flame flicker and twist and settle all around
them.

They picnicked by the brook, leaning against two sides of a great gray-barked sugar maple. They talked. Leaves drifted down around them now and then. One settled in zigzag arcs to land in Sarah's lap. She held it up to the light. Her face went sad again.

"What's wrong."

"Oh, I'm sorry. It's just my autumn mood."

"It really makes you sad?"

"Yes. It's . . . It's beautiful, but it's what everybody says it is: the death of the year."

"Winter's the death. Autumn is just middle age. I consider the distinction to be very important."

"It's— Oh, come on, James. You're not that old."

"My point, exactly. But 'that time of year thou may'st in me behold . . .' "

"And you don't like it, do you? I mean, I don't see you fallen to the 'sere and yellow leaf,' but if *you* do, you're not very happy about it."

"No. But I'm enjoying it anyway. I know what's coming, and I *don't* like it. But I guess I've learned to accept, because the alternative is to poison my enjoyment of now. Don't do that, Sarah."

"Maybe you're right. I know that's what's usually regarded as wisdom. But . . . I guess I feel like Dylan Thomas: 'Do not go gentle into that good night. . . . Rage, rage against the dying of the light.' "

"Rage. . . ."

"What?"

"I admire— I respond to that love of life. Sure. But rage against something you can't do anything about? Anger about a situation, anger that leads you to do something that changes it, that's positive. But rage is blinding and consuming, and when it comes

from something you can't change, then I think it
finds other objects. I think it becomes a habit, even
an end in itself.'' Suddenly he was sorry the subject
had arisen. This was not the time. ''I don't know.''
He focused on the flashing stream.

Sarah was ready to retort, but caught the change in
his mood. She studied him for a moment, then let the
argument slip away on the water.

For a long time they were content to sit silently in
each other's company.

When they were talking again Sarah mentioned
Franconia College. ''I couldn't finish at Smith, or
matriculate anywhere else—I'd changed my name,
had no records. I was hiding. But Franconia was
loose enough that I could sit in on courses. It was a
pretty strange place—some people absolutely stoned
all the time.'' She laughed. ''One time there was a
school talent show, and one couple—I guess it was
what they thought they did best, and they did it, right
up onstage in front of everybody! But there were
some good people too. Some brilliant people.

''One of the weirdest things about it was where it
was. The college had gotten the old Forest Hills Hotel.
You probably saw it when you came into town, that
huge white building up on the hill? It was one of the
old grand hotels. Very fashionable in the last century—
I guess in this one, too, up until the Second World
War. Anyway, there we were, longhairs, antiestab-
lishment, antielitist, doing our thing in that monu-
ment to the gracious living of the leisure class.''

''Is it still there? The college, I mean.''

''No. Funds ran out. It folded about ten years ago.

The hotel is still there. It's derelict now. Would you like to see it?''

"Sure."

They parked off the road, just past the driveway. "The police might come if they saw a car there. You're not supposed to go in." They walked across untended lawn.

The old building sprawled, vaster close up than it appeared from below, a long spine running east to west, transverse wings at the ends, another making the central section. "Whited sepulchre" came to Marley's mind. But the hulk seemed less a house of the dead than a dead thing itself. Loosened clapboards, splintered, hanging, scattered among the ragged weeds, were like tattered strips of shroud. The dull, chalky whiteness was stained with black patches of mildew, red-brown streaks, gray of weather-ravaged wood where paint had sloughed, colors of dessicating bone. Four broad steps led up to the entry porch. They were cracked; dead leaves and sand had collected in their corners and rotted, and weeds grew out of that humus.

"I'm sure the doors are locked. People get in through windows around the back."

"Have you been in?"

"Not since the college closed. But a friend of mine has. They've been selling it off in pieces, and he bought an old sink with porcelain knobs. And I guess kids get in."

At the east side a portico had fallen. Fluted columns sprawled where they had toppled. Made of once finely jointed hardwood, they were cracked;

milkweed grew up through them. A Corinthian capital pedastaled three beer cans.

"Sic transit gloria mundi," Marley said.

"I know a woman in town who tells of coming here for tea with her grandmother. On the veranda. I can just imagine it: Lapsang-Souchong and cucumber sandwiches, white eyelet lace, big hats. Pleasant. We don't have 'pleasant' anymore. If we have a good time, it's a kick, or a gas, or it's intense."

At the corner they found a window that had been smashed. Jagged fangs of glass threatened them should they attempt to enter through it. Marley found a stick, broke most of them away. "Watch out, there may still be some splinters." He went in first, helped Sarah over the sill. Shards cracked under their feet.

"This was the library."

Books still were stacked in corners and along one wall. *"Census of 1960,"* Marley read.

Sarah offered, *"The Federal Code."*

"Need a Detroit phonebook? Nineteen sixty-eight."

Dead facts moldering, Marley thought, and wondered what crops would grow from them if they were composted.

Torn ends of dangling wires showed where fixtures had been ripped from the ceiling. They seemed a hazard, not electrically, but as though they might, like tentacles, entwine and trap someone who blundered into them.

Along one side of the room, remains of large glass globes, milk-white, once a string of giant pearls, hung in a row at the ends of the thin black rods. Each one had been smashed, Marley assumed, from some hatred of their delicacy and geometric perfection. He thought of his goblets.

"There's a stairway through here." Sarah pointed toward a set of glass-paned double doors. She went through. Marley followed, and when he released the doors behind him, spring-loaded hinges made them swing back and forth with a *whump, whump* that seemed menacing in the mortuary stillness.

Broken plaster and glass from light bulbs littered the stairs. Marley and Sarah made their way up carefully, but there was a tiny crackling at each footstep.

"This was the lounge for us. It must have been the lobby." A thick red carpet still covered the floor, stained and torn, humped in places over warped floorboards. A forest of square pillars, leaves carved on their capitals, held up the paneled ceiling. Marley imagined the hotel bus drawing around the curving drive, the guests entering leisurely, the army of porters with portmanteaux.

They went up another floor. Confronting the stairway, big as life, stood the painted figure of a woman. Two-dimensional, orange, naked, with legs apart she proudly presented her pubic hair, unashamed that her head was bald. Inscribed above her: IF JUST ONE WOMAN TOLD HER STORY, THE WORLD WOULD CRACK. The woman's mouth was open, and jagged shapes in yellow, red, green, and violet crashed behind her.

Farther along the corridor, notices were still pinned to a bulletin board.

"I guess the money finally all ran out one day. Students were told the college was closed and wouldn't reopen, and that was it. They just walked out and left about everything.''

The broad corridor ran the building's length, rooms opening right and left from it. Everything felt cold. Marley had twice visited morgues. He recognized the chill and stillness, and suddenly wished they hadn't come.

"This was the dean of students— Look at that!'' Papers lay heaped on the floor, spilling from boxes in one corner. Sarah went to them. "It's all the students' records! They've just left them here! They shouldn't have done that!''

"Maybe it's nothing confidential."

"Let me see." She went down on her knees, scanning papers.

"Probably no one cares now anyway." Marley wanted to go on, but Sarah was engrossed.

He left the room, wandered down the corridor. A line of movie film trailed along it, turned at a staircase, and wound on upward. He wondered what event whose motion made it worth recording had been frozen into split-second sequence and, so reduced, abandoned.

He stepped into a room. Its high walls met the ceiling gracefully at a heavy cornice. Tall windows looked out upon the lawn. Not a large room, really, although it had a generosity of proportion. He walked carefully to the center of the room over a carpet that might once have brought inside the rich and restful green of summer. Now, sun-bleached and stained, it suggested slime on stagnant ponds. What he could see of the flooring looked sound, but there was a sense of dry rot in the wood everywhere. He drifted to the adjoining bath, saw the scars where fixtures had been ripped away, went back into the corridor again.

Doors were open, at least ajar, as he went along, and he could see some part of every room. Most furnishings were gone, of course, but odds and ends enough remained to give a sense of hasty flight, as though in terror. One room contained a broken chair, another a wastebasket; a single athletic sock hung on a doorknob. But what lay in them all was emptiness. He couldn't any longer imagine the genteel guests, or even the free-style students. It was not their ghosts that troubled him, but an instinct that all those rooms could not be vacant.

At a transverse corridor he turned left, went to the high windows at its end. They looked south, down the valley where Sarah's cabin hid. The view was spectacular: Franconia Notch and the mountain ridge to the east, a lower range of hills to the west. At that distance the trees blended together into washes of color—rosy on the lower slopes modulating to golden above, and then to evergreen at the tops. He tried to enjoy it, but the cold was seeping into him, the silence, the feeling of the emptiness becoming positive. He had been uneasy. He began to be afraid.

He should not have left Sarah alone.

Marley turned. Back at the main corridor he paused and looked both ways, listened. He heard nothing, but had the sense that there had been some sound. Well, of course, he told himself, Sarah had made a noise. That explanation didn't satisfy. He tried to recreate in his mind's ear what must have been received subliminally.

The swinging door! The double doors at the bottom of the stairwell—that *whump, whump.*

Marley tried to convince himself he was being ridiculous. Distant from the doors, he couldn't have heard them swing even if they had. The spookiness of the building had set him on edge, made him hallucinate.

Or— Had being on edge made his senses sharper?

He started back toward the dean's office.

"Sarah?" He called quietly so that she might hear, but not loudly enough, he hoped, to alert anyone else. "Sarah?" He hadn't realized he'd wandered so far from the office. He walked faster. "Sarah?" He rushed in through the doorway.

She was not in the office.

"Sarah?"

Marley checked the adjoining room, wheeled back and into the corridor again. He forced himself to pause. Took a breath. Listened. Over his heartbeat he heard only sinister silence.

Softly, as though stalking, he crossed to the opposite room, paused by its half-open door. He put his back to the corridor wall beside it, pressed his palm against the door, swung it in. He could see no one inside. He rolled around the doorjamb into the room. He prowled across it, toward the connection with its neighbor. The corner of his eye caught the motion before he could be pounced upon. He sprang, whirling, arms coming up crossed in front.

He confronted himself in a cracked mirror.

He had to get control of himself.

He passed carefully into the next room, back to the corridor again. Hopelessness began to settle into him like the cold. How could he find her, search every room, fight whoever might wait behind any of the countless doors?

He breathed deeply and slowly, then held his breath and listened again.

Footsteps. Faint, but he was not imagining them. They came from the floor above, from the far end of the corridor.

Rapidly, quietly, keeping close to the lefthand wall, he went to the stairway that he and Sarah had used. Also faintly but unmistakably he could hear someone moving below as well, not on the stairs, probably in the lobby.

Moving fast but testing each step to see if it creaked, Marley made his way up. Unable to be cautious any longer, he sprang out into the hallway. Sarah stood there twenty feet away, silhouetted against light from far end windows. He dashed to her, seized her arms.

"Are you all right!"

"What's wrong?"

"What are you doing here?"

"I came up—"

"I couldn't find you."

"I came up to see—"

"Let's get out of here."

"What's wrong?"

"There's somebody here."

"What! Who!"

"I don't know. Come on!" Grabbing her hand, he hurried her back to the stairway. "This was a stupid idea. We never should have come here. It's a perfect place—" He didn't want to say it.

He kept them to the wall going down, peering

around each turn. Now that he'd found her, his panic
abated. He was able, as usual, to be keyed but controlled. Hoping that whoever hunted them wouldn't
know where they were exactly, he made them creep
quietly as they could, given his sense that they must
flee.

They passed the lobby level, at the end of the
building away from where he had heard footsteps,
and reached the lowest floor again. It was at ground
level to the south, below grade on the north side.
They had come down at the end of the building
opposite the library; the corridor to it passed through
darkness. Marley turned the other way. Light, reflected from the room that opened there, filtered into
the hallway through an arch. He started toward it.

"No," Sarah whispered. "That's the kitchen. It's
below ground level. The windows are too high."

Marley had released Sarah's hand. He took it again
in his left. She held tightly to him. They started
toward the library.

Light from the kitchen, and more faintly from the
library, struck doorjambs, outlining black holes into
deeper darkness.

"I don't like this, James," Sarah whispered.

"No."

He moved on the balls of his feet, breathlessly, set
to dodge or spring. They came abreast of the first
doorway. The door stood open, but they could see
nothing within. Anything, anyone, could crouch there.
Nothing lunged at them, so Marley went on. Then he
paused. Nothing had sprung. Might that be but to
strike from behind? He'd had no strong sense there of
anyone lurking, but waves of danger from some-

where were rising in pitch. He wanted a weapon, if only a club!

The light at the long hall's end narrowed their pupils, made their present darkness deeper. They went three eggshell steps. Just ahead, the next two doorways, not quite opposite each other, gaped. Marley stopped. He could see nothing, hear nothing; but the silence was thick, and threat a pressure. He stepped, stopped again, leaned against it, trying for courage to force himself forward. He could not.

He gripped Sarah's hand even tighter. Her arm was as rigid as his. He pulled back against it. Eyes darting between those doorways, ears pricked for a sound behind, they cat-footed carefully backward; then back again. They feared to rush away lest the sound draw whoever lay in wait. Marley chanced a slight noise, pulling Sarah quickly by the opening they'd passed. Again, nothing sprang at them.

As they distanced themselves from the darkest place, they felt relief enough to turn toward each other, to move sideways and quicker. The sum of threat kept constant though—as that from the paired doorways faded, the fear that they'd been followed down the stairwell swelled. Marley pulled Sarah around him so he'd be the closer when they reached it again. No one was there.

There seemed no choice but to go back up to the lobby level and then to break out onto the front porch.

Marley had heard footsteps at that level though. He paused on the lobby landing, listened. He heard them again. Someone—he sensed more than one—was coming directly toward him.

Instantly he whirled, pushed Sarah ahead of him up the next flight of stairs. He knew she was frightened, but she was keeping her head, moving quickly but still with all possible quiet.

Out again in the corridor of the second floor, Sarah paused, questioning by a glance which way he wanted them to go.

Marley had only an instant for thought. Better not to be caught in the corridor or trapped in one of the paired rooms along it. To the right he could see the arched entrance to a large room, and another doorway within that. He jerked his head in that direction.

Several doorways opened from the room beyond the arch. A heavy table stood in the center of the large space and workbenches had been built against the walls; all were splotched and streaked with garish colors. The wing must have been used by the college for art classes.

Marley pictured dragging the table to barricade a door. But he rejected the notion. Like most people, he assumed, he sometimes had a nightmare that a horror stalked him. He would flee, try to hide, but finally would turn, and, shouting defiance, would charge. The tactic always worked, because he woke then.

Now, as in his dream, he had had enough of fear and flight; but, awake, he had no illusion that a shout would shatter his enemy. He looked around for a weapon. Little that he could see was movable. Three large jars of pigment stood on a shelf over one bench. On another, brackets supported a four-foot-long roll of kraft paper.

"Get a jar," he whispered. "Two, if you can." In

two strides he crossed to the other side, lifted the roll of paper. Getting the jars down, one held under each arm, Sarah turned and stared in bewilderment when she saw Marley start back toward the corridor. But though she didn't understand his plan, she followed at once.

The pipe that ran through the length of the roll, on which it had turned, projected at either end and gave Marley a grip for each hand. What was left of the paper must have weighed thirty pounds. He lifted it, resting it on his head as he stood with his back to the wall next to the archway at the head of the stairs.

People could be heard coming up now. And then there were whispers.

Marley set himself. He would pivot into the opening and hurl the roll down the stairs. Then he would either grab the jars from Sarah and throw them, too, or simply leap feetfirst down upon his enemies.

The multiple footfalls, the whispering, came closer, from halfway up the final flight. Marley pressed the roll to full arm's length over his head and spun on his left foot.

Two shrieks and a high-pitched ''Jesus Christ!'' as Marley suddenly loomed in the doorway.

Something in the tone of the whispers, perhaps a suppressed giggle, must have alerted him even as he had moved. He was able to balk, staggering, but holding on to the heavy roll as the first boy threw himself backward, knocking his companions down against the handrail.

Marley righted himself, threw the roll sideways into the corridor, and—in continuous motion—bounded down four steps to grab the first boy by the shoulder. "What the goddamn hell—"

"Oh, Jesus! Please! Please!"

The boy clutched the railing to keep from falling backward. He could not have struck at Marley from that position if he'd wanted to; but he seemed too terrified to think of fighting. The same was true of the boy pressed against the wall behind him, and of the other trying to rise and run from the step where he'd collapsed. All three of them must have been about twelve years old.

Marley gave the boy one violent shake, then caught himself. He relaxed his grip enough so as not to be hurtful, nodded twice, and made his voice calm, even though his heart still pounded.

"Okay, son. Okay. It's all right. Now, what are you doing here?"

"Please, mister. I'm sorry. We were just . . ."

"Yes?"

"We—" The boy's eyes widened still more as he focused on Sarah's silhouette: a shape—with those jars under her arms—as grotesque as Marley's must have been.

"It's all right," Marley reassured the boy, and patted his shoulder without actually releasing him enough so that he could bolt. "What are you guys doing here?" he asked again.

"We—we saw you come in, and . . ."

The second boy, either naturally braver or more confident because not in Marley's grip, finished for his friend. "We thought you were coming in to make it. We thought we'd give you a scare."

Sarah stepped to the head of the stairs, looking as

though she would heave the jars down upon them. "Why you damn nasty little perverts!"

Marley smiled at the boy, chuckled. "Well, we weren't; but you did." Then he made his voice serious again but not unkindly. "That wasn't a nice thing for you to do, was it?"

The boy under Marley's hand agreed at once. "No, sir. We're sorry."

The third boy sat very still, looking at the steps, not looking at Marley at all, possibly convincing himself they might all believe he wasn't there.

The middle one wasn't brave enough for defiance, but didn't say his amen to Marley's moralizing.

"I don't think they're sorry at all, James! I think they're vicious brats, and they ought to be taught a lesson! I think you should take them down and lock them in that room in the cellar!"

The first boy protested again. "I'm really sorry, lady! Really, I'm sorry!"

Marley put his head to one side and looked sternly at the second boy again, as though seriously considering Sarah's suggestion. He must have been convincing.

"I *am* sorry. I am. I'm sorry! I mean it!"

"Okay. Now, you guys get out of here as fast as you can." They started to move, but Marley held them in place for another moment. "And while you're going, you think about what would have happened if I hadn't been able to stop myself from throwing that roll down on you. Or if I was still as mad as she is. Or"—he suddenly made his voice hard, mean, and loud, ending in a shout—"if you met somebody in here who wasn't a nice guy like I am!"

The boys scrambled over each other and bolted down the stairs. They could be heard running without pause across the lobby and down the other stairway to get out through the library.

Marley went up, took one of the jars from Sarah. "I think maybe we shook them up enough so they won't do that again. Putting them in the cellar was a great idea. They really thought you meant it."

"I did mean it! Those little bastards! They—I— oh . . ." Sarah fumbled with the other jar. It slipped from her shaking hands, dropped, and broke apart, spilling a mound of blue powder.

Marley set down his jar and caught her in his arms. She buried her face against his shoulder, weeping.

"Sarah, Sarah. It's all right. There, there."

"Oh, God! I was so frightened!"

"Me too." He held her tightly.

"Okay. I'm okay now." She raised her head, wiped her eyes with the back of her hand, but didn't push away from him.

"Come on, let's get out of here." He released his arms from around her and took her hand. She gripped back as firmly while they went through the building and out into the warm sunlight.

Only then did they speak again.

"I'm sorry I was so foolish," she said, not looking at him.

"What do you mean?"

"Going to pieces like that."

"Sarah, don't be ridiculous. You were terrific! All through it. Naturally you'd have some reaction after, but *I'm* the one who should be feeling foolish. As a matter of fact, I am. I made up the whole thing. Obviously we were never in any danger.''

''Well, we thought we were. How could we know it was only kids?''

''Why should we have thought it was anything else? Anything dangerous? Nobody knew we were there—I mean, nobody whom we have reason to fear. The natural, sensible thing to do when I heard somebody would have been to call out, 'Hello, who's there?' But I let the place get me on edge, and then spooked both of us. I—I'm sorry.''

''Now who's having a reaction? Come on, James. If people have already tried to kill you because . . . And you think . . . Well, I'm certainly glad you were on edge. You just stay that way!''

They had stopped halfway along the driveway back to the road and Sarah's car. Sarah was facing Marley directly, looking directly into his eyes. Her eyes had that evaluating look, then, as she spoke again, one of valuing.

''You were very impressive, James, trying to get us out of there without confronting whoever it was, turning to fight when you couldn't. Resourceful—making a roll of paper into a dangerous weapon. And the way you handled those kids—I really *could* have locked up the little bastards in the cellar! You were very nice. You have nothing to feel foolish about, James. You're a very impressive man.''

CHAPTER 9

Marley looked through Sarah's collection of tapes, put one into the machine. She was in the kitchen making salad for supper. Without speaking she nodded in agreement with his choice: Mozart, the C major piano concerto. She finished and came back into the living room just before the second movement started. As the first motif began its ascension he smiled, and she smiled in return and said, "Yes. It doesn't matter about *Elvira Madigan*—that it's been popularized. It's still the best."

"Yes." They were looking eye into eye again. "Of course, Number Twenty-seven is probably more nearly perfect, altogether." He qualified their judgment—from critical honesty? Or lest he lose himself in the luscious music, the honey sunlight, the sense of her liking him?

Sitting beside Sarah on the drive back to her cabin from the college, Marley had realized that his curiosity about Sarah, his appraisal of her as attractive and interesting, had been superseded—overwhelmed, in fact. He wasn't in love, he told himself; he told himself he couldn't be in love with a woman he'd known only two days. But no matter what he told himself, he knew what he felt.

The sun was setting over a hill to the left, out of sight from the cabin; but its last glory glowed in the orange and yellow trees. The closest one, a maple, showed separate leaves against the paling sky. Then, as though to the stately pace of the music, light in the foliage lifted ahead of rising shadow, like the soul imagined, and expired.

"Look!" Marley pointed. At eye level a huge, dark bird, broad-winged, slowly stroked its way across where fields below lay hidden by the nearby trees.

"It's a heron."

"Yes."

"He comes by here often this time of year. They nest in some of the marshes around; but they come into the meadows in the fall."

"Yes. I used to see them at home—in Vermont."

Sarah had come to the window too. She turned away, her arms folded against herself.

"What's wrong?"

"Nothing. The same thing. It always makes me sad to see them. Summer's over, winter's coming: It's as though they bring winter."

" 'If Winter comes, can Spring be far behind?' "

"Yes. Up here, yes."

Marley watched the heron out of sight. "It doesn't seem to bother him."

"Why should it? He's going to Florida, or someplace."

"He's not in any hurry to get there. I guess that's one of the things I like about them. I mean, some of the other birds—the flocking ones—seem to get frantic when it's time to migrate. He just takes it as it comes."

She looked at him steadily again. "Yes. You would admire that."

She smiled at him, and Marley had to pretend to peer after the heron, sure that his awareness of potential romance, the possibility of love, was mutual. The attraction each felt for the other was becoming plain in their looks. Too plain too soon: he would have to tell her about himself first.

"And then, of course, I had a tour in Vietnam."

"With the army?"

"Yes. The work with the Friends came later."

He had gotten to it gradually, naturally. Last night she had led their talk; tonight he did. Not straight through. They digressed, took up whatever thought his story brought. But he kept the thread, strung the years on it. Family, childhood, adolescence were told during dinner; college over coffee. He'd bought tenderloin steaks at the local market, and wine. They ate in the living room, from the slab table, sitting on cushions on the floor: awkward, but cozy with the doors of the wood stove open so they could see the flames. They had finished eating, but had wine left to linger over. He took the story on, getting now to the point of it. Yale had meant ROTC; that's how he'd afforded to go there. Then obligatory service, the tour in Germany, and then . . .

"I see." She looked away from him for a moment, then smiled. "I thought you were going to tell me you were married. I knew you were going to tell

me something." She touched the back of his hand.
"Lots of people went to Vietnam, James."

"I went twice. I mean, with the army. I liked it."

Sarah's smile was gone, but she did not turn from
him.

"I liked it a lot. My company . . . We were a
special group. They sent us in where there was a
special problem. We saw a lot of action. I liked
that. I liked killing people." He would not let himself look away from her either. His eyes kept trying
to shift, to be drawn to the firelight, flame reflected
flickering in wineglasses, anywhere; but he held them
steady for her to look into. "I felt . . . I felt *ecstasy*
when I could build up anger and then release it in
some . . . ultimate and violent . . . To have an enemy, and *destroy* him!"

A log settled in the stove. Marley looked toward
the sound. He couldn't tell if Sarah had also. Her
eyes were still fixed on his face when he turned back.
He tried to hold himself to them, but the momentary
shift seemed to have broken his resolve. He looked
back to the fire.

"You don't seem to be that sort of person," she
said after a while.

"No. I don't *seem* to be. I try not to be. Oh, I'm
not—I wasn't a psychopath! Nobody had to worry
about me when the moon was full. And I never did
anything sadistically. I might never have known if I
hadn't gotten into a war. But I did choose to stay in
the army, and chose to go Rangers; and I did volun-
teer for a second tour. And then I found out why."

"How?"

"I just realized. Nothing dramatic. No particular

atrocity. I killed people in combat. They tried to kill
me, did kill my men, some of my friends. But it was
just your everyday war. And one day I realized I
liked it, and why."

"What did you do?"

"I quit. They sent me to the chaplain, and the
army shrinks. They certified me. And I'd paid my
dues. They gave me a medical discharge."

"And then you worked with the refugees."

"Yes. But that's not the end of it. I have to tell
you all of it, Sarah.

"While I was doing that I met David—David
Cheyney. Most people don't know it, but he's a
Friend; and he puts a lot—both money and his own
time—into things they do. Anyway, we got on. I was
able to handle some logistical problems over there,
and he offered me a job working for him. Most of
what I do is— It's interesting but not dangerous. Last
month I was in Bolivia. David's trying to get a road
built to a ranch he owns there, and for some reason it
just wouldn't move. Well, I found out eventually that
there was a feud between the contractor's brother-in-
law and the regional administrator's cousin. And before that there was a guy in California who wanted
David's backing on a computer venture. David had
all the technical and financial data; but he just wanted
a gut response to the man."

Marley recognized the temptation to go on telling
her the good things, the safe things. He made himself
turn back to the point.

"But sometimes there is some danger. It's only
happened about half a dozen times in the past ten
years. And—less often than that—there can be vio-

lence. In the past ten years I have killed three men. The last two were totally in self-defense. I shot one man while he was trying to shoot me, and the other—he was trying to run me off the side of a road, over a cliff, and, purely trying to evade him, I did it to him. But the first one . . . was different.

"It was one of the first things I did for David after I came back. David suspected that the manager of one of his farms in Arizona was embezzling. I found out he was. He was involved with a woman—his secretary. It was one of those love-fear things. He abused her, but she couldn't leave him. Well, I got to know her, and we got along, and finally I persuaded her to give evidence. But he found out, and got to her first.

"I was just going to her place to pick her up. When I got there I found her. He'd tried to make it look like a rape and robbery, but I knew. So I went after him. I didn't go to the police, I went after him.

"I found him in his office. He was going on just as usual. He was going to try to brazen it out. But when he saw the way I was coming, he lost his nerve. He went for a gun in the desk, but I threw the desk over on him before he could get it. And then I beat him to death.

"One of David's lawyers got me off. Temporary insanity. The jury didn't care. They were with me anyway.

"Maybe I *was* temporarily insane. Maybe that's what that rage is. But it wasn't that I was blind with it. I knew exactly what I was doing. And I had it for forty-five minutes, from the time I found her until I got to him. And I loved every minute of it.

"And I've hated it every minute since then. It's never happened again. The other two . . . It was nothing like that.

"I've thought about doing some other work. Doing something where there wouldn't be any danger, any chance . . . But I decided it was better this way. So that I'd know.

"It seems to be something in the past, now. And I feel good that I'm able to say that. I'm pretty much at peace with myself. But I wanted you to know."

Sarah put her glass on the table, sat in stillness, one hand holding the other. Finally, she said, "What do you want me to say to you, James?"

"I . . . whatever you feel like saying, Sarah."

"You want me to forgive you."

"I hadn't thought of it that way. But you're probably right."

"Why? Why me?"

"I guess because of what *you* were doing during the war. Because of who you are, what you are."

"How do you know what I am? You've known me for only two days."

"No. I've been getting to know you for . . . I know you from way back. I know you in pigtails. I've read your prize poem. I know . . . I know I'm falling in love with you, Sarah. And I think you're falling in love with me."

He could look at her steadily again. It all had been said, more, sooner than he had expected. He could lean back against the frame of the couch, one arm resting on one drawn-up knee, and look at her and wait for whatever she would say.

Sarah looked beyond her clasped hands, or into herself.

He could feel his heart pounding, knew his hand would tremble if held outward; but he could wait.

Finally, speaking very quietly, she said, "I can't forgive you, James. It's not my place to forgive. And even if it were, I couldn't say, 'It's all right; it doesn't matter; the slate's wiped clean; forget about it.' What you did was wrong, and obviously you know that or you wouldn't have had to tell me about it. So I can't *forgive*." Then she looked at him again. "But I accept you. Whatever you may have been. . . . I know you've changed that. I know what you are now; I know what you want to be. I—" At the end of it suddenly she was shy and looked down again.

She ventured a glance; he was staring at her. Away again, then she forced her eyes back and returned his look. He was still waiting for her. She came forward to her knees, put her hands on either side of his head, and kissed him gently.

At last his passion could be loosed. He clasped her, startling her with his intensity and strength.

"Wow!" she gasped when at last he let them breathe. "I never guessed you had all *that* hidden back there."

"I save it till it's wanted."

She looked at him, seeing through to another level, then grinned. "It's wanted."

They held each other there until the last piece of wood in the stove broke.

"I'd better fill the stove." Sarah extricated herself. She closed the stove's front doors to make it airtight for the night, filled it from the top with logs from the rack. When she shut the loading door the room was dark but for skyglow through the window wall.

She stood for a moment, looking at Marley. He got up, went to her. They embraced, and then she turned and—without either of them speaking about it—they went together toward the loft. The ladder to it was narrow, and Marley stayed close behind her, his hands on the pipe railings, arms extended on either side of her. Halfway up she paused, leaned back into them and against him, tipped her head back beside his. He kissed her neck. And then they went on up to her bed.

"Jesus Christ, they're screwing!"

Marley came awake instantly, tried to move. Sarah lay on his left arm, hers across his chest, her leg over his, her sweet weight, unheavy on him while they'd slumbered, now pinning him down.

Light, voices. Someone was in the cabin!

He wrenched, rolled, looked down from the loft, perceived two men, tried again to rise, then froze, focus fixed by the binocular stare of the shotgun where one man's eyes should have been.

"Caught in the veritable flaming deliciousness. Sorry about that." The other man spoke. He held a handgun, not pointing it. Marley recognized the voice from the cornfield. The man's eyes, though screened behind aviator glasses and narrowed by mockery, seemed more threatening than the gun-barrel openings. Marley kept his own eyes on that greater danger, tried as best he could to match the man's casual assurance. That was difficult since the man looked

like a devil-may-care flying ace—wide jaw with deep
lines beside his mouth, those glasses, the once-again-
fashionable brown leather flight jacket, turtleneck
sweater—while Marley lay naked under the bedclothes.

"Mal?" Sarah came slower to consciousness. Startled by Marley's movement, she propped herself,
trying to see past him, trying to comprehend.

"Sarah." The man nodded, twisting shoulders
slightly, swinging his arm. Downlight, highlighting
skin tight over face bones, cast shifting shadows,
sharp edges that cut his mock bow's humor, just as a
glint on the silver pistol barrel flashed a threat bely-
ing his ease.

"Hi, Sarah." The other called without shifting his
sight from along the shotgun.

"Dennis? Mal, Denny, what are you—?"

"We'll talk about it, Sarah. Come on down. I
said, come down. Slowly, Marley."

Marley sat up slowly as directed, keeping the sheet
across his lap. He reached for his trousers.

"Leave them!" The command whip-snapped. But
for that, he gave everything an ironic drawl. "It's
okay, Marley. We all used to skinny-dip together.
We don't have any hangups about bodies."

In that combination of command and sarcasm Marley
smelled the man's assumption that other people were
his inferiors.

Marley managed the smile that always made him
look well-meaning and harmless, and now, he hoped,
must seem idiotically ingratiating. He rose, started
down the ladder. Air at loft level was as warm and
gentle as lovemaking remembered; but each succes-
sive tread brought colder reality. Malcolm stared at

him, smiling lopsidedly as he descended. The look was not lascivious, rather an enjoyment of Marley's presumed embarrassment. The man didn't smell of after-shave this late at night, but Marley knew him anyway as the one who'd played those clever tricks in his apartment.

"Come on, Sarah! We've all seen it. You don't have to be shy with us."

"A lot of things seem to have changed, Malcolm." Sarah got out on the opposite side of the bed, took her robe from its peg, and put it on without haste before turning. Then she came down too.

As Marley reached floor level the man with the shotgun lowered it to his waist and stepped back to be out of lunging range. His appearance remained the same though: eyes large, dark, and close-set to a thin nose. He reminded Marley of a lanky hill man he'd known. The identification was unnerving, since that man could shoot a squirrel from a tree at forty feet with a hip shot.

"You guys really are persistent. How did you find us?" Marley tried to make it sound like a compliment.

Malcolm had been watching Sarah. He snapped his head in annoyance at the interruption. "Shut up. I didn't come here to talk to you, Marley. I've *already* talked to you. I told you. I warned you. Twice, which is at least once more than a man with any smarts should need. Denny, put him in a closet."

"Sure, Mal." Dennis kept his gun trained on Marley, never losing aim but for fractions of seconds while checking the room. "Where?"

"What's that back in the corner?"

"The bathroom," Sarah answered.

Malcolm took one step to look; that was enough. "Window." He scanned the living room. "That's why you've got your shit all over the place: no closets. I thought it was just you being you. What's that? Trapdoor?"

"The cellar."

"Yeah? I didn't know you had one. We checked all around outside when we were seeing how to get in here. We were going to come down the chimney, for Christsake, until—just for the hell of it—we tried the front door." Malcolm went around Dennis, lifted the trap. "Yeah. Super. Okay, Marley. We'll call you when we need you."

Partly from shock, more from control, Marley had been without emotion. He could not allow fear or guilt to immobilize him, to divert his attention from any opportunity. For a moment, though, he did look like a Last Judgment sinner sentenced to the crypt. Then he tried to look like fury controlled while crossing to the trap, and with as much dignity as a naked man commands, descended into the dark and cold. Malcolm closed the trapdoor down after him.

"Okay, Sarah. Let's rap. Nobody 'raps' anymore, but for old time's sake, we'll *rap*."

Marley could hear well through the floor. He heard the voices—"Come on, sit down"—footsteps, chair scrape.

"What is this about, Mal?" In Sarah's tight voice Marley heard fear, and resolution not to let that show. Love for her strength surged in him. He had to save her.

"We'll get there, Sarah. Let's just shoot the shit first, okay? I mean, it has been a long time."

"It's a little hard to believe we're just old friends chatting about old times, Mal, when you're holding that pistol."

"Oh. Sorry. Sure. I'll put it in my pocket, okay? It was just for effect."

Marley could begin to see. The cabin floor above was single-planked: two-by-eights laid directly across the joists. A construction sound enough, but quick and dirty. Shrinkage had made narrow gaps between the boards. Cold air would come up from the cellar; light filtered down. He stood on one foot then the other on the chill concrete. His skin had goosepimpled, and soon the cold would penetrate and set him shivering. But he stood, letting his eyes widen to see by that little light, thinking.

". . . worked in the natural foods store down in the village until . . ."

He had no plan. But he had begun to hope when Malcolm ordered him closeted, put out of sight as unworthy of attention. And to have been put into that cellar, that treasure house of tools, that potential arsenal! He had felt like shouting, "Don't throw me into that briar patch!"

". . . artists-in-the-schools program. I've been getting fourth-graders to write poetry. Malcolm, you don't care about this. Why are you—"

"I do. Sarah, I really, really do want to know what kind of life you've gotten into, and how you like it, and whether it's rewarding and fulfilling, and all that shit."

Marley told himself he merely had to figure what

to do with his resources. Obviously, he could not conceal a weapon against the time they called him back among them. Refusing to come out, springing on them from hiding as they came down, would be a tactic they surely would anticipate. Might he find some projectile, fabricate some launcher, lift the trap but an inch?

Dennis spoke. "I mean, it blows your fucking mind, Sarah, to hear about people. You know what Bobby Atkins did? He went to fucking Harvard Law School. Okay, work within the system: He goes home to Mississippi to be a public defender. You know, they assigned him to defend the fucking Grand Dragon's Asshole of the local KKK! No shit!"

Dennis's voice was louder than the others. It came from almost above. Marley peered up, trying to see between cracks. At the distance above his head they were too narrow for that, but the lines of light were blocked by an irregular patch. It moved as Dennis gesticulated. "Jesus, I'd liked to have seen that sucker's face when he realized his ass was in a black man's hand."

Sarah and Malcolm probably were on the couch or rocking chairs. Dennis must be sitting on the loft ladder. How could any of them be reached?

Malcolm took up the line again. "So, you see, we do want to know about you. How about it? You still think it's a gift to be simple? Still getting your strength from the land, your hope from the hills, and all that shit?"

"I live here."

"Yeah. It's nice. Cozy. Simple, honest, but comfortable."

The first shiver ran up Marley's back. He tried to relax into the cold instead of tensing against it. His eyes were accommodating rapidly. He scanned the ceiling, noticed an irregularity, felt it. A nut. Swept his hand over. Another one. Of course. He'd seen the bolt heads from above. The loftladder was bolted through the floor.

Marley spun toward the workbench, the tools and supplies strewn near it. He went on the balls of his feet, minimizing contact with the cement. Was it only cold, or damp too? He had to connect without danger to himself, come instantly through the trap at Malcolm. He swept over what hardware he could see. A wall outlet, not heavy enough. Mousetrap. He picked it up; right idea, unreliable practically.

At the far end of the bench: a wooden box heaped full of junk. Marley snatched things out using both hands, afraid of noise. Doorknob. Padlock Drawer pulls. Broken blockplane. Sash weight. He tried frantically to deduce some machine by recognizing the true purpose of parts disguised as other things. He emptied the box, didn't find it.

As he looked over the pile he kept himself alert to the conversation—to any sounds—from above. He needed to have the clearest image possible of everyone's position there. He needed to have some sense of the shape of the talk, of how much time he had until it would reach the inevitable conclusion.

He heard rocking from time to time. Sarah wouldn't be doing that, so Malcolm must be in the chair. Marley couldn't tell whether the rocking was an expression of Malcolm's ease or of his tension.

"Great view from here, I imagine. Sense of the

seasons." Malcolm seemed genuinely appreciative.
"You feed birds?"

"Yes."

"I thought you would. I do too. I'm in the city, so
all I get is sparrows; but I get a charge. What varie-
ties do you get?"

"Chickadees, nuthatches, woodpeckers, warb-
lers. . . . Mal—"

"Terrific. Picnics? You go on picnics?"

"Yes."

Again Marley looked over the odds and ends on
the table, fighting against hopelessness. What has to
happen? An image came. He put the empty wooden
box upside down on the floor near the cellar ladder.
He found first a narrow chisel, then an ice pick,
jammed the points of each hard into the box so the
tools stood erect about four inches apart.

"Yeah. Remember the great picnics we had? Down
by the river. Mount Tom. Sugarloaf, over in Sunder-
land. A loaf, a jug, and thou and Herbert Marcuse
singing in the wilderness. That was real. That may
have been the most really real thing we all did. And
you've hung on to most of it, haven't you?" Malcolm's tone conveyed admiration and some envy.

"I guess so."

Marley snatched up the coil of two-conductor wire.
Where among the jumble on the bench was the tool?
He rummaged with his eyes, saw, grabbed the strip-
per. He snapped two lengths, stripped bare leads at
each end of each. Very fast, but holding himself just
back from frantic haste that would make him fumble.
Quietly he connected a wire of one cable to each
ladder bolt, bending the leads, twisting them with

fingers, afraid pliers might scratch and sound against the metal. Then he took the other end, twisted one wire around the chisel blade and the other around the icepick. While the frame and railings of the loft ladder were metal, the treads were wood. Each side, then, would constitute a separate line. Marley had to hope that Dennis was touching both.

Malcolm rocked again. "Nice life, Sarah," he said in a tone of sincere approval. Then, "So how come you want to leave all this? You're going to leave, aren't you."

"Lead 'em on and chop 'em off. You haven't lost your touch, Mal. The smiling cobra. What have *you* been doing since you didn't get to be commissar?"

"I am an entrepreneur. Denny and I are entrepreneurs."

"What do you mean?"

"We buy and sell."

"What?"

"Whatever you want."

"You mean you're pushing shit?"

"You mean, do I stand around playgrounds hooking toddlers? Do Mr. Smith and Mr. Wesson sell Saturday night specials on street corners? We are businessmen!"

" 'Property is theft. The root of all society's evils is the profit motive.' "

"It's true. The analysis was absolutely correct, Sarah. Our only error was in believing we could change it. We couldn't. Maybe the next time the cycle comes around . . . A hundred years, maybe only another generation . . . I pass on the torch. As some wise man said—it may have been Marx—

Groucho, that is—'If at first you don't succeed, try
and try again. And then quit, there's no sense being a
damn fool about it.' The system is shit. But we
didn't have big enough shovels. So, if we're going to
have to stand in it, we might as well grow tomatoes.''

Marley picked up the other cable, bent the stiff
wires at one end into loops, separated them. There
were C-clamps hanging above the workbench. He
grabbed one, clamped the cable to the bench, the
looped end projecting out eighteen inches.

Snatching the other end, he bent each section of
bared wire back upon itself, making hooks. He approached the entry panel. Of course, the main should
be pulled for safe work. But the spring-loaded switch
would bang like Dennis's shotgun going off and all
the lights would go out. He'd have to work hot. He
stood for a moment looking, took a breath to steady
himself. There would really be no danger if he was
very careful. All those foolish amateurs and over-
confident professionals who worked hot and electro-
cuted themselves did so only because they weren't
careful enough. He separated the wires farther to be
sure they wouldn't touch anything accidentally.

Even though he had stood on tiptoe, cold from the
floor had made his feet ache. Now he had to stand
flat to be steady. Because of greater contact, and the
slight draft from the foundation wall, his shivers
became a steady quivering.

Malcolm asked, ''Cold, Sarah? Or withdrawing?''
Sarah must have tucked the lapels of her robe more
tightly around her. ''Well, don't be too judgmental. I
mean, you didn't answer my question, but you are

going to leave your treehouse for the Ten Broeck millions, aren't you?''

''My daughter needs me.''

''Sure. Okay, okay. Your daughter needs you, and she can't possibly come *here,* now, can she? Okay. Whatever. But Sarah, that kind of makes a problem. For Denny and me.''

Marley took a deep breath, willed himself still. Very slowly he brought one lead over the eighth inch of bare wire that showed beyond a terminal connection on the panel. He took a breath again, and suddenly pulled down, making contact. Keeping the connection tight, he hooked the other wire to another terminal. He now had a 240-volt line.

''How would my coming back make any difference?''

''Well, they want us; but I don't think they've been looking very hard for a long time. I mean, the evidence they had wasn't certain, and it's pretty cold by now. But if they've got you— Then if they get us they've got us, you get me? As I said, Denny and I are men of substance in the community now. We're not into bugging out.''

''I wouldn't tell them anything, Mal. I told you that then, and now I would have even more reason for keeping it all—''

''You'd have even more reason for not wanting to sit in the slammer.''

''They wouldn't—there's no charge against me.''

''There will be—at least contempt of court if you refuse to give evidence. Maybe accessory after.''

''Part of the arrangement with Mrs. Ten Broeck—''

"Don't count on it. Or, at least *I'm* not going to count on it."

Half-following the talk, as he had been, Marley knew it was almost over. But now he couldn't hurry. He came back to the clamped cable cautiously. He freed the clamp, holding the cable in his left hand steady and away from him like a snake held behind its head. Clothing wouldn't have protected him from its touch, but nakedness made him feel more vulnerable. Without taking his eyes from those deadly fangs, he picked up the sash weight and sidestepped slowly to the cellar stair. The cable was stiff enough so that he could hold it about two feet from its end, but not more than that, and still control it accurately.

Conversation had halted. Sarah must have been looking directly at Malcolm with one of her long stares. "Whatever it takes," she said at last. "That's what you always would say when we argued about what to do.' 'If the cause is right, then, whatever it takes.' And how about you, Denny? How do you feel about killing me?"

Marley stepped onto the bottom rung with his left foot, up two with his right so his leg was cocked under him. He got his cheek up against the floorboards, trying to see back toward Dennis to check his position. With one eye to a crack between boards he could make out enough of the man's figure to see that Dennis was sitting on the third step of the ladder, one leg bent and resting on the second step, the other extended to the floor. He was leaning against the left railing, cradling the shotgun against that arm, his right hand hanging from the opposite rail.

Marley shifted position, extended the cable, locating one looped wire around the chisel handle and the other over the icepick.

"Ah, shit, Sarah," Dennis drawled. "I mean, Jesus Christ."

Marley took a final deep breath, let half out, and dropped the cable. Vibration hummed from the electrical panel, and in the living room lights dimmed.

As he banged back the trapdoor and came up, Marley caught sight of Dennis shooting upward as his muscles went rigid. His left shoulder caught under one stair railing, his right hand clutched the other one, unable to release. Eyes huge, lips drawn back, teeth clenched, hair standing, his body strained against the current's grip. The shotgun slid downward, clattering and spattering sparks as it struck railing uprights and bounced away. Blue smoke began to rise from Dennis's hand and shoulder.

Marley's focus snapped toward Malcolm who was already on his feet as though shot up by the surge galvanizing Dennis. As Marley's shoulders came above the floor, Malcolm dug in his pocket for the pistol.

Marley hurled the sash weight and continued bounding up his ladder. Two steps to floor level, and he was in a crouch, driving like a sprinter.

The weight spun end over end across the room. Marley's aim was true, but Malcolm saw the missile coming, lurched away. It hit only the side of his left arm, the sleeve of his jacket. Thrown off balance, though, his pull at his pistol was awkward. The hammer caught in the corner of his pocket. He fumbled, freed it.

But Sarah flung herself upon him. Even as Marley hurtled across the room, as Dennis's body finally fell forward, she sprang up on the couch and threw herself at Malcolm. Her full weight struck him just as the pistol came from his pocket. He was thrown, toppling backward, Sarah falling with and on him. Instinctively, as he was pulling the trigger, his right arm flung out to break his fall.

He didn't get to shoot again. Falling backward, his head struck the floor, and the flash that must have come in his eyes seemed to blind him. For one instant he was stunned.

Marley was there then, clutching Sarah's shoulder, trying to drag her off. She struggled against him, not really aware. But his pulling shifted her focus to the side. She saw the sash weight, grabbed it up, her arm going high in the same motion, and smashed it down against the side of Malcolm's head. She would have struck again, but finally Marley was able to seize her wrist and hold her.

CHAPTER 10

For an instant she struggled against his grip, then was aware. Marley felt energy leave her arm, not so much draining off as recalled to some readiness inside her. She let him help her rise, gave the sash weight to him as though he were her assistant. She stepped away, adjusted her robe, seemed to wait for him to carry out his tasks.

Marley knelt, laid the weight beside Malcolm. Sarah had swung full-strength. "Slapped that horse—smack!" he remembered. The skull cracked, blood had spread. Malcolm's head, high white forehead highlighted, seemed to lie on crimson satin. Marley closed the man's eyelids.

Part of his mind running things to be done, Marley paused, looking up at Sarah. She had not turned away.

"Are you all right?"

"Yes." Her voice was firm.

"I've got to cut off the power."

"Yes."

"Just for a minute."

"Yes."

Could she be so self-possessed? He was, of course, but by discipline.

When he ascended again from the cold, feeling freed from the tomb, he found Sarah turned to the window. In the moment of shutoff and disconnect she might by faintest starlight have seen outside. Now the glass was black mirror. He could see himself, white, naked. He wanted his clothes, not from modesty, but partly to seem less vulnerable, and mostly to put on the world again and move in it. But he stopped, watching her, trying to see what she watched. In a moment her eyes focused on his reflection. She knew his mind.

"I was seeing the heron."

"Ah. What were you thinking about it?"

"I wasn't thinking about it."

"Ah. We'd better get dressed."

"Yes."

Dennis lay sprawled all gangly, limp as though that killing current had been all the animation of his lifetime discharged in one brilliant bolt. Marley knew they should leave everything undisturbed for the police. He and Sarah stepped over the body.

"Do you want me to drive?"

"No." Sarah looked startled that he should have asked.

Yet he stood by her side of the car while she got in and inserted the key. Then he went around and sat beside her. She fired the engine, and they started slowly down the track through the woods.

The car's lights reflected from dew or frost on leaves. Shining on tree trunks, they cast strange shadows that swung and seemed to bar the way or twist it.

They drove all the way to town to telephone. There seemed no urgency, and they were reluctant to wake neighbors along the road. Marley called the emergency number, reported the two homicides. The offical voice of the man on the line became yet more precise, and Marley gave his name, and spelled it, and said where he was, and promised to wait.

A sallow waning moon slumped above the rumpled ridge to the east. Marley got back into the car.

"How are you?" he asked once again.

"I'm really all right."

"Sure?"

"Yes. I . . . Perhaps it hasn't hit me yet. I . . . numb." Then, for the first time, she looked at him with the kind of concern he'd shown for her. "You keep asking, you must . . . How are you?"

"Okay."

"Are you sure?"

"I'm sure." He turned from her to stare through the dusty windshield at that moon. "This isn't a new thing for me, you know."

"I know. That's why I asked. I'm sorry."

"It's all right. Understandable you should ask. No, no psychopathological kicks this time. Just ordinary . . . like taking out the garbage. Sort of thing I can do every day and not think about."

"I'm sorry, James. I asked only because I know there's something you're afraid of in yourself and I was concerned that—"

"Don't be. I've got it all under control now. I can

kill people now without being the least bit angry at them.''

"Why are you getting angry at me?''

"I'm not!''

"You are! Why!''

"*I'm not angry!* I'm not angry. I'm just . . . after-shock. The more you keep calm during the crisis, the more reaction you have after it's over. I'm sorry, Sarah.''

"Yes. And I know you're sorry, James. About doing it. But what other way was there?''

"There wasn't. That I could see. Or can see. And I'm glad it didn't make me feel good. But . . . I guess I don't like the idea of not feeling anything either.''

"Well, obviously you do. Feel. Badly. So.'' She touched his hand, and he took hers and gripped.

"Thanks.''

Then she freed her fingers. "I don't. Feel anything.''

"Numb. It'll come.''

"I don't know. I should, shouldn't I? I didn't have to . . . hit him. You were there by then, weren't you? I didn't do it deliberately. I . . . instinctive. Fighting for life, saw something to hit with—''

"Don't.''

"Grabbed it—''

"Sarah, don't.''

"I want to. I *don't* feel bad about it, James. And I want to understand that.''

"You're still in shock.''

"I don't think so. I don't think that's it. I think it's because . . . They were so *different*. I didn't know them.''

"It was self-defense, Sarah."

"Of course it was. That's what I'm saying."

"You have to believe it. You'll remember them, and then you'll—"

"I *do* remember them. I do. So well. We were all so close then, back then. I remember, and—oh!—I'm so sorry. For them. For what they'd done to themselves. But not . . . what they'd become, what they were going to do, but not what I—you and I—we did to them."

"Right."

"I know it's right! You don't have to keep reassuring me!"

"Not now. Okay. But tomorrow. Or tomorrow night. Next week, when you wake up cold in the middle of the night, and it's all happening again, and you *do* have time to think about it."

"I don't think so."

"I *know* so. I've—"

"Don't! Don't try to tell me you've been there so you know what *I* will feel! You're not me."

"Of course I'm not. But I know you; and I know—"

"No you don't! You don't know me, James. Not that well. We are alike in many ways. We think many of the same things. But we're not the *same*."

Sarah held Marley's eye, but then there was a flash and they both looked aside. Again light struck the railings of the little bridge over the river behind Main Street. A car must be approaching.

"Police," Marley said. "Tell them the truth, Sarah. Everything."

"Of course."

"I mean everything—any detail they ask. They'll

separate us to take our statements. This is a clear-cut case. They probably won't even ask for an indictment. As long as they are convinced. There mustn't be any discrepancy to raise any kind of unnecessary suspicion."

"I understand, James."

He took her hand for a final squeeze as the police car came over the bridge. As it turned in the intersection and came up behind them, Marley got out.

The policeman sat in his car for a moment, checking them over, then got out too. He paused, looking over the roof at Marley—keeping his car between them. It was a white car, with a star and GRAFTON COUNTY SHERIFF lettered on the door, so Marley knew the man was police even though he had on a T-shirt and a red and black checked jacket. Must have been what he'd grabbed first when called from bed. Marley might have known anyway by the man's care. He was sure that though awakened suddenly and sent out half-asleep out of uniform the man would remember his gun. Marley made his face pleasant, moved slowly around the side of the Scout to be in plain view.

"Morning."

"You Mr. Marley?"

"That's right."

"You reported a homicide?"

"I did."

"Where did this occur?"

"At Sarah Klein—Sarah Cameron's cabin."

"Sarah?" The policeman seemed suddenly to recognize her in the car.

"Hello, Ray." Sarah got out. The policeman came over to her and Marley. "What's this about, Sarah?"

There was real concern in his voice and face now, but Marley saw—even through the man's glasses—the narrowed look that would overlook nothing. He was a big man. Marley opened his own eyes, more innocently, wider.

"Two men, they broke into my place. They were going to kill me—us. I knew them and . . . It's a long story, Ray; but they were going to kill us; but we were able . . . We killed them."

Ray rocked back ever so slightly. "You're telling me that you caused the deaths of two people?"

"That's right, Ray."

"Well, now, Sarah, I don't want to alarm you. If it's as you say—they broke in with intent to cause you bodily harm—then I'm sure there's nothing for you to worry about. But under the circumstances I'd probably better advise you—both of you—that you have a right to remain silent, and to have the advice of an attorney—"

Marley had heard it all before, but he tried not to show that.

He could see her clearly, her figure, her slim silhouette, through the cabin window, small across the distance from the dirt road, but clearly her. He stared steadily through the cruiser's back-seat window, unwilling to break the line of sight connecting them. Ray had "suggested" they leave the Scout and ride with him; he had opened the front door for Sarah; there wasn't room for three in front because of the radio equipment. Marley had gotten into the back. He had sat forward, hand on her seat-back.

Ray hadn't asked about the killings during the

drive. Marley knew he wouldn't while they were together. Ray had reported in, called for backup. He'd asked if Sarah was warm enough, put the heater fan lower when she said she was. He'd offered that nights were pretty chilly now, asked if she had her wood in for winter. He'd asked if Marley had been there before, said since he hadn't he must like the foliage. Small talk, to put them at ease. Marley believed the man was kindly, thought that was nice of him while he was really letting intuition decide how suspicious to be of the stories they'd tell.

When they got to the end of Sarah's road, Ray formally asked her permission to enter the cabin.

"Of course, Ray."

"I'd like to have one of you come with me. It'd be more according to the rule book if you came, Sarah; but if you'd rather not . . . Mr. Marley could—"

"Right." Marley started to open his door.

"I'll go. It is all right, James."

Marley still sat forward, his hand where it had been when he'd slipped fingers down behind her shoulder. He tried to remember her warmth against them. He almost got out of the car, to be beyond the barrier of door and window. He could see her figure, back to him, standing, watching, arms folded. He saw Ray kneel beside Malcolm's body, then go out of sight to Dennis. They would be back soon. Once Ray "officially ascertained" the men were dead he would get Sarah away from "the scene."

Another cop, the backup, was coming up now from the highway with flashers on—warning the squirrels to clear the way? Blue light burst between tree trunks, flaring harshly against foliage across the gulley that seemed to flinch from every sweep. Marley followed his progress without shifting his eyes. He knew he would be given to this one while Ray kept Sarah.

Since he knew how it worked, he shouldn't worry. It would take what was left of the night, and all day; but open and shut as it was, no more. It wasn't going to be really long. But however long was too long. The excitement of new romance made every moment away from her painful.

"You know Sarah well?"

Ray seemed to mean no offense—making conversation while the stenographer rolled her machine out—so Marley took none. "I think so."

"Nice girl."

"I think so."

"Works steady. Not on food stamps, like some of the ones stayed around after the college folded. Works up at that Robert Frost museum in town. He used to live here."

"I know."

Ray stifled a yawn. "I sure hate these things. You get a homicide, you know it's going to be at least thirty-six hours straight."

"You get many up here?"

"No. This is only the fourth I've ever been involved in."

"You seem to know how to handle them."

"Well, it's just routine police procedure. Same as in an auto accident where there's loss of life. Or burglary, anything. Find out what happened. Get the stories. Check the facts."

''I wouldn't think you had a lot of crime around here.''

''We don't. People here are pretty peaceable for the most part. But anytime you have people you're going to have a few rotten ones, and some trouble-makers. And domestic problems—you know what I mean. And there's going to be accidents.''

''So there's no way we're ever going to get rid of the police.''

''Well, say, it's a good thing. Otherwise some of us would have to try to make an honest living. No, you're always going to need the police. Not because people are so bad, but because they're people.''

''You're pretty philosophical about it.''

''What's the alternative?'' He got up from the end of the table. ''Well, she should have your statement typed up for you to sign before very long. I wouldn't think there'd be any problem about your leaving then.'' He paused at the door. ''I could put you in a cell if you'd like to lie down, get some sleep.''

''Going to take more than an hour?''

''Wouldn't think so.''

''I'll wait here.''

When the man left, Marley let himself sink back. He pulled over another chair, put his feet up. He was tired. The backs of his eyes felt dry. He was getting too old for all-nighters. He should retire.

He let the thrill of finding Sarah sweep over him again, let himself fantasize love and a life with her. They would marry. He would sell the condo. Just from that and his investments he and Sarah could have a comfortable simple life in the country. He could probably work for David occasionally for luxuries—travel money, whatever.

They could walk in the woods in the summertime. Picnic in meadows. Wildflowers he'd put in her hair. Wine and love in the grass by a river. Fireside in winter. She'd write, he'd read. Brahms. Holding each other when the wind blew.

Thinking about that warmed and soothed the ache of separation from her. He did ache, and knew that was ridiculous. They'd been apart for a mere twelve hours, and she was probably in the very next room. A flash of excitement went through him, and he tried to see by it through the wall. He longed to be in bed with her—not for the sex, though that would be fine, but for the holding close. He slouched lower, put his arm on the table and his head on his arm. He thought about that holding, felt it, and dozed, smiling.

Going under for even that little time restored the edge, so he was alert instantly when Ray came again. And he knew there was trouble.

Ray came around, put the typed statement before him, a ballpoint next to it. "You want to read that over, and if it's correct, sign it?" The man's expression was noncommittal, voice neutral as ever, but there was a tightness in it.

Marley picked up the stapled papers, began to read. *Before describing the incidents that took place last night, I'd like to give some background.* As he'd started to tell it for the record. "Did you reach Mrs. Ten Broeck?"

"I hear so, and that she confirms that you're working for her."

Marley went to the second page. "Illinois State Police?"

"Yeah. Confirmed the attempt on your life."

Marley read through to the end without further question. He put the paper down.

"What's wrong, Ray?"

"Are you in agreement with what's written there? Is your statement correct and complete?"

"Yes. What's wrong?"

"Then I'll ask you to sign it, if you would." Ray returned Marley's steady stare. Marley smiled, picked up the pen, and signed.

"Okay, there. Now, what's wrong about it?" Had Sarah differed on some detail? She wouldn't have lied—no reason. And she wouldn't.

"Nothing. It's not about this. But it seems there's an APB out on you from Massachusetts. Town of Northampton. I'm afraid I'm going to have to take you into custody, Mr. Marley. It seems you're wanted for questioning in connection with another homicide. A professor down there—name of Bascaglia."

Marley prowled the cabin. Everything in it was Sarah's—was her. He wanted to learn about her, but he didn't want to pry. He compromised: He'd study everything she'd exposed of herself for anyone to see, open nothing. He picked up a book. No title, figured-cloth binding. He opened it. As he suspected, it contained pages bound for its owner to write in. He thought it might be her poetry. It was her diary. He was tempted mightily to read and know her, almost felt he had the right, but he closed it and put it down again.

A nightgown hung on a peg by the bed. It surprised him. He always slept nude. She had, of course. Sleeping alone in a cabin, she might need nightclothes, he thought, but he would have thought pajamas. The nightdress was practical flannel, but frilly at the neck and cuffs, tiny flowered print. Its femininity pleased him yet seemed out of the directness of her character. He took it in his hands, then put his face against it to breathe her scent.

Tacked above her dresser was a photo of her, arm in arm with a good-looking man. Marley was momentarily jealous. But he knew there had been other men. He would have assumed so, had known by her lovemaking there must have been. Her lovemaking pleased him. And it was one more expression of the strength, maturity, wholeness of her that he loved. A logical man, Marley accepted that in loving her he must accept the life that had formed her. He did hope, though, that when they were married she would discard the picture.

He played the Mozart concerto and then other tapes, without listening to them. He tried to read. Mostly he sat staring through the window, thinking about her, missing her.

Wind in the night had stripped the leaves from many trees. Gray trunks and branches muted the brilliance of those that were left—silver beneath an aging beauty's auburn. In shifting mist and drizzle, color came and went like scenes from happy dreams: veiled, vivid, vanished again.

At noon he found some cheese and bread and beer, and ate standing at the counter looking out. Before he was finished he saw the car coming up the winding track to pull in behind his at the turnaround.

He recognized the man who got out and surveyed the cabin, then started to cross the gully: Letterman, the FBI man from Chicago. Marley hadn't expected him to come there, but wasn't surprised either. Marley took another sip of his beer, then went to the door. He opened it as Letterman came up onto the deck, but waited for him to speak.

"Hello, Marley. How's the Lone Eagle?"

"Clifton." Marley nodded in greeting, but took just a moment before stepping back to allow Letterman to enter.

Letterman gave his own stiff nod as he passed Marley. He walked on into the center of the cabin, secured his flanks before turning. "A couple more notches on your gun, I hear."

"You've heard, so you know the circumstances."

"Yeah. You keep trying to quit, but they keep coming, trying to outdraw you. Let me see it. That's the ladder?" He approached the ladder to the loft, studied it, but did not touch the railings. "Where's the cellar?"

Marley indicated the trapdoor.

Letterman opened it, peered down. "I'm really pissed off at you, you son of a bitch, but Jesus!—put you down in the cellar and you still blow them away." He closed the trap again and looked around, taking in all of the cabin.

"Nice place. Cozy. A little out of the way."

"Sorry you had to come here. I didn't really expect to see you."

"No problem. I just thought I might as well check

it all out myself—make sure there aren't any loose ends, wrap it up. Got to Northampton yesterday, thought I might as well come up here today. Nice drive. Nice to see the leaves." He went back to the window, near Marley, who had stayed by the door, and looked out as though that vista were the more important reason for being there. But his expression suggested that he was not so much enjoying the splashes of color as inventorying them. "Great view from here."

"Yes. Even better when it was clear."

"I'll bet. Still nice though." Letterman continued speaking without turning to Marley. "Lucky you could stay here while you had to wait. Sarah's gone to Mrs. Ten Broeck's?"

Marley assumed Lettermen knew, but played it his way. "Yes. They aren't going to seek an indictment—in fact, they said they'd recommend against it. But the grand jury doesn't meet for another three weeks. She told them her daughter needed her, and she called Mrs. Ten Broeck, and her lawyer called back, talked to them. So they said she could go as long as she kept in touch."

"I guess I'll have to go over there to see her."

Marley took a beat, tried to ask as though simply curious. "Why do you need to see her now?"

"Wrapping it up."

Marley couldn't maintain the tone of disinterest. "Why don't you leave her alone? It's over now, and she's been through a lot."

Letterman turned to Marley that look of counting the leaves, then said, "You did get involved, didn't you?"

"Yes. I did. I am."

"Yeah. I read your statements." Letterman scanned the cabin again, taking in the loft and bed without making a point of it. "Well. *Mazel tov*."

"Thanks."

"You didn't get much time together."

"No. They kept me at the jail Monday night—the detective didn't get up from Northampton to question me until late Tuesday morning. Sarah thought— We thought there was no point in her waiting, too, while they checked me out; it was better for her to get over to Mrs. Ten Broeck's to see Melissa."

"Just the weekend, then."

"Yes. Sometimes it happens that way, Clifton. Sometimes it doesn't take long."

"That's what I hear." Letterman turned to the window again.

"They wouldn't let me go with her—didn't charge me, but wouldn't let me leave the jurisdiction. That was kind of annoying, you know."

"Standard procedure."

"Sure. One of the possible standard procedures. Sarah did state I was with her Friday night. They said they just wanted to confirm at the inn where we had dinner. And with you. I get the idea it was mainly with you."

"Yeah?" Letterman continued watching the store of leaves diminish.

Marley didn't know why he was being played. Impatience to be with Sarah made him uncharacteristically unable to outwait the other. "So, you've corroborated my story? Is it all right for me to go now?"

"Sure. You didn't need me. That pushing into Bascagalia's place the other week could have meant your ass, but you've established your presence in Franconia at the time he was killed. And it all hangs together the other way: They heard you were still looking for her, decided to find her first, went to Northampton, made him tell where she was, came here. I corroborated, but the locals in Northampton were satisfied already." That subject seemingly closed, Letterman turned away from Marley and ambled to Sarah's writing table. He looked down at the papers there before continuing. "I just asked them to have you kept here until I got here."

"Why?"

Letterman poked at a page or two on the table, then cleared a corner, turned, and sat on it, facing Marley. "I thought there might be something else you know you haven't told me. Like you didn't tell me you'd found Sarah. Like you didn't tell me Bascaglia was in touch with those guys. If you'd told me he put them on to you—back in Illinois— If you'd told me he knew where they were, I'd have gotten it out of him, taken them."

"You wouldn't have gotten it out of him."

"I'd have given it a damn good try."

"I think he'd have liked that."

"Professional martyr?"

" 'Name names, reveal whereabouts, betray your comrades': If you'd pushed him hard enough, he'd have made saint. They had to burn his feet to break him; what could *you* have done?"

"I might have gotten something he didn't know he was giving me. I might have gotten something without him even knowing I was there. Who knows what I might have gotten if you hadn't been playing like your game was the only one in town? From now on, Kemo Sabe, you play with the team or we're going to put you on the bench.''

Marley wouldn't accept the position: called on the carpet, the superior officer sitting. He moved in to make Letterman look up to him. "Why is there any 'from now on' in this? They're dead, aren't they? Was anyone else involved?"

"Not that we know of. Not in the raid. Malcolm and Dennis must have been the ones who took out the gate guards. A kid named Stickney drove the truck. They found enough of his fingers to make the ID. I don't know if he meant to be a Kamikaze or if he was supposed to aim it and jump. But planning it, making the explosives—there probably were accessories. That's what we want to know.''

"What do you care about accessories now? If there were any.''

"Tidiness.''

"It was a long time ago. There were things done on all sides. Let them be buried.''

"No way. I mean, it can't be done. They get up and walk in the night.''

"Come on.'' Marley tried to use the scorn of superior height.

But Letterman wouldn't wilt. "They walked in on Bascaglia, didn't they? In the middle of the night? Why? You weren't after them. You're just trying to help this kid. Okay. But everything's got a past. If you don't get it laid—not 'buried,' but laid to rest—it comes for you. Isn't that right? You know about that, don't you, Marley? Isn't that right?''

Eye to eye. Marley might have outstared him on bluff, but he couldn't evade his own self-knowledge.

''What do you want to know?''

''Has Sarah talked about the Westhover thing? Mentioned anyone else who might have been involved?''

''No.''

''You're sure?''

''I'm sure.'' Marley spoke firmly, but he turned to look from the window again.

Letterman studied him for a moment. ''You're not sure.''

Marley looked at leaves falling and knew winter would come. ''Do you think Brooks Ten Broeck was involved?''

''Why do you ask?''

''It was after that night that he disappeared, wasn't it? Was Brooks involved?''

''Not that we know of, but that's one of the things we want to know. It's possible. Supposedly he stayed with Sarah in the nonviolent faction. But he must have had some reason for taking off. What did Sarah say about him?''

''She said he was dead.''

''How!''

''She didn't say.''

''How did she know?''

''She didn't say. She said it was the night Melissa was born, that's all. I didn't know that was when the raid happend; but it was, wasn't it?''

"Yeah. Did she say anything else? About any of
it?"

"No. Why is Sarah so important?"

"She seems to have been the mother confessor.
Even after they splintered up. Mrs. Ten Broeck had
her away and under care for a week before the raid,
so she couldn't have been involved to the point of
being an accessory. At least, we'd probably never
prove it. But we figured they must have told her
enough that she could put us on to them, maybe even
give evidence."

"Hearsay."

"Who knows? She must have thought she had
something, to disappear. They must have thought so,
since they didn't want her found. So if she does tell
you anything, don't hold out on me."

Marley looked at the black-green evergreen stee-
ples constant among the fading foliage.

"I mean it, Marley. I don't want you screwing
things up anymore."

"I haven't screwed anything up! I made those two
surface—without meaning to. You hadn't been able
to do it. And I got rid of them—God help me—and
saved the taxpayers a lot of money. I wish now I had
told you about Bascaglia knowing where they were,
but there isn't any harm done . . ."

"Yeah. Bascaglia. Just a little harm there. If I'd
had him in custody—or even under surveillance . . .
You know, Marley, a piece of Bascaglia *is* yours."

At last! The accusation came from outside, where
Marley could fight it. "He called them into this! If
he'd just told me when I first asked him! When I

went back! If he hadn't . . . What happened to
Bascaglia is not my fault!''

Letterman asked quietly, ''You believe that?''

For a long moment Marley concentrated on the
mist outside, believing he might transcend the sense
of self and rarefy into oneness with it. ''No.''

Letterman waited as long. ''So, *is* there anything
else you'd like to tell me?''

''No. Not now. I mean I don't know anything to
tell you.''

''But if you should, you'll be in touch.''

''I will.''

''Good. Where you going to go now?''

''Back to Boston. I've got to change clothes, check
on some things.''

''You'll be seeing Sarah?''

''Yes. I'm not sure when; I'll have to call her.
Soon.''

''Okay.'' Letterman nodded, and almost managed
a friendly smile. Marley had none in response. ''What's
the matter?''

''I just . . . I'm sorry they got to him.''

''Yeah.''

''I don't mean just the pain. Well, of course, that;
but it must have been twice as bad . . . finally, to
have to tell them.''

''He must have tried pretty hard not to tell them.
Judging by the damage they did.''

''Yes. That's what I mean. He had to suffer so much
because he wouldn't tell, and then he had to suffer
because finally he couldn't take any more and did tell.''

''They must have killed him right away, then.''

''Well, that would have been a kindness.''

CHAPTER 11

"James?" She sounded excited that he had called.

Hearing that, hearing her voice, hearing her speak his name, thrilled him. "Hello, Sarah." He separated the words, hoping that deliberateness would send a special meaning.

Sarah dropped the pitch of her own voice to return it to him. "Hello, James."

He paused to allow time for the exchange of imagined looks, of touches. "How are you?"

"Fine. Wonderful! I can't believe it: Mrs. Ten Broeck has been charming. She had a little speech ready about the past is past, and she's been falling all over herself to make me feel welcome. She's taken me shopping for some new clothes, and we're going— How are *you?*"

"Miserable."

"What's the matter?"

"I'm not with you."

She used silence, too, then, "Yeah," then paused again for them to savor. "How are you otherwise? Where are you?"

"In Boston. Letterman had them stall me, keep me up there, just to make a point so I'd be more 'cooperative.' "

"There's no more suspicion about you . . . about Robbie?"

"No. It had to have been Malcolm and Dennis. I think they've closed it. At least I'm not involved."

"I called Smith to find out. They did torture him?"

"Yes."

"Oh, God. Oh, poor Robbie."

"I guess he tried very hard not to tell them about you—to protect you."

"Yes. But I don't know how he knew. I knew if they—the police—if they ever were looking for me again, they'd go to him, so I never told him. I'd go down to Northampton and see him sometimes, but he'd never know until I got there, and I never told him where I came from."

"He must have found out essentially the same way I reached you, through those friends you did tell."

"Still, it's my fault."

"No. No, it's not, Sarah. You did everything you could— What they did is not your fault." He waited to hear if he'd convinced her.

"I'm glad we killed them," she said finally, and he didn't know what to answer.

After a moment he said, "Letterman said he's coming over to talk to you."

"I know. He called. Mrs. Ten Broeck's lawyer is handling it."

"I don't think you have anything to worry about."

"I'm sure not. Now."

"Sarah, was Brooks . . ."

"What?"

"Nothing. We'll talk about it when I see you. When am I going to see you? I could come over there. . . . I have to finish some things here, but I could be there the day after tomorrow." He tried to make the suggestion sound casual. While driving to Boston he had planned how to dispose of commitments, what clothes to pack, thought about how long the trip would take, what time he could start, how many hours until he saw her.

"I'm not going to be here. I'm going to be in New York—the city."

"Why?"

"Mrs. Ten Broeck wants me to take Melissa and move down there—she has an apartment. She thinks too many people here know about Melissa, and that we could get better help there."

Marley paused for just an instant to control incredulity, even horror. "You're going to live in the city?"

"I don't know. I said I'd go and look at it."

He didn't trust himself to pursue it on the phone. "How is Melissa?"

Silence for an instant. "All right, I guess. I haven't . . ." she said hesitantly. Then, more rapidly, but in a tight voice, "She's visiting an aunt and uncle—Mrs. Ten Broeck's nephew. Mrs. Ten Broeck thought it would be better for her not to be here right now . . . 'Till I got settled.' "

"Mrs. Ten Broeck seems to have everything planned."

"Yes. She would, of course."

"How do you feel about that?"

"Furious! What would you expect! I almost— But I didn't know. . . . I'm not going to let her run over— I wanted to establish right from the beginning that *I* am Melissa's *mother*, and I am going to be the one . . . But I didn't want to start off with a confrontation either. And she really was being so nice and conciliatory. And— Oh, I was so disappointed; I was looking forward so much— But I . . . I guess I'm kind of afraid too. What am I going to say to her? How am I going to explain . . ." Another hesitation, then in a small voice, "What if she doesn't like me?"

"Sarah, I told you. She'll love you: You're just what she's imagined. You're just going to tell her the truth. That's close enough to what she's made up. She'll love you."

"I know. I guess I just got scared. Anyway, I accepted putting off . . . just for a couple more days."

"I think you should see her as soon as possible."

"I will."

"Well, when am I going to see you?"

"Could you come down to New York?"

"Possibly."

"There's a memorial service at the Smith chapel for Robbie day after tomorrow. I'm going, and then going on down to New York. Could you meet me, go down with me?"

"I guess so. I—I don't think I'll go to the service. I . . . could I meet you afterward?"

"It wasn't your fault either, James. James?"

"Where shall we meet?"

"Do you want to wait for me outside the chapel? The service should be over by three."

"Sure. See you then." He couldn't pretend there was anything else that needed to be said to keep in contact. "I love you, Sarah."

"I love you, James."

For several moments after hanging up he kept his hand on the receiver, as though—if she did too—they might still somehow be touching through the line.

Marley missed the scent of leaf smoke. There were laws against it now: no gathering leaves into piles at curbside for giggling kids to tumble in, pushing one another to a cushioned fall, burrowing into, erupting scattering, having to rake again, finally to fire the heaps and leave them smoldering at twilight, the dusk thick with their tang. Down along the walk beyond the chapel a crew of groundsmen windrowed leaves with one machine and vacuumed them up with another. Exhaust from the gasoline engines probably polluted less than burning leaves, but Marley would have preferred the smoke.

He sat on a bench where he could see the chapel but still feel distanced from it. He'd worked it out that way. He had caused Bascaglia's death, but at a remove. Walking along a way he had a right to go he'd dislodged a pebble that struck a stone that knocked a boulder down on someone who shouldn't have been where he was. Bascaglia had known those men were killers; he'd protected them. Marley might have some responsibility, but not all—or even most. He wasn't *guilty*. He'd worked that out, and in time he'd believe it.

The groundsmen would have their work to do over again. Although more leaves had fallen than remained on the trees, many yet held to the last of life. With sun behind them they glowed their gold and orange, demonstrating how to go out in style.

Finally the doors of the chapel opened. Marley stood. He was sure Sarah would be able to see him from the steps. People came out. Most of the faculty must have been there, and many students. Despite his distance, Marley could tell one set from the other by clothing alone. Though properly rumpled and tweedy, the teachers were dark. Most of the men wore ties, most of the women skirts. The students had come as they were: jeans and jackets, sweaters, some brightly colored. They seemed to feel no incongruity though; needed no uniform to grieve. One girl in gaudy green and yellow stripes came past him sobbing blindly on another's scarlet shoulder, she weeping too. Marley almost wept himself, scanned for Sarah. Two men came, one nose-blowing, the other staring straight ahead dry-eyed. Then two women, handkerchiefs in hand, dabbing. Next, another woman, strikingly dressed in a smart black coat with padded shoulders and wide puffed sleeves, her head of twisted tendriled curls held high. Two girls, chattering, apparently unmoved. Three together, silent, tear streaks down their faces. And then a mass of mourners close together. Marley swayed back and forth, trying to see Sarah among them.

"James?"

He snapped to look at the fashionable woman who'd accosted him. He couldn't believe she'd spoken with Sarah's voice.

"What's the matter?" she asked him.

"Sarah? I didn't recognize you. You look so different. Your hair."

"You don't like it?"

"I . . . I guess it's just so different."

"You don't like it."

"It doesn't look like you."

She set her jaw, took a breath, then decided to be good-humored. "It doesn't look like I used to look. It looks like I look now."

He was outraged that even she should tamper with her perfection. He smiled. "I like the way you used to look."

She still spoke lightly, but lost her smile. "I like the way I look now."

He caught himself. It wasn't the time to pursue the point. "How was the service?"

"Sad."

"Yeah." By understanding, by touching her arm, perhaps he could draw off some of her sorrow.

Perhaps he did. She slipped her hand under his arm, leaned on his shoulder. They walked with the mourners, then turned aside to a narrower path.

"He was a wonderful man."

"Yes?"

"He was a great teacher. He made poetry seem exalted and yet natural, accessible. And he made you believe in yourself, in your own possibilities. Nothing was impossible."

"Yes."

She had wept: Her eyes were puffy. They filled again. She brought from her pocket a wadded handkerchief. Marley had a clean large one, gave it to her.

"Thanks." She wiped her eyes. They walked on. "I can't believe it. I still can't believe it. That this is what would happen, to Robbie; Mal and Denny becoming what they'd become. Me. Killing each other! If you had known us then . . . We had such hope." She put Marley's handerkchief into her pocket. She shook her head, negating. "We were so foolish."

"You have to have hope."

"Even foolish hope?"

"Yes. Better, of course, if it's not foolish."

"Yes. But you don't know."

"You can try to figure the odds."

"Sometimes they're all against you. If we'd figured them better, seen that, maybe we wouldn't have burned ourselves out fighting them."

"Maybe you wouldn't. Burned out, I mean. Maybe then you'd still be fighting." He thought of Francey, the potter.

She pulled away from him. "Is that supposed to make me feel bad?"

"No. No, Sarah, I didn't mean—"

"Because I don't!"

"I wasn't criticizing. I just. . . . You seem pretty sensitive about it."

"Of course I'm sensitive about it." Then she put her arm back through his. They strolled again along the path, among the cadmium-crowned black-trunked trees. Already the groundsmen's tidied lawn was littered with leaves. "And I do feel bad. We had such a beautiful vision of how the world could be. And we couldn't achieve it. And I guess I'm always going to feel that if only we'd done something differently, or

tried harder . . . But that way madness lies. That's
what Brooks . . .''

After a moment Marley prompted, "Brooks?"

"It doesn't matter now, I guess, who knows about
it. Brooks was killed at Westhover."

"He was." Marley already had come to know it,
without telling himself he did.

"Yes. I've never— You're the first person I've
told, James; in all these years. I tried to tell her—
Mrs. Ten Broeck—but she wouldn't listen. I wouldn't
tell on the others, Mal and Denny, even though I
thought they were wrong. And I didn't want Brooks's
memory. . . . I guess it doesn't matter now, but I'd
like you not to tell.''

"All right, Sarah. I don't think, either, that it
matters now. What happened?''

"It was crazy. He must have been crazy. I should
have seen it. I should have said more to. . . . After
the invasion of Cambodia the spring before, the escalation, it seemed that nothing could stop the war.
Nothing we could do—had done—was any use. We
had been into civil disobedience already: sit-ins, block-
ading. . . . When we got back together in the fall,
the group split. Malcolm, Dennis, Bill Stickney, a
couple others. They wanted direct action, 'to bring the
war home.' The rest of us— It was against everything we believed, I believed. Using violence to
impose your will was exactly what— I knew what
they were planning; I tried to convince them. . . .
But I was sick—I mean physically—and it was almost time for Melissa.

"Brooks was beside himself. The war, what Nixon
and Kissinger were doing— Brooks was the sweet-

est, kindest man I've ever known, and he was in agony over what they were doing. And with Melissa coming, I guess that made it more intense. He felt he had to do something for her, take more responsibility for the world she was going to be born into; I don't know, something like that. If I'd been with him I could have helped him; but I let Mrs. Ten Broeck get me away. In the week I was gone, Brooks went over.

"He went on the raid. He went in the truck, with Bill. I don't know what happened, exactly. They had some kind of device. They were supposed to aim the truck, and it would keep going straight, and they were supposed to jump. But something happened, and it blew up too soon."

"How do you know about it, Sarah?"

"Mal told me. He was on his way west, going underground, but he stopped at the hospital. I couldn't believe it. About Brooks. Not just that he was dead. I . . . I . . . That was hard enough. But that he had gone with them! I try—I tried to understand. I understand it must have been something like what I just told you. I guess I understand that; but I'm not sure I'll ever really understand."

Marley thought perhaps he could. "If he had reached a certain point of—what did you say?—agony, anguish, and it turned into a certain kind of anger, Sarah . . ."

"But, oh! That it could happen. That even Brooks— What hope is there for us if even the good people can't keep themselves from doing evil?"

Marley felt the weight of her hand on his arm. He put his own over hers. "I'm sorry. That must have been a terrible time for you."

"Yes. It was." Then she pulled herself erect again. "But it's over. It's over. That time was terrible; and wonderful too. We tried, and failed— No. We accomplished some things, but failed at others, failed ultimately. I have sorrow for it, and regrets—and happy memories too. But it's over. And I have a new life now."

"Yes."

"I think I have a right to it. I tried, I worked, I put myself on the line back then."

"Yes."

"And I suffered for it. I've had to give up so much. And now I think I have the right, when I have a chance. . . . Oh, James, it's beyond a dream! Mrs. Ten Broeck's apartment is on Park Avenue! I take it she has a whole floor! She has a season subscription to the Philharmonic, and the Metropolitan Opera; she says she hardly ever comes down to use them anymore, so I can. All the theaters, the art shows! She says she knows a publisher who might be interested in my writing—at least, I might work with him, meet people. She's accepted me. She really has. She's giving me money—a trust fund or something. Her lawyer has to explain it to me. It's money that would have gone to Brooks. She's giving it to me! Can you believe it?"

"Not easily."

"I know. She's being just wonderful to me. Oh, I don't think I misjudged her. I don't think she's really a very nice person. It's just that she has accepted me, out of necessity or whatever, so since I'm in the family she's giving me what I'm supposed to have."

"A big jump up from a cabin in the woods."

"Unbelievable!" Then she caught his tone. She stopped, faced him. "That's over too, James. It was wonderful too. And I have no regrets about my life there—except maybe that it went on too long. I grew there. Grew up. But it was time for me to move on, to do something, be someone else."

"I know, Sarah. I knew that. I was hoping you'd be doing that with me."

"I hope so too, James. I want to. You're not happy about this. Why not? Now I'll be able to do things, learn things—become like you. You're so sophisticated, so cosmopolitan. I've never been anywhere, never done anything. How could you be interested in me?"

She faced him directly, looked directly into his eyes as she always had. Not flattering him, not asking for flattery. Direct, honest, open, true, deep, essential—and in that, simple. All the virtues he'd seen from the first, when she'd looked at him from the photo.

"Maybe I'm not as sophisticated as you think."

"I think you are. Maybe you just enjoyed the novelty."

"Whatever the reason, Sarah, you are very . . . special . . . to me."

"You are special to me, James. I felt that from the beginning. But sometimes . . . sometimes I think you're inventing me. We really don't know each other very well. It's been so quick."

"Are you changing your mind?"

"No. Are you changing yours?"

"No! Why?"

"The way you've been looking at me."

"I'm sorry. You look so different. Your hair . . .

you're wearing makeup—more than before. I . . .
I'm not used to it. I really didn't recognize you at
first.''

"And you still don't know if it's really me, do
you?''

"I guess not.''

"That's what I meant about inventing me. This
kind of makeup wouldn't have been appropriate for
Franconia. It is appropriate for New York. I'm going
to live in New York now. If I go back to visit I won't
wear it. But I live in New York now.''

"I see.''

"And I don't think I'm any different. I may look
different, and I will be doing different things. But
I'm the same person.''

"I hope so. I liked that one a lot.''

"Thank you.'' She smiled at him quickly, and took
his arm—turning him to walk back the way they'd
come. "Are you coming with me?''

He held his arm tight, to press her hand against his
side. She responded, keeping her arm against his.
She was there, close; and yet she was gone, leaving
him hollow. "I've been to New York,'' he said.

"A nice place to visit, but you wouldn't want to
live there?''

"I don't even like to visit it much anymore.''

"I see. Will you visit me?''

"Of course. Will you visit me?''

"Where? Boston?''

"Actually I've been thinking of leaving Boston.
Getting a place farther north—probably back in Vermont. Oh, of course I'd still take trips to the city,
travel. But I was thinking of living in the country.''

"I see. Yes, James, I would visit you. But we hadn't been thinking about visits, had we?"

"No. At least, I hadn't."

"So what do we do? Is one of us supposed to give up?"

"No. Maybe we'll find a compromise. Or one of us might change. Or decide it's worth it—that wouldn't be the same as giving up."

"No. Perhaps not."

There'd be a way. He would understand her need, make some adjustment, and she could forego—

"But I am going to New York today."

"Yes. How are you getting there?"

"By car. Mrs. Ten Broeck's chauffeur brought me over, and he's waiting to take me down."

She made no point of being waited upon, but Marley thought, as she said it, that even her voice was richer. "Very nice," he said.

"Yes. I could go with you, if you'll take me; have him go on ahead. Mrs. Ten Broeck said that I should use the car in New York."

"Very nice."

"James, don't make me angry at you! I am not going to be your woodland nymph! I have come into good fortune, and I am going to take advantage of it and enjoy it!"

"Fine, Sarah, fine. Do."

"Stop smiling! Don't smile at me like that, James! I hate that smile. *That* smile is the one you use to pretend you're not angry, to hide what you're really feeling."

"It works!"

"Not on me!"

"It works on *me!* I'm just seeing a whole beautiful dream go up in a puff of— Of what is it you're wearing? Chanel? And I'm feeling kind of bad about that. And kind of angry too. And I find it's better not to let myself feel that way."

"Why not! Can't you be angry without killing somebody? You can. James, you're a good man. You're a good and wonderful man. Why can't you trust that part of yourself?"

"I—I told you."

"That was in the past. It's past. You've conquered that. You know it. You've proved it."

They had halted on the path, facing each other. Her face was toward the sun, bright. Her eyes were bright, looking at him, looking into him; brighter, clearer than by the firelight; seeing deeper and more clearly. Accepting him, loving him.

Marley's own eyes filled. He couldn't speak.

After a moment Sarah took his arm again and they walked.

They reached the main path again. "Are you going to come with me?" Sarah asked.

"I think not today. I think I'd better get used to a new idea about you, about us. It'll come"—he smiled at her—genuinely—"but it'll take a little while."

They walked again, in silence, apart though she kept her fingers around his forearm. They came to a street, and she nodded, and he saw the black limousine farther along.

The chauffeur had the rear door open when they reached him. Marley wanted to nod, to signal that he would do the service, to send the man around to his place. But he felt constrained. He and Sarah stopped.

She took her hand from under his arm, then put it back on top.

"Will you call me?"

"Yes. What's the number?"

"Oh, I don't know yet. I'll call you."

"I'll be home tonight. If I'm out tomorrow, you can leave a message."

"All right."

He wanted to kiss her. To embrace, clasp, kiss her with passion. But the chauffeur was there.

She kissed him. On the cheek.

He wouldn't say good-bye.

She smiled, got into the car. Marley stepped back to let the chauffeur close the door between them. As the man went around to the front, Sarah suddenly lowered the window.

"Oh! I almost forgot!" She rummaged in her bag, which she'd left in the car. "I wrote you a poem."

"You did?"

"It's about the great blue heron. Here." She handed him a folded paper. He started to open it. "Don't read it now!"

"Why not?"

"I'm shy. It's about you. Read it later, when you get home."

Her hand was over the top of the window. He put his own on it. Then, knowing he had to, he stepped away. Sarah looked back at him, while she could, as the car drove off, whipping up a trail of whirling leaves.

CHAPTER 12

I sometimes see evening like a Great Blue Heron
shadow meadow, field to field,
with steady beat,
my heart unsombered by purple wing
of cloud spread hill to hill.
I watch November plumage rise and sweep
the night and winter after
as Heron flies from sky to sky,
serenely.

Marley had it almost by heart. Restraining himself,
he hadn't read it there on the campus, or when he
returned to his car. He drove all the way back to
Boston, parked, went up to the apartment, hung up
his jacket, made a drink, settled into his chair. Only
then he unfolded the paper and read. He had to read
it several times. Then he was very pleased, since
she'd said she'd written describing him.

The sorrow, sense of loss, seemed lessening now.
The two Sarahs—the old and the new—were both in

his mind, where he could merge them. Part of him tried to erase the new, to pretend a persona had been put on like a silly hat, and Sarah would take it off again as soon as he'd laughed and she, by the very act of wearing, had proved it wasn't her. He knew better though. He had made her up, at least in part. Or, rather, there were parts of her he hadn't known, hadn't allowed himself to see. That was it, more accurately. He hadn't been wrong about her; only incomplete. Which meant the things in her he loved, the things in her from which she loved him, too, were hers in truth.

In those things, those parts, he had hope. His fantasy of vows exchanged in the green shadow of a summer tree, of a life with her like walnut, must go on the shelf with Pooh and Santa Claus. In reality, he would visit her and go to those concerts, the opera, the films, and enjoy them. And she'd visit him, and walk, and watch the sun set behind the hills across a meadow, drinking wine the long summer evenings, and truly enjoy that too. Perhaps, in time, they'd do more and more of one or the other (or both) together. Or, perhaps their together would ever be one-day-two-days-a-now-and-then-weekend. That wasn't what he wanted, but was better than he had.

Even though knowing it almost by heart, he read the poem over again to see it in her simple, graceful hand.

He didn't want to cook his supper, but didn't want to leave, in case she called. He made himself an omelette, the easiest thing. He read, or tried to read. Each half hour, quarter, five minutes, finally, seemed more certain to be the one when the phone would ring.

He rationalized, first, that she'd been in traffic, or stopped for supper, gotten there much later than he'd estimated. And then that she would—naturally—take time to explore her new apartment, unpack, put away her things to make herself at home and not a visitor, see every room, admire the costly bric-a-brac, appreciate the paintings, look from every window at the city lights like trays of diamonds. Naturally, she'd do that first, not first go to the phone to talk to someone she'd seen four hours before.

By ten o'clock each second seemed the one for the second ring, the first already willed into his hearing. Perhaps her phone, in an unused apartment, had been disconnected. Marley checked his own, got the dial tone, wondered if a defective line might let that reach him but block incoming calls. He knew that was foolish.

For another hour he tried telepathy: by longing enough for her, to force her to call.

Perhaps, he decided, she's simply gone to bed. She was grieving and excited too—emotionally exhausted. He could surely forgive that, understand. She'd told him she loved him, given him the poem she'd written just for him. She might forgivably think she'd displayed enough affection for that short day.

He went to bed. It took another half hour to give up all hope, but finally he slept.

He woke at five. It was dark, and he slept again till seven. For a while then he lay awake, hallucinating her

warmth, her weight, her dear self pressed against
him.

He got up, breakfasted, rambled his rooms, intensely aware of himself, his solitude. He sorted his
laundry, balanced his checkbook.

If he called Information, he could get her number.
He'd known that, of course. But she'd said she'd call
him. He didn't want to . . . pester her.

The phone finally rang at 11:10. Marley had it on
the second ring.

"Hello!"

"Jim—James? This is Cliff Letterman. I'm in New
York."

"Oh. How are you, Clifton?"

"Fine. I'm . . . Ah, I was supposed to meet Sarah
this morning at Mrs. Ten Broeck's lawyer's office.
Ah. . . . James, I've got bad news. I don't know
how to . . . I guess I'd just better say it: Sarah's
dead, James."

Marley heard. He knew what the words meant,
what *dead* meant, what it meant to say "Sarah's
dead." He'd been told a fact which he understood.
There wasn't Sarah anymore.

"James?"

"How—?"

"I'm sorry, James—"

"How? What happened?" There were more words
to say, more facts to learn. One said them, asked;
one wanted to know, all the while knowing the only
word was *dead,* the only fact was *no more Sarah*.

"We don't know. A mugging, apparently. She
went out for a walk last night—last evening."
Letterman spoke more easily, as though focusing on

the little facts he knew kept him from knowing what they meant to Marley. "Someone must have forced her into a car. Her body was found about 2:00 A.M. on the Henry Hudson Parkway. She'd been shot, several times. Her clothes were ripped"—he rushed on—"but she hadn't been actually . . . molested. They must have— There must have been more than one to get her that far. They must have intended . . . But she must have fought, and they shot her. I'm sorry, James."

"Yes. What . . . ?"

"Yes?"

"What . . . ? Where . . . ? Ah . . ."

"She's . . . her body's at the city morgue now. I wondered . . . Ah . . . Her purse was there—at the scene. Billfold. They'd cleaned it out, but threw it— She'd made a note with the lawyer's name and number, so the police called. And he called me. And Mrs. Ten Broeck. He's handling all the . . . arrangements. But nobody here is really able . . . I never even met her myself; and neither did he. And he thinks Mrs. Ten Broeck is too old, and we shouldn't ask her if we can get someone . . . So I said I'd call to let you know and ask you. . . . Could you come down and identify the body, James? I'm sorry."

The T was running. People were getting on and off, going wherever they were going. Marley got on, rode to Logan. The Eastern shuttle was flying. Travelers came and went. Marley boarded. The world was going on, a lesser, poorer, sadder world, but going on. Life went on, only Sarah was gone. Life went on, even if it had no point.

To distract himself he took a magazine from the seat-back pouch. Inside the front cover a stove like Sarah's held flame without heat, falsely claiming it could make his home cozy. On another page a couple who weren't him and Sarah stood by a waterfall like one he knew and would never show her. He started to read about prospects for peace, read over twice. He put the magazine away, tried simply to clear his mind, and slept. He had ten minutes' blessed oblivion before they landed.

"Hello, James. How are you?"

"Okay, Clifton. I'm okay."

"Good flight?"

"Yes. Perfectly smooth."

"You don't have a bag?"

"I'm not staying."

"Ah. Yeah, sure. Okay, I've got a car right out front."

Letterman seemed ready to run interference, to guide Marley along the corridor like someone blind. But he saw Marley handling it, and fell in stride.

Letterman must have shown the cop his ID. The car stood in the loading zone, unticketed, untowed. They got in and headed into parkway traffic.

". . . probably take us as long to get in as it took you to fly down." Letterman tried to be conversational, but soon gave it up.

The traffic was heavy, but moving fast; set-jawed drivers cut each other out. Some did it viciously, some with panache, some (as Marley saw their faces go by) as if they really didn't care; but all of them raced for the prize of arriving six car-lengths ahead of the others. Just as many fought past each other to flee the city these hustled for. They all stank the air with their passing.

Some too old or weak, tired or injured, had fallen out of the herd, and been set upon by jackals. Hulks of cars, stripped of wheels, headlights, any part of use or value, lay like carcasses here and there along the sides of the highway.

For a while the route that Letterman took ran between lines of tenements. Their grimy windows stared at each other with the dullness of prisoners chained in rows.

When they reached Manhattan, Marley saw men barnacled in doorways, covered with gray mold and rotting. He saw the towers, too, of course: high and bright as the crown of a medieval queen holding her skirts up and mincing around the dogshit in the rushes.

New York.

New York had killed Sarah. Had it been in his power, Marley would have rained fire and brimstone until nothing remained but slag, and then spread salt on that.

"Yes. It's Sarah. Sarah Kleinhagen, also known as Sarah Cameron."

"Thank you, Mr. Marley." The man covered her face so white, so cold, so fair—the face that was not Sarah's face, eyes closed, not keenly perceiving. He covered the face that Marley would never see again, and always see, the dead face of bone and flesh less real than the image alive ever in his mind.

Seeing her face, the form of her body under the sheet, caused Marley no pain. Pain would come from *not* seeing her, from seeing her in memory or in vivid might-have-been and not in fact.

"Thanks, James. I'm sorry."

By not seeing her in his mind Marley might not suffer so. "I appreciate that, Clifton. So, where does this leave you?" Keep the mind busy. Let the man roll that body not Sarah now back into its cabinet. Turn and walk out of the room that was cold and silent as a life alone. "Do you still have an investigation?"

"I guess not, now. I'm sure there were some other people involved in the raid who knew about it, helped set it up. But I don't see how we'll ever identify them, ever prove anything if we did. Unless Sarah told you something . . . ?"

"No."

"About Brooks Ten Broeck, maybe?"

"No."

"Well, it wouldn't matter if she had. It'd be hearsay unless we had an actual statement, and we'd still have to dig up some corroboration."

"Yes."

"You want to go straight back?"

"Yes. If you don't mind. I could take a cab."

"Come on, James."

"You said the lawyer would be handling the 'arrangements.' Do you know what . . ."

"I don't. I think he'll call you, probably tonight, for the address of Sarah's family."

"I wonder if they'll take her back now. Well, are you home to Chicago, then?"

Marley chatted with Letterman on the drive to LaGuardia. He bought a *Times* and worked on the crossword puzzle during the flight. He arrived in Boston at the rush, so getting on and off the T without being trampled kept him occupied. He ate a sandwich in a delicatessen on Boylston. He never drank liquor when really depressed, so he allowed himself only a beer with the sandwich, didn't drink all of it. He considered trying to distract himself further, but decided he was going to have to face it eventually. With the feeling a man might have whose final appeal has been denied, Marley turned himself in for solitary confinement.

The phone was ringing as he came in the door. It was Mrs. Ten Broeck's lawyer. Marley gave him the address of Sarah's family, and warned him about their attitude toward her. The man was thoughtful enough to call back an hour later to say the Kleinhagens would accept the body and bury it. That would be something they knew how to do from practice, Marley thought.

A little later Mrs. Ten Broeck herself called.

"Harriet Ten Broeck here, Mr. Marley. I am so terribly . . . terribly . . . sorry about this dreadful, tragic occurrence."

"Yes. So am I, Mrs. Ten Broeck."

"Yes, I know; I know you must be. Sarah . . . I inferred from various things she said that the two of you had developed an . . . affinity."

"Yes."

"I am so, so sorry. And after all of your efforts to find her. Such an incredibly difficult task."

"Yes."

"I was so grateful to you. So very grateful. And now . . ."

"Yes, Mrs. Ten Broeck. Thank you. What's going to happen with Melissa now? How is she? Have you told her?"

"No. She is away still, visiting my niece. That is, in part, why I have called you. I wonder if I might ask you . . . I am most reluctant to tell Melissa what has happend in actuality: That her mother was found, and then . . . murdered. I think that would be a terrible blow to her, and—as you know—her condition is delicate at this time. Furthermore, as we had had some most unfortunate words about her mother, I would prefer not to be the one to say that she is . . . Melissa seems to like and trust you, Mr. Marley. Could you . . . would you . . . write to me, and to Melissa, and say that you did locate Melissa's mother, and discovered beyond doubt that she had died? Without specifying how it . . . or that the death was recent? That would not involve any untruth, you see; but I believe it would inform Melissa in the least painful way of what she must be told. Would you do that, Mr. Marley?"

"Yes. Yes, I can do it that way. That probably is the best thing."

"Thank you so much, Mr. Marley. I was sure you would understand. Oh, this is such a dreadful . . . dreadful . . . business. I feel so very bad, myself. I feel very much responsible. If I had not urged her to go down to the city . . . But it seemed such a good idea. But if I hadn't . . . If I hadn't set you to finding her at all . . ."

If he hadn't found Sarah, she would still be alive.

"But I tell myself, no, there is no direct connection. One can't hold oneself responsible for ramifica-

tions that could not be forseen. Who knows what
. . . accident . . . might have befallen the poor woman
this very day, in the place where she was living, had
she *not* been found.''

"Yes. I'm sure you're right, Mrs. Ten Broeck.''
Marley found some solace in her rationalization, but
he preferred to deflect his thought from the accusation altogether. "What will happen to Melissa now?
What will you do?''

"Time must tell; time must tell. She does seem
much improved, however, Mrs. Gaskill is a jewel.
They get on very well, and Melissa seems much
calmer. And she and I have somewhat reconciled. At
least we seem to have made a truce. With care for
her and some greater stability in her life . . . I am
optimistic, Mr. Marley. I truly believe she soon will
be better.''

"I'm glad to hear that.''

"Yes. Perhaps one day you may visit Melissa. I'm
sure she would like that. And thank you again, Mr.
Marley. Thank you. I can never tell you how grateful
I am for all you have done.''

Sleep, that knits up the ravell'd sleave of care,
Marley quoted to himself. The organism takes care of
itself. He had felt the heavy hand come over his eyes
by 9:30, before he had finished the letter to Mrs. Ten
Broeck and Melissa. As soon as he'd stamped it, he
went to bed and slept. He dreamed, but not of Sarah;
woke several times; but by a simple directive to
himself did not think of her, and slept again.

When he woke at last, past eight, the wound he
had expected to ache seemed barely tender. He felt

refreshed, relieved—almost joyous—at the lack of agony. He breakfasted, took his laundry out and left it, returned to putter around his apartment. By 10:30 he knew that grief would be not just as bad, but much, much worse than he'd expected. Like a clever torturer, it was going to let him revive, regain some strength, before tormenting him on and on. At eleven o'clock, beaten insensible again, he passed out on his couch for thirty minutes.

After lunch, to counter the solipsism of sorrow, Marley went for a walk. The wind was chill, but wan sunlight warmed the aged brick facades a little. They seemed to take it as do pensioners sitting side by side on a rest-home porch. Some had crimson ivy pulled like shawls around them.

A newspaper page blew down the street, tossed and tumbled in the gutter, that might yesterday (he thought) have headlined, *The Secret of Life Discovered!*

He crossed into the Public Gardens, where late the swan boats swam. No one lolled on bench or lawn, no couples lingered by tulip beds. People passed him hurriedly, hands in pockets, shoulders up, hunched within their separate selves.

The trees were tattered. Only the oaks had leaves, ragged, dessicated as pressed flowers from a belle's bouquets, testifying pathetically not to former beauty but to its loss.

Marley ate dinner out. He had to look at his plate from time to time to remember what he was chewing.

As he was crossing, a car came fast on his right, turned left, and nearly hit him. ''You fucking son of

a bitch!'' he screamed, ''I'll kill you!'' and slammed
his hand down on the fender as it passed him. The
driver didn't stop.

He sat in his chair, relaxed, quite calm, practicing
not being there, not thinking, numbness. He wasn't
good enough at it yet. He put his head back, his
palms over his eyes.

It wouldn't always go on this way, he knew. He'd
get over it in time or he'd kill himself; but this
wouldn't go on. It helped to realize that, and he slept
again, for ten more hours.

Again he woke, again felt her absence vividly
along the length of his body. He rejected trying to
protect himself from pain by putting her out of his
mind. Only there could he have her with him now.
He would rather remember and accept, learn to en-
dure the pain of loss, than lose her altogether. He
wanted to recollect every instant they'd spent together. Suddenly he realized he could have more of
her than memory.

Her cabin seemed abandoned. Even seen from the
turnaround, across the little gully, it gave a sense of
emptiness—not merely of no one home just now, but
of being long unlived-in. Marley had been prepared
for the possibility of meeting someone there: some
friend of Sarah's, member of her family, police,
someone sent to look after or collect her things. But
the lack of smoke from a fire within warming against
the chilly wind, the dull, dead leaves, wet from
recent rain and matted over deck and steps, some

stuck to the window and piled against the door, showed no one was staying there or had gone in or out for days.

Marley slowly walked the path to the cabin. On either side, in the area cleared of trees, plumes of goldenrod had drained to tan, stalks of steeplebush turned leather-brown. Across the valley, the trunks of trees, now bared by loss of foliage, hatched the western hill with strokes of black and gray. Inside, though, the feeling changed. All her interests, tastes, her treasures and fripperies, still sprawled and cluttered. A paperback novel lay open, facedown, the story in suspended animation. Anyone entering (who didn't know) might have called, "Sarah?" and settled to wait.

Marley heard her refrigerator running. He thought of shutting it off; but that would mean cleaning it out, then checking the cabinets for perishables, and then . . . what? Her clothes? Her towels and bedding? It wasn't his job. He hadn't come to pack her life away.

He had come for her poems. He gathered the folders: twenty years of writing, everything since she'd started in high school. He'd looked at only a few. Now he'd read them all, perhaps be able to interest someone in publishing some. Perhaps he'd have those he liked best printed privately. He didn't consciously think of that as atonement for bringing Sarah out to die.

To be certain he had them all, he checked the papers on her writing table, the shelves nearby. Again he came across her diary. He had been tempted to read it before; now he was not. The only Sarah he'd known, wanted to know, was her of those few days they'd had together. He put the book with the poems. They were meant for the world; he would be her messenger. The diary held her private thoughts; he would guard them for her.

What else might he, should he, take of her for memory? Nothing, or everything. Standing, then, in the middle of the room, he looked once more at the kitchen where they'd cooked together, the couch and table where they'd eaten, where he had confessed and she absolved him by knowing him and yet loving; at the bed on the loft above him; at the stairway, the cellar trap. He turned, finally, to the window that had shown them the vibrant glory of autumn foliage, and now looked over a bleak woodland waiting for winter.

He read three of the poems that night, when he'd gotten home to Boston, and three each night after. He'd work through them slowly, he decided. He got back to a routine that passed for living. He called David's office, but David was in Tokyo, and no assignment for Marley was anticipated. Marley made some long-deferred repairs around his apartment. He visited the galleries on Newbury Street, had lunch with a friend. Evenings were the loneliest time, and now that the days were growing shortest there was much of them; so he ate in restaurants. He saw George and Gwen one night; took out a woman he liked, not romantically, another. He went to three films in four days. He was grateful now for the city; to have been alone and mourning without its distractions would have been very hard.

Sarah's image never faded, but gradually others could be superimposed. He would never "get over" her; but (as he'd known when he went for her poems) while losing her would always pain him, he hoped he could come to accept the loss and yet find joy remembering. If what he had heard could be believed, he might even again meet some woman who would attract him.

Marley finally began to think he had himself under control, believing he would—in time—find pleasure in living. He felt that until he received Melissa's letter.

He came in from the thickening dusk, collected his mail, and climbed the stairs looking through it. Melissa's name on an envelope corner caught his eye, pleased and excited him. Evidently, from the return address, she still was visiting her uncle Richard. He went into his apartment, but stopped in the foyer, tore it open and read.

As he'd have expected, she thanked him for looking for Sarah and expressed her disappointment and grief. As he hoped she would, she accepted losing her fantasy about her parents' life together. But he wasn't prepared for her joy, could never have been prepared for the reason for it.

"But I guess it doesn't really matter," she wrote, "because half of my dream is coming true anyway! MY FATHER IS COMING HOME!!!"

CHAPTER 13

Marley must have known, must have known what Melissa was really telling him, must have known intuitively, instantly, because shock readied his body for violence. Though he read on through the final sentences, then walked ever so slowly into the living room and sat, still staring at the letter all the while as though he saw it, his heart raced, his lungs pulled more air, he felt the chill thrill of adrenaline. Outwardly somnolent, he slumped. His conscious mind trudged through "But Sarah said . . . How could he? Why now?" But his body must have known at once. It shook him—his fingertips first, then the whole hand holding the letter—until he roused.

He knew. Oh, God! He understood. He understood it all, oh, God! Deceived, used, betrayed— He'd betrayed— Oh, God!

He could have screamed, risen up screaming in his guilt and shame and rage, lashed out, seized up and smashed his chair, made mayhem room by room, staggered through the shambles, howling and battering hands and head against the walls.

Marley pulled his hand across his brow and down

over his eyes. He took one breath very deeply, held, and let it out. He swallowed, then stared at his hand, controlled the shaking to a minor quiver.

He scanned the end of Melissa's letter again. "Gray called . . . will explain it all . . . coming home on Wednesday . . ." He checked the date at the letter's head: three days before today.

Today was Wednesday.

He looked at his watch. Just past five. Four hours (or a little more) to get there. No need to rush, he easily could arrive at a reasonable hour. For several minutes more he sat, quite calm now—deadly calm—thinking. Then he hung away his overcoat, changed to a heavy sweater and country shoes, and got Sarah's diary from his study. He opened it and read the date of the first entry, to be sure: She'd started keeping it three years before. He put it into his windbreaker pocket.

Before getting his car Marley walked up to Boylston and bought two sandwiches and two half-pints of milk to have on the way. He topped up his gas before getting onto the turnpike.

He drove carefully all the way, keeping his speed down to the limit, checking and signaling before passing. Once someone cut him off, but he only braked and smiled: no blaring the horn, no shouting obscenities.

No screaming, no smashing unfeeling objects, no rushing wildly this way and that, no howling out torment. Keep it in. Marley knew how to maximize wrath.

For a little time the last twilight tinged the sky a dirty violet in the west toward which he drove. Then the hand of night, thrusting out ahead of him, descended to crush the color down. He hurtled along the highway within it, isolated and encased in darkness, in the steel shell of his car, in the harder armor of hatred.

Windows across the house front beaconed, proclaiming the prodigal son's return. Marley cut his own headlamps, crept up the drive by the yellow-eyed glow of parking lights. The Ten Broecks knew now he was coming, of course, an unwelcome guest at the feast. He had had to wait at the gatehouse for the permission to enter that, however reluctantly given, couldn't be refused. Still, he wanted for himself the sense of quiet inexorability that came from looming out of darkness, from hearing the weight of his car, heavy but slow, crush the gravel in a rolling, softly grinding crunch. He coasted around the final curve, quietly came to a halt. The well-tuned engine barely hummed under its half-heard rapid ticking. Marley sat for a moment, staring at the house, centering and steadying his anger. Then he shut the motor off.

The cedar shrubs, which would be evergreen throughout the winter, still flanked the downstairs windows, but the mums had been removed when they'd lost their bloom and become unsightly. Marley pressed the bell and waited until the butler came.

"Good evening. It's James Marley."

The butler's reserve expressed annoyance for the household. "Come in, please. Wait here, please." But at least he went to the drawing room to announce Marley.

Then suddenly Melissa dashed out. "Mr. Marley!

Mr. Marley! My father's home!'' She ran to him, threw herself upon him, hugged him. "My father's back! Did you get my letter? My father's come back again!" She bounced up and down with excitement.

It seemed that every time he saw her she wept, but this time her eyes were bright with overflowing joy. Her joy might have melted Marley's heart, if anything could have.

"Yes. I got it just today. It's wonderful news, Melissa." Because he liked her, because she touched him, there was a little sincerity somewhere in his broad smile.

"Come on! Come on in! Come meet him! He just got home this afternoon." Clutching Marley's hand, Melissa dragged him after her. "Mr. Marley, this is my father! Father, this is Mr. Marley!"

Brooks Ten Broeck rose from the couch. Melissa must have been sitting beside him, Marley imagined, big-eyed, doting, hanging on every word from her hero returned from the wars. Marley wondered what he'd been telling her. Mrs. Ten Broeck sat in her wing chair.

Brooks was clean-shaven now; his hair, still curly and full, was shorter; his forehead high and pink. Once, he'd been a year younger than Sarah; it seemed he'd slipped past her and reached middle age first. The youthful chubbiness had started to settle to pouch and paunch. He wore a plaid shirt, but even at home a jacket and tie. Though he arranged himself to meet Marley pleasantly, with a smile as sweet as his reputation promised, the lines around the rosebud lips were those of a man who has tasted life and found it corky.

"Mr. Marley, I'm so glad to meet you."

"It's a real pleasure, Brooks."

Brooks smiled, Marley smiled.

Mrs. Ten Broeck didn't bother to smile. "Your calling is an unexpected pleasure for us, Mr. Marley."

"Good evening, Mrs. Ten Broeck. Yes. I hope I'm not disturbing you. When I got Melissa's letter saying Brooks would be here today, well, I just had to come right over and meet him."

"Melissa wrote that Brooks was coming?" Mrs. Ten Broeck shifted her displeasure.

"Yes." In her happiness Melissa missed the hint of censure. "I wrote to thank Mr. Marley for . . . for finding . . . for finding out about Mother. And I just had to tell him about Father! I knew he'd be so pleased! Isn't it wonderful, Mr. Marley!"

"Incredible!"

"That was very . . . thoughtful . . . of you, Melissa dear."

"Won't you sit down, Mr. Marley?" Brooks gestured vaguely, and Marley went around and took the other wing chair again. "I'd like to thank you myself for all your efforts."

"Yes, I'm sure you would."

Brooks had waited for Marley to sit, then started to take his own seat again. Marley's tone caught him half down, and he held for an instant. But Marley kept up his interminable smiling, so Brooks settled. Melissa came back beside him.

"It is incredible," Marley said, "your coming back now—after all these years—from the dead, as it were."

"Yes. It's . . . it's a very long story."

"I'm sure. Where have you been? If you don't mind my asking."

"In Switzerland. I don't mind at all. I have a little gallery there. Paintings, objets d'art, sixteenth and seventeenth centuries, mostly."

"Fascinating. It must be, I mean."

"Interesting, yes."

"But you decided to come back."

"Melissa. Gray convinced me Melissa needed me."

"Yes. And we can all see how much your coming back means to her. You haven't seen her or written in all these years."

Melissa didn't hear that fully as rebuke, but sensed enough to come to her father's defense. "Father couldn't! He couldn't let anyone know. . . . Because he thought the government thought— Because he was against the war."

Marley nodded to assure her he understood. "I understand. I *know* what your father did against the war." Then he turned at once to Mrs. Ten Broeck. "But, of course, you knew."

"Of course." She smiled smugly. "Of course I knew. And I told everyone that I knew." She drew herself even more upright. "Everyone thought I was merely a dotty old woman." Her eyes gleamed.

Brooks had caught what Marley had said. "You say you know about my . . . antiwar activities?"

"Oh, yes. That's why I was so very surprised to hear of your return—as from the dead, as I said."

"I *told* you Brooks wasn't dead."

"Yes, Mrs. Ten Broeck, you did. And I didn't believe you. That was very foolish of me, and I'm very sorry for it. But now I know the truth." Marley's hands were in his lap, the left clasping the fisted right. That way his fingers didn't tremble, and he could appear at ease.

Mrs. Ten Broeck relished her triumph. "Yes. It has been very amusing to me—"

But Brooks interrupted her. "Gray." He only lifted a hand, and she stopped, catching the nuance of warning at once. Marley realized more fully how much he'd misjudged her.

Brooks looked at him for a moment, then shifted focus to Melissa, touched her arm. "Melissa, Mr. Marley and I, I think, have some business to discuss. It has to do with things I still have to keep secret. You understand, I have to. Could you, please, for a little while, go up to your room, or somewhere?" He was very good about it, good with her, not dismissive, but asking with regret as though he'd miss her more than she'd miss being near him.

Secrets, his secret life, were part of her fiction of him. Though crestfallen, she accepted her responsibility to help him keep them. She glanced at Marley, but he nodded back as though to reassure that he was in collusion with her father, not a threat. "All right, Father."

"Just for a little while."

"Sure." She gave Brooks a quick kiss on the cheek.

He seemed both startled and pleased, kissed her brow, then gently guided her away.

"It's nice to see you again, Mr. Marley. Thanks again for trying to help me."

"My pleasure, Melissa. It was a pleasure for me."

Conscience, care for her, tried to touch him, but his heart was hardened.

Brooks waited until she'd left the room, and for another moment after. "Well, Mr. Marley? What do you know about what I did?"

"I know you were in the raid on Westhover."

"I was not. That is not true."

"It's not?"

"It is not."

"Sarah said you were."

"That woman—" Mrs. Ten Broeck began, but again Brooks stopped her.

"She did?" he asked.

"She did."

"She was mistaken. She was telling you a falsehood. Perhaps she believed it, but it is not true."

"She said Malcolm told her."

"That's what she said? Well, if that's what Malcolm told her—if that's true, then Malcolm was lying."

"Why would he lie to her?"

"I would have no idea."

"But you weren't involved in the raid."

"I was not."

"Then why did you run away? Why have you been in hiding all these years?"

"I was afraid. I was afraid of being accused of being involved in that raid—just as I have been."

Mrs. Ten Broeck seemed willing to let Brooks carry it, but was unable to resist saying once more, "I told you."

"But you weren't accused. You haven't been accused for fourteen years, yet you stayed away, in hiding, not even letting your own daughter know you were alive!"

Brooks took a deep breath, let it out in a long sigh. "I was very, very much opposed to the war—as, no doubt, you have heard. I was involved with a group that fought against it by radical means—radical, but nonviolent. I was arrested several times. None of these actions had the least effect.

"I became increasingly distraught over that, over the fact that not only were we not stopping the war, it was being escalated. Then our group divided into factions, as you know; and one turned to violence. I opposed their methods yet shared their goals. I was torn apart, in a state of near nervous collapse. When they made that raid on Westhover, bringing the conflict in my values to a crisis, the collapse occurred. As part of it, I was convinced I would be identified with them. There may have been some rational basis for my fear because of having been associated with them before; but irrationally, I realize now, I feared because of that part of me that identified with their goals, and therefore with them. *I* judged *myself* guilty by association. Do you understand? I fled. Gray got me out of the country in secret. I spent several years in a private institution in Europe.

"When I emerged, the irrational part of my fear was gone, but I still believed I might be falsely charged. More than that, though, I found I had developed a disillusionment with—a revulsion against—my former ideals, and the places and people associated with them. That included—indeed, was focused on— Sarah Kleinhagen and my daughter by her. It is a testament to the healing powers of time that I now am able to be with Melissa, look at her, even to think of her without a feeling of almost physical sickness.''

"She idolizes you.''

"Yes, it would seem so. I like children. Several . . . I am a sort of honorary uncle to the children of several of my friends in Geneva. Melissa seems— essentially—to be a lovely child despite the . . . behavior problem Gray has told me about. I'm sure Gray is right: That my return will bring Melissa's problem to an end. No doubt I should have come back sooner. I simply couldn't.''

"Yes. I know.''

"*Now* you know.''

"Yes. Well, that would seem to explain everything, wouldn't it?''

"I hope so.''

"Yes. I'm sure you do, Brooks. I mean, it's a good story, coherent.''

Mrs. Ten Broeck could no longer restrain herself. "Far more coherent, Mr. Marley, than the wild lies that woman—''

"That woman—Sarah—would never lie! But *you* have lied and lied and killed—'' Marley caught himself, released his clutch on the chair arms, set again his increasingly inane smile. "It's a coherent story, Brooks, but it just doesn't answer all the questions. I mean, if you were going to come back, if you'd gotten over your 'revulsion' and you were going to come back for Melissa's sake, what was the point of hiring me to find Sarah? What was the point of continuing to keep your existence hidden until she was found?''

"Mr. Marley, you understand—''

"I do! I do understand, now. I understand why Mrs. Ten Broeck hired me instead of going to professionals, to an agency, where there would have been several people assigned to the case, where there would have been records. I understand that you couldn't come back while there were still people alive who knew you'd been on that raid."

"I was not on the raid. The story is that I was killed on the raid? Well, obviously, I was not killed; obviously, the story is false."

"Only the being-killed part. You were there, but you escaped."

"That is not true. No one who knew me would ever believe it."

"Sarah believed it."

Silence. Mrs. Ten Broeck scorned, stiff and superior as an archaic statue set with glittering agate eyes. Brooks rubbed his fingertips together, back and forth; otherwise he seemed placid. It didn't matter anymore what Sarah had believed.

Marley felt himself spring upon them, felt his hand seize a scrawny throat and clutch, shake, and snap the neck; felt stiffened fingers spear flabby flesh and tear. "I believe it," he said quietly.

"I'm sorry you do, Mr. Marley."

"It's obvious that woman told him these lies to get his help in extorting as much as she could from me. She threw herself at him, and he's besotted!"

Marley felt the brittle face bones crush as he pounded them.

"Gray, please. Mr. Marley is clearly very upset. I understand, Mr. Marley, that you developed a . . . relationship with Sarah. I am very sorry that . . . that things have turned out as they have. But your suspicions are groundless."

"Your story is bullshit. It's full of holes. Why try to find Sarah? Why come back now?"

"There are explanations—"

"Bullshit!"

"Mr. Marley, if you don't want to hear them, if you won't believe . . . Well, I'm afraid you may justly be accused of bias."

"Other people—"

"Other people will believe what I tell them, or, at least, they will have no grounds for not believing. What grounds do you have? You *say* that Sarah *said* that Malcolm Grandgeorge *said* . . . Who can believe that? No court, no jury. You have no *evidence*."

"You killed her, Brooks. You murdered Sarah. It wasn't more than one man, who just happened to be driving by when she just happened to decide to take a walk, and forced her into a car without anybody noticing. You got her to come out somehow, and she got into the car and drove all that way with you because it was *you*."

Brooks shook his head; lamplight flashed on his glasses. Marley saw the lenses smashing, shards being driven back into his eyes.

"You killed Robbie Bascaglia. It wasn't Mal and Denny— He *didn't* know where Sarah was. What he knew was where *they* were. But he wouldn't tell even you. Did he figure it out? That you wanted to set them on to us? Or was he just not revealing 'whereabouts' of anybody to anybody? *You* knew where she was, because I'd found her for you."

"Fantastic, Mr. Marley. This is all a fantasy of

bereavement. You have nothing to substantiate what you are saying.''

Marley forced himself to pause, to smile a bitter smile at Brooks. It wasn't time to kill him yet. Some remaining scruple, some vestigial wish to overcome his rage, made Marley need to know it all, to prove himself completely justified.

"No. No, and without something concrete, something Sarah'd put in writing, something that could be checked on, you'd probably sue me for libel if I even suggested it.''

"I hope we wouldn't do that, Mr. Marley. Doing that, after all you've been through, would make me feel very bad.''

"You really are so sweet, Brooks. Of course, that's what makes this all seem so incredible. Tell me. . . . I guess it's the only satisfaction I'm going to get: How could anybody who's as sweet as you're supposed to be do what you've done? I mean, interpret 'what you've done' however you want. Let it be ambiguous. You know. You let Sarah give up Melissa, go away. Stayed away yourself for fourteen years, whatever else you may have done. What you told me doesn't cover it.''

"What I told you is the truth.''

"I need to know some more. I need to hear it, more, to be satisfied.''

"There is no need to tell Mr. Marley anything, Brooks.''

"Let me at least try to understand, Mrs. Ten Broeck. Don't you owe me that?''

"We owe you nothing, Mr. Marley.''

"You do. You do, Brooks. You owe me at least a

sense of understanding. How could *you* have done what you've done? They say, 'To understand all is to forgive all.' '' Marley knew—who has sinned, and longs not for forgiveness? Marley knew about that, but in case that wasn't enough, he added, "I've got to have some satisfaction, Brooks, some understanding; I can't let this go until I have it."

Brooks studied Marley for another moment. "What I told you is all there is to tell: fear, a sense of guilt, revulsion.

"I was not on that raid. How could anyone imagine it? Could anyone imagine *me* involved in trying to blow up a bomber with a truck full of homemade dynamite? Imagine *me* assigned to shoot anyone who tried to stop it? Absurd. Absurd. I would have been paralyzed—by conflict in my values, by fear. At the first sight of interference I would have jumped from the truck and fled.

"Imagine, then, my disillusionment if I had done that: with my ideals, with myself. Imagine how I would have felt, knowing both that I had allied myself with evil, and been unable to carry out my part because of cowardice. Imagine my self-loathing; and then my realization that if even such a person as I . . . Sweet. Yes, everyone always said I was so sweet. I was. I was so sweet the tears of a single child could melt me. And if *I* could be so corrupted and so weak, what absurdity to believe the world could be transformed, that people can change—except for the worse.

"What revulsion I would have had then for my former ideals, and for anyone who reminded me of them. My former lover would have been a constant rebuke, my daughter a living accusation of guilt.

"I would have seen that the world is as it is, and one must live in it by its rules. There is no need to do gratuitous harm, but no reason not to do whatever is in one's interest.

"But this is all imagination. This is what I imagine I would have felt if I had been involved in that raid. But I was not, and there is no evidence to the contrary."

Brooks continued to look at Marley levelly, calmly. Marley nodded slowly.

"Whatever. 'If there is no God, anything is permitted.' Kill Sarah. . . . Use me. . . ." Marley's voice shook with the anguish and anger that tremored his whole body. He held his breath, stiffened himself. "You're wrong. There is evidence. Sarah's diary." He took it from his pocket. "She put everything in it." He held it open at arm's length before him, so Brooks could see what it was, recognize the handwriting. "About Westhover: What she knew of the preparations, what Malcolm told her."

Mrs. Ten Broeck reached, even though too far away.

Brooks shook his head. "It's still hearsay."

"Give that to me!"

"It doesn't matter, Gray. It's not evidence."

"It gives details that can be checked, corroborated. More than that, it establishes a motive. There's no such thing as a perfect crime, Brooks. Not when they know who really did it, what to look for. They'll check Bascaglia's place again."

Mrs. Ten Broeck struggled to rise. "Mr. Marley, give that to me!"

"They'll find . . . dandruff. Lint from your socks. You had to come into the country, before. False passport? Still had your beard? It doesn't matter. When they know they're looking for you, they'll trace you."

"I'll pay you!"

"No, Gray!"

Marley snapped back to her, "How much?"

"A hundred thous—"

"He's bluff—"

"Half a million!"

"I'll pay!"

"It's a trick!"

"Yeah!"

Mrs. Ten Broeck had heaved herself forward onto her feet. She stood rocking, as though preparing to throw herself at Marley as soon as she had her balance. Marley came up, too, and Brooks.

"Yeah." Marley held the diary up by his head, waving it. "This must really be valuable if the Ten Broecks will put out half a million dollars for it!"

Silence then as Brooks and Mrs. Ten Broeck contemplated her mistake and Marley savored his triumph.

He knew now, certainly, by their own admission. Now no compunction need stay his vengeance. "You killed them. You killed her. You used me to find her. *I* found her, *I* brought her out for you to *kill!* She was . . . I loved . . ." His voice shook again and grew tight with the breath filling his chest for screaming, for screaming before he hurled himself to beat and rend. "You murdered Sarah! You—"

"Ahhhh!" Mrs. Ten Broeck shrieked, staggering backward, hand clutching her chest. "Ahhh—ahhh—ahhh!" She reeled, tottered. "Pills!" She gasped. "Pills!"

Brooks lurched to catch her, but she twisted away from him.

"Ahhh! Pills!" Arm outstretched, she wavered toward the secretary.

Brooks stumbled half a step toward her, then halted, petrified with shock and fear.

Still gasping, Mrs. Ten Broeck reached the secretary. She almost fell against it, fumbling at a drawer. She got it open. One hand on the writing leaf for balance, she reached inside, clutched, then pivoted and pointed the nickel-plated pistol straight at Marley.

CHAPTER 14

"Put that book down! Put it down, Mr. Marley! I have waited . . . too long . . . for Brooks to come home. Put it down."

Light from the nearer couch-end lamp shone softly on her face, flattering away the lines, the lies that years had told about her: that she was old and therefore frail and foolish. The pistol waved in her outstretched hand, but she steadied herself against the secretary, and Marley was sure she'd hit him if she shot.

He stood frozen, no more than fifteen feet from her, in front of his chair, just the step forward from it he'd taken on springing up. Brooks stood stunned, too, perhaps five feet away.

Marley considered moving left to put Brooks between them as a shield, and rejected it.

"Put it down!" she said once more.

Instead, Marley extended the diary to the length of his arm, his other hand going up beside his head. "Okay, Mrs. Ten Broeck, okay. Take it easy." He went forward a reassuringly cautious step. "Okay, Brooks, you win. Here." Another step.

"Put it on the couch!"

"All right, Mrs. Ten Broeck. Take it easy." Ever so slowly Marley pivoted a quarter turn toward the couch. He brought his right foot forward, weight on it, reaching far over to lay the diary down.

Suddenly he half-lunged, half-fell, springing crashing into Brooks, bear-hugging, knocking him off balance. They staggered together, Brooks trying at first to free himself, hands on Marley's shoulders, pushing away. Marley rocked back enough to get his footing, keep them from falling. Lifting most of Brooks's weight, he swung to shield himself. Ungripping his hands, he clubbed Brooks once—side of head with heel of palm—then clasped around again, getting Brooks's arm pinned beneath his own.

Mrs. Ten Broeck had tottered fully upright, lurching from side to side, trying to aim at Marley.

But Marley kept swinging Brooks. Brooks pounded with his free fist at Marley's shoulder, at his head. Marley sheltered his face against Brooks's cheek, against his neck. Mouth to neck, Marley bit. Brooks shrieked. Marley tasted blood with savage ecstasy.

Brooks clutched at Marley's head, grabbing hair, yanking to tear him away. Again Marley unlocked his grip, caught Brooks's arm, forcing it down and back to pin it like the other. Brooks struggled, trying to twist, to kick. Together they staggered, nearly falling, knocking off the table lamp. It crashed, base smashing, bulb white-flash popping.

Heaving Brooks around again, Marley kneed him, bulling him, forcing him back toward Mrs. Ten Broeck. Too late she realized his intention, staggered sideways trying to slip by.

Brooks was heavy; but Marley, taller, hunching, driving like a football lineman, toppled him, ramming the two of them, intertwined, into her, crushing her against the wall.

She half-gasped, half-screamed. Brooks screamed, "No!" found the panic-strength to straighten, forcing Marley backward.

Marley let himself be pushed away, let his knees bend; then, lifting Brooks, recoiled and threw their bodies at her a second time. Again she gasped. Her arm flung back, struck the wall; she dropped the pistol.

At the side of his vision Marley caught a glimpse of another figure, in a white jacket, arms raised. Still struggling to hold Brooks, he tried to turn to avoid an attack, but none came. The old butler, shocked and horrified as he was, had more wit than to throw his frail self into the melee. He spun away and dashed out of the room again to call the guard at the gate. The door that he flung open in haste bounced closed again.

Taking advantage of Marley's distraction, Brooks twisted, wheeling the two of them away from her. As they pivoted along the wall, Marley's back was slammed against an upper corner of the secretary. Paralyzing pain shot across, down his arms, stunning him, breaking his grip. Brooks jerked himself free. He threw up his arms and struck down wildly, both fists together, at Marley's neck and shoulder. He struck again, flung up his arms for another blow; then spun, scanned, spotted the pistol on the floor.

Still half-blinded with shock and pain, Marley—looking under an arm feebly raised to shield himself—

saw Brooks stagger, stooping, for the gun. He threw himself, tackled.

Brooks hit the floor, arm outstretched. His left hand closed around the weapon. As he fumbled for a firing grip, Marley scrambled up over his legs and fell upon him, one hand grabbing his forearm. Brooks forced his arm down, forcing Marley's back. Suddenly Marley shifted, getting his other arm free, grabbing Brooks's wrist—thumb pressing into tendons. Brooks screamed in pain, tried to snatch his hand away even as Marley shoved it. The pistol was flung from his grip.

Brooks writhed, legs churning, kicking, kneeing. Marley had to roll away. He set to fling himself back on Brooks, but Brooks twisted, scrabbled, got half up on knees and forearms, scrambled toward the pistol that had landed just under Mrs. Ten Broeck's chair. He groped, found it.

Marley knew he could neither rise and spring on Brooks nor lunge far enough to reach him in time. He threw himself sideways, knocking away the end table, rolling behind the end of the couch.

Brooks swung around, came up sitting.

Marley catapulted forward, still on his knees, shoved the couch with all his strength to slam against the far end table and topple its lamp. Again the pop and flash; at the same time Brooks fired twice and Marley rolled forward to hide behind the couch's back.

Darkness absolute. Marley tried to hush his desperate lust for air as he heard Brooks's gasping and Mrs. Ten Broeck's moans. Brooks's weapon would be of no use if he didn't know where to aim.

"Father!"

Marley realized it was the second time she'd called; the first more muffled—from farther away—had come after the shots.

If he could creep around the couch in silence . . . He pictured the layout of furniture.

"Father!" Running, coming down the stairs.

If he could come from the end opposite where he'd last been seen . . .

Running along the downstairs hall. "Father!" Melissa threw open the drawing room door. Light struck in from the hall, diffused and dim across the room, but sufficient to see by. The door banged against a rubber stop, bounced, starting to swing closed. Melissa stood at the threshold, surprised by darkness inside. The heavy door swung to seal the room again, but she stopped it with an outstretched hand, pushed it back more slowly.

Brooks staggered to his feet, staring toward the light as though it were his enemy. Marley, more aware, rolled against the back of the couch.

Melissa stood in silhouette, her shadow, only, venturing in. Her father, his back to a chair, was staring back at her without recognition. The hand holding the gun was shaking; his whole body was shaking.

"Father! What's wrong? What's happening?"

Brooks must not have heard her questions, only the questioning tone. If he knew at all who she was, he must have known her only as his accuser. Now she had opened the door, let light reveal him. In the moments of darkness he must have felt senselessly secure, like a child covering its eyes with its hands, and thus invisible.

He pressed back against the chair. It barred him.

Not knowing consciously what he was doing, he slid to the side to escape the trap. Not knowing consciously, he raised the gun at the dark shape in the doorway.

"Father!"

He fired.

Melissa screamed and staggered backward.

Brooks fired again, wheeled around the chair, dashed to the terrace doors. They were locked. He rattled the handle frantically.

Marley hadn't been able to see any of it. He heard Brooks shoot, then run. He came up to his hands and knees, peered over the couch.

With a scream strangling in his throat Brooks flung himself against the glass doors, cracking mullions, smashing panes, showering them out into the slates before him. He lurched through, wavered but an instant, then ran to his right.

Marley spun around to look at Melissa. When he saw her backed against the wall in the hallway, hands over her mouth in shock and horror, but standing, unhurt, he sprang like a sprinter after Brooks.

He saw no movement, listened. Yes! Footsteps, running, on the flagstone path. He dashed across the terrace, down over the steps in a bound, toward the sculptured trees by the side of the house. As he reached them he leapt sideways onto the lawn so his own footsteps would not clatter.

Brooks's steps, muffled through foliage, were moving off to his left. He turned that way, around a great, dark, needled tree, meaning to cut in at an angle. But another tree spread in his way, its limbs outstretched to those of a third, planted closer to the path again. He remembered that two serried rows of trees stood guardians of order there, requiring all who went that way to keep the proper path.

Marley returned to it, loped into the turn of the tennis courts. Once past the lines of trees he paused.

All the stars burned icily. He could see the tennis lines, the fence stanchions, the flat courts, empty. The path ran along one end, up to the huge, ghostly eminence of the conservatory. It turned there, along the courts' side. Against and within the black of farther trees, Marley could barely see the roofs of other buildings, presumably the garages, toward which Brooks must be headed.

He ran along the end of the courts, turned along the side. He stopped again. The garages were partially screened by bushes and trees. Brooks, though panicked, was armed. If fear abated enough, he might hide and wait.

Marley listened. Silence. No running, door banging, car starting. He sank to his haunches, knowing that from certain angles his figure would show against the lighter fields of tennis courts and conservatory.

Silence.

No. He became aware that from somewhere behind, softened by distance, there came a steady rushing, roaring sound. Not natural, not wind or waterfall. Part of his mind tried to place it while he concentrated ahead for sight or sound of Brooks. He saw nor heard none.

Oil burner, furnace, heating system, from the conservatory.

He looked back toward the vast glass structure. Its whitewashed panes reflected starlight, glowing softly;

the building's curves clear, sharp against the black sky, it was—and yet, so pale, was not—a fairy Xanadu, a magic palace carved of ice around a tropical forest. A cozy refuge from winter's cold. A place for a child to play hide-and-seek. He suddenly knew that Brooks, terrified, would go to ground there.

Marley rose into a crouch, made his way across the lawn toward one end of the conservatory. He might be wrong, Brooks might still be ahead.

As he approached, the noise was louder. It came more clearly as he circled the conservatory. He saw a small, solid-walled attachment to the great glass house. A door stood open; the sound came from within.

Marley entered carefully, though certain Brooks would not be there but farther inside, in the jungle.

In the darkness he could sense only that the room was large. From the far end the furnace roared, burner and fan forcing hot air through ducts. He had no fear of being heard there. Even a shout would be thundered over, even a gunshot.

The entrance to the conservatory proper showed as a rectangle infinitesimally brighter than the darkness around it. Marley crossed to it. Whitewashing that made the glass luminescent from without kept it almost black within. Concealment favored Brooks this time. Armed, in the darkness, Brooks could wait for Marley to come up close, where bad aim wouldn't matter. Marley felt along the wall by the doorway, found a row of switches. He flipped the first.

Light flashed on in the room behind him. He struck the switch again as he dropped to the floor.

He scrambled to the side, waited, then reached up, pushed the second switch. It controlled a row of lamps hanging on drops down the length of the conservatory. The next two switches controlled two more. Work lights. They revealed the greenery. In a center island-bed, palms rose to reach the middle dome. Lesser trees grew around them, and broad- and cut-leaved shrubs masked the lower trunks of all. Another bed flanked either side, filled with vegetation growing as much as eight to ten feet high. The walks between them had wavy margins to give a slight meander, a sense of natural woodsy ways.

Lit from above, the paths were clear; but shadows cast from the foliage downward made hiding places, hardly what Marley wanted.

There were more switches by the door, and he tried them.

Light came on from below.

Yeah! he thought. He turned the downlights off.

A jungle illuminated, a pleasantly exotic place for party guests to stroll. Spots and floodlights along path edges, and back in the beds, here tickled out a feathery fern, there shot up the palm trunks' curve to skyrocket out and down on fronds. Five-leaf clusters of schefflera, silhouetted, became black hands. Bamboo stalks were ribby streaks, some light, some dark, set off against each other.

Marley, stepping onto the path, stood in twilight; only soft reflected glow shone on him.

He paused. He had sensed from the moment of Brooks's crashing through the drawing room doors that the man was terrified out of his reason. However calculating he might have been when committing crimes on his own terms, his reaction to discovery and physical attack was mindless flight and hiding—as it must have been those years ago at Westhover. Marley understood that Brooks would shoot if cornered, but would not plan an ambush nor reveal himself by firing at a distance from cover.

Despite his rages, Marley could think that way, assessing the situation tactically.

He went back to the utility room. Unafraid now of revealing himself, he turned on the light. He scanned the shelves, workbench, tools. A long-poled pruner stood in a corner. He considered it.

Though his pulse pounded and blood sang, rage never fevered him out of *his* mind. He knew now he had Brooks cornered. He could call the police.

The pole wasn't really long enough, and would encumber him. He looked further.

He should call the police. This was Tucson all over again.

He didn't see what he was looking for. He went back into the conservatory. If he couldn't find the right device, he'd just have to be more careful. He'd counted shots. Brooks had only two bullets left.

This was the rage he hated in himself, that he'd fought all these years and thought he'd conquered.

He saw the hose. Attached to a faucet, it coiled on a reel that would pay it out. Just take the nozzle end and walk. He took the nozzle end, turned on the pressure.

Twisting the nozzle brought a fine spray first, then a stream. He adjusted it for the longest distance, greatest force, shot it at the nearest greenery. The water lashed outer leaves aside, penetrated. Passing across a light, it seemed to kindle, becoming a line of liquid fire. As though seared, the leaves and lesser branches jerked and twisted, trying to escape it.

Methodically, he played the stream down the left side-bed as far as it would reach, then swung it over to work along the right side of the center. When he'd done both sides of the path as far as the stream allowed, he went onward slowly.

The lights shooting upward cast shadows on the dome. Lit from different sides, one tree would be projected into two, in separate places. Shorter bushes, closer to the lights, grew monstrous, looming over trees. Confusing images, one upon another: a phantom forest, a sense of jungle wildness, fearsome mystery, made more vivid than the real vegetation. The swirling shadows, the streaking flashes of light, twisting, writhing, were the spirit of earthquake and hurricane, terrifying. As Marley moved along the path, here and there a spotlight beam would catch his figure, throwing his shadow huge and solid stalking through chaos.

One-third of the way along the path the side-bed divided, making room for double glass doors, one front entrance to the building. Another set was symmetrically placed another third away. Brooks crouched closer to the second one, in the center island, under an elephant ear. Twenty years or more since he'd played hide-and-seek there; the plant—his friend, his protector—had grown as he had, could shelter him still.

He huddled on his knees, head down on his fists on the ground. He knew Marley was there in the building, heard a strange hissing, rushing, slapping

noise, without understanding what it was. He was
terrified. Perhaps somehow his dear plant would hide
him if he made himself small enough, still enough,
and trusted it. It had saved him so many times in the
past.

The noise came closer. Little light taps sounded
over his head. Wincing, he felt icy touches on the
back of his neck. He dared a tiny peek to the side,
under and through the sheltering plant. The leaves of
plants beyond his own stirred, flapped, jerked frantically from a scatter of sparks. They came at him
more and more, smashing away his shelter, striking
him, burning cold.

Marley thought he saw Brooks crouched there in
the center island. He crept cautiously forward, the
stream steady, its pressure greater with every step.
He did see him. Brooks saw he saw him. Marley
aimed the water lower, on Brooks himself. Brooks
flinched from it, rising on his knees, staggering upright, one arm raised across his face. Brooks twisted,
tried to dodge, to back away. He stumbled over the
great gnarled stalks of the plant, lurched forward to
keep from falling.

Marley closed on him slowly, jabbing the water at
his face, his gun hand, but mostly at his left side.
Brooks shied from it, letting it herd him outward. He
staggered, stumbling into bushes. To move to his
right seemed the way of escape. Then he was on the
path.

Water drops covered Brooks's glasses; he had to
keep his left arm up in front of his face to shield it
against the constant stinging stream. Brooks twisted

and turned, backing, but wouldn't turn away completely. He had his gun.

Fifteen feet away Marley moved steadily, using the water as a lance. In desperation Brooks threw up his arm to fire; but Marley parried, knocking the gun hand just enough so the shot went wild. In the instant the water was off his face, Brooks looked above his arm, trying for better aim. Marley threw the nozzle upward, and Brooks jerked back as water hit his eyes. The second shot missed Marley too.

Marley smiled, not knowing this time that he did. He shut the water off at the nozzle, dropped the hose.

Brooks backed away, not turning, watching Marley stalk him closer, fascinated as a monkey by a snake.

Marley came on slowly, sensing what Brooks was feeling. Slightly crouching, weaving side to side as he walked, ready to spring either way, he closed the distance.

In the classic pose of horror, Brooks had both hands lifted, warding off what was in front of him. Marley's smile widened; he was grinning. He took another step: just six feet away now. Should he lunge from there or, keeping the rhythm, walk up to Brooks and slowly take him by the throat?

Brooks flung his right arm up and hurled the pistol straight at Marley's face.

The blow didn't stun Marley completely; but he didn't remember falling or seeing Brooks turn and run. He simply found himself sitting on the path, watching Brooks run out through the second set of doors. Then he had difficulty seeing anything. He put his hand up and wiped at his eye.

He realized he was bleeding. He felt his forehead,

wincing, poking at himself more gently. His skull
didn't seem to be broken, though it hurt enough that
it might have been. Blood streamed into his eye
again. He wiped, and saw his hand covered with it.
Beginning to think, he found the hose, started a gentle
spray, washed over the wound and his bloody face,
then held his handkerchief tight to staunch the flow.
He staggered up onto his feet.

That Brooks could shoot six times and not hit
anyone, then bring him down by *throwing* the thing!
"Son of a bitch!" he screamed.

Giddiness passing, Marley lurched out after Brooks.
Coming from light, he could see nothing. Which
way? He had no memory of the sound of Brooks
running past him, outside, toward the garages. Perhaps he had gone back to the house. Stumbling in the
darkness, Marley found the path.

Cold air cleared his head. He trotted by the tennis
courts, hearing nothing. He went on steadily, relent-
lessly, silencing the rage that shrieked at him to run
headlong, wildly, and the conscience begging him to
stop. Conscience did call to him, tugging at his
coattails, like the tearful daughter in a temperance
play. Like the rum-besotted father, he shook her off.

Light from the drawing room shone across the
terrace. It showed a shape huddled on the flagstone
steps. Marley thrilled as a wolf must when a deer
sinks in the snow. Then he saw it was two people:
Mrs. Gaskill, holding Melissa across her lap, a blanket draped around both of them.

"Where's Brooks!"

"Mr. Marley!" Mrs. Gaskill held her voice low,
but it carried the snap of a shout. She threw up one

hand, tried to keep Melissa close with the other. But Melissa raised her head.

"Mr. Marley? What's happening? Father . . . Gray is . . ." Her face shone from crying. It twisted again, and she seemed to strangle as she said, "Father . . . Father . . . He tried to . . . *shoot* me!" The horror overwhelmed her, and she sobbed.

Mrs. Gaskill pulled her back to her bosom, stroking her head, holding her tightly, rocking.

Marley started to demand once more that Brooks be delivered up to him. But as in the play, the little girl's tears finally broke the demon's grip. He let himself down on the steps beside the other two.

Mrs. Gaskill stared at him, astonished, and he realized his face and hand were smeared with blood. She said nothing, obviously unwilling to rouse Melissa again.

In barely a whisper, more mouthing than speaking, he asked, "Police?"

She nodded as she rocked.

"Mrs. Ten Broeck?"

She shrugged.

"Ambulance?"

Again nodding.

"Is Brooks inside?"

She shook her head no.

The cold air on his wet head and face, his sweat-soaked back, gradually chilled him. He stared at the darkness, not trying any longer to see Brooks in it. The police would find him sooner or later.

That dull cold air was winter's air. Not crisp, invigorating now, it settled like hopelessness from the blackness between the isolated stars: those stars that

foolish people speak of reaching, to symbolize their
aspiration, and—so saying—show it doomed. He'd
failed to murder Brooks, but he'd failed to keep
himself from wanting to, from trying. If Brooks were
in his hands that moment, he still would kill him. He
would wrestle him, clasp him tight as though to
crush, then hurl them together into hell to freeze
eternally in the lake of ice, both damned.

Marley, chilled in body and spirit, rose, stood for
a moment without plan, then wandered forward through
the break in the hedge toward the pool only because
that was the way he faced. When he reached its edge
he turned right only because he couldn't go forward
anymore.

The pool was sealed for winter. A plastic cover
stretched across it, pitched shallowly over some kind of
framework.

When Marley reached the end of the pool he turned
and kept going along it. It was a line he could follow
without having to think.

Metal clips held the cover along the sides of the
frame. Laces tied it at the corners to rings set into the
stonework.

Marley turned the next corner, continuing his list-
less circumambulation.

He stopped.

Pulse beginning to rise again, he went back to the
corner. The lacings there weren't tied. He pushed at
the cover with his foot. It had slack for a little space
until the sides were clipped again to the rail. Some
steps led down. It was the shallow end.

No, Marley told himself, Brooks wouldn't do that.

He'd keep running. He's gone; he's hiding in the woods. You're not going to catch him.

Marley looked back and forth. He saw, on a stanchion by the hedge break, a set of capped, outdoor electrical switches.

No, don't do it, he told himself. Let him be in the woods. You don't want to catch him.

Marley went back, flipped the switches. Pool-wall lights came on under the plastic. He went slowly around to the loosened corner again.

Don't do it. Don't look, he told himself. If you catch him, you'll have to kill him.

He lifted the plastic. There wasn't enough give for him to look far under, but a man—even a pudgy one—could squeeze through. Marley had to turn away, go under backward, down the steps. He wasn't worried that Brooks, if there, would attack him.

The lights for swimming at night reflected from blue-glazed tile. With the water drained, though, the space seemed not aqueous but airy. Even the canopy above was blue, so the men seemed to float in a void. Marley turned, crouched below the covering. At the diving end Brooks clasped his knees close to his chest, huddling in a corner. Marley seemed huge in his sector of space, Brooks tiny in vastness.

Hunched, arms swinging apelike, Marley sidled down the sloping floor until he could stand. As he came upright, so did Brooks—pushing himself hand over hand up one wall.

Brooks faced the side wall, tight to it. Like sky solidified, the wall would not let him through; but he pressed himself against it, standing absolutely still, as though believing he might blend with it and not be

seen. Only his eyes blinked, visible through the thick
lenses as he stared at Marley.

For several moments Marley stood as still, then
stepped one step forward, slowly. Then another.
Brooks's hand slid up and down the wall beside him,
as if searching for some chink, some crack where he
could liquefy and flow out.

Another step. The floor pitched downward, in-
creasing the sense of space, and Marley felt himself
swelling to fill it.

Brooks groaned, trying to force himself more tightly
into the corner. He rolled, his back against the end
wall now, sweeping the arm backhanded up and
down. The only breaks in the pitiless surface began
above his head, a rising metal ladder. He seemed
suddenly to think of it. Turning, he reached. The first
step was just beyond his upstretched hand. He jumped
once, and again.

Marley reached out and touched his shoulder. Brooks
froze, then all at once went limp. Hands against the
wall, cheek against it, he slid down, crumpling on
his knees. Marley stepped to one side, grabbed
Brooks's collar and necktie knot in his left hand, and
swung him around.

Now he could draw back and punch, blow after
careful blow, bashing that face methodically. He could
jerk that head from side to side, smashing, wall to
wall. Betrayal, sorrow, love lost, hopes unfulfilled
and dreams destroyed: all hunted down and in his
hand. He could at least wreak bloody vengeance.
Vengeance for Sarah. He saw her face, for Sarah, her
eyes, for Sarah, Sarah!

CHAPTER 15

Twigs of some shrub outside the window, leaf-less, lifeless, dull red-brown as old blood, swayed stiffly now and then. A shudder might sweep across the dun-colored lawn. Otherwise, all lay still, waiting for a shroud of snow.

Marley faced the window from the couch. The director had taken an armchair to his right.

"Her father's death . . . An almost ultimate blow for her." Dr. Bishop shook her head in sorrow, then tapped her folded glasses against her palm as if to call sympathy to professional attention.

Marley nodded, not looking at her. He was staring out at the gray and lumpy sky—not looking at it either.

"Very unfortunate, very difficult for her. On the one hand, Mr. Ten Broeck's suicide—before even being brought to trial—confirms for her the allegation that he killed her mother. And that man at Smith. Which shatters her idolization of him. On the other hand, it may seem to provide a model for her as to how to deal with—escape—an overwhelming situation."

"Do you think she might . . ."

"We're very apprehensive. I don't think it's to the point that she has to be watched continually, but we're monitoring her—discreetly—we're monitoring her carefully."

"She knows about everything, then?"

"Yes, of course. I think that's generally the best way. And there would be little we could do if it weren't. We have newspapers here; the students have radios: Trying to make them aware that there is a world outside themselves is often an important part of their therapy.

"Melissa gets through the day, more or less; goes to her classes. But . . . Well, you'll see: There's a dullness, a listlessness. She doesn't want to visit Mrs. Ten Broeck, which is understandable, of course. And I understand that Mrs. Ten Broeck probably wouldn't know her anyway. Apparently she's recuperating as well as can be expected from her injuries, but has lost all will to live. Still, if Melissa would want to see her, or, on the other hand, *refuse* . . . But it doesn't seem so much a refusal—out of anger—as a lack of feeling. I'm afraid— Totally disillusioned, isolated, feeling she has no one, no one loves her—and that horrible trauma of her father *shooting* at her! I'm afraid she finds very little to go on living for."

"Do you think she can leave, if she wants to?"

"Coming to believe that someone cares for her would be the best thing possible for her. The process would have to be gradual, of course. But any relationship that gives her a sense of self-worth again, of being loved . . . I would certainly encourage that."

"I understand that Sarah's mother has inquired

about taking custody. Her uncle—her granduncle—
seemed adamant against it. I know he's Melissa's
legal guardian now, but if it would be best for her,
maybe . . . What do you think?''

"I don't know. . . . While Melissa might receive
some of the affection she needs there, putting her
into a totally new environment, with people she doesn't
know . . . And since her grandparents and her mother
were estranged, I don't think it would be a good
thing for her at this time.''

"How do you think she'll take me?''

"I really don't know, Mr. Marley. She has only
barely alluded to you; and, of course, I had no reason
to discuss you with her. Frankly, I shall be interested
to know. As you suggested, I have not told her you
were coming. One never knows—I certainly don't
believe in playing tricks, but I thought it might be
more useful to have her confront you in person rather
than getting it all worked out first in her head.''

"I'm pretty scared about this.''

"Yes. I imagine so. It's very good of you to be
making this effort.''

"Well . . .''

"Yes. I'll send her in. I won't stay with you,
but perhaps we could talk again for a few moments
afterward.''

"Thank you, Dr. Bishop.''

He rose as she did. Then not knowing why he did
so, he took cover, standing behind one of the
armchairs.

Not institutional in atmosphere at all, the pleasant
parlor in a country house was large and unconfining,

with furniture cozied in the center. Marley took no cheer from the chintz or flowered wallpaper.

The door opened, Melissa came in, saw him, stopped.

"Hello, Melissa."

He could read nothing in her expression beyond surprise. Gathering more courage than he knew he had, Marley stepped from behind the chair. "How are you?"

Melissa turned aside, going to the window.

The thinness of her face appalled him. Her hair seemed wiglike, so dark against her pale skin, its curly fullness out of scale. She faced the window, the late November bleakness; but he sensed there might have been a brick wall there for all she saw.

"Melissa, I—I wanted to see you, so I took a chance and came over."

The pale light of that overcast afternoon was cold, like that of the morgue's fluorescents. Melissa's face looked as colorless as Sarah's had.

"I . . . I was hoping . . ."

The little daylight left would dim soon, so slowly, and she would stand on in darkness, never knowing.

"Melissa . . . Melissa?"

He wished that she would shout in anger at him, hate him. Anything alive.

It wasn't going to work. He wasn't going to reach her. "I'm sorry. If you don't want to see me, I guess I understand. I just want you to know, at least, I'm sorry." He started around the couch toward the door.

"You did find my mother." She didn't turn. Her voice was flat.

He halted, struck motionless with hope. "Yes."

"What . . . what was she like?"

"She was beautiful, Melissa. More beautiful than in the picture." His hand came up as if to sculpt Sarah's face in the air, and Melissa turned and seemed to see it. "And intelligent, and . . . she understood things. She could look at things, at people, and see things in them, behind them. When she looked at you, you knew she was . . . *seeing* . . . you. I . . . When she saw something good in you, then you felt you had to live up to it. I guess that's what thinking of her, remembering her, meant— Has come to mean to me. I—I have her poems, if you'd like to read them sometime. They might give you an idea."

"Yes. Please."

"I brought one with me today. I thought it might . . . It's the last one she wrote." He took the folded paper out of his pocket. Melissa came away from the window, and he extended his hand so she wouldn't have to come all the way to him at once.

She unfolded, read. "I don't get it."

"Read it over some more, later."

"What does it mean?"

"It's about accepting things, and going on."

"Well, thanks."

"Melissa . . . I . . . I am sorry about everything. I wondered, well, how you feel about me."

"I don't know."

"I wondered . . . if you . . . blamed me."

"I don't know. Yeah, I guess I do. But I don't know. I mean, I know you didn't mean . . . And it was my—*him*. And her. They . . . He—" Her face wrenched, but she didn't cry. "Mr. Marley, you found out. . . . You knew. . . . How could he! How

could *he!* How—how—'' She began to rock and
twist, the final word a moan.

He caught her, held her. Tears came into his eyes,
but not to hers. She caught quick breaths, but not the
one that would trip and spill her grief. After a minute
she quieted, and Marley took his arms away. He was
filled with fear as he began to hope again.

"You going to be all right?"

"Yeah. Sure."

She was sinking back into despondency. He went
on, trying to sound calm. "I thought . . . I wanted to
ask you if you'd . . . I've talked to Mrs. Gaskill. . . .
I thought—if you wanted to—you and she could
come and spend Thanksgiving with me, in Boston.
Would you like that? We could do some things."

"I guess. Yeah, sure. But I don't know if—"

"I've talked with Dr. Bishop. She thinks it would
be all right. I'll come get you next Wednesday, then.
Okay?"

"Sure. Is Thanksgiving next week?"

"Yes."

"Oh. Sure. How is Mrs. Gaskill?"

"She's fine. She's . . . she's really a wonderful
person, especially when you've . . . got trouble. I've
been—I've seen her several times lately. She'd like
to see you."

"I'd like to see her. That would be nice."

"And if you, if that works out, maybe Christmas.
If you want to."

"Yeah. Maybe. Why?"

"Well, I'm kind of lonely these days myself, and I
thought, well, you probably are too. I thought you

and I and Mrs. Gaskill, we . . . It would be good for all of us.''

"Yeah. Sure.''

"And . . . Well, I guess I like you, Melissa. So . . .'' He knew he shouldn't go too far, but couldn't help himself. "I've talked to your uncle Richard. He's agreeable that if . . . Maybe we could work something out on a longer-term basis. If things work out. If you want to.''

"Sure. I don't know.''

He doubted that she'd really heard him, understood. Perhaps it was better if she hadn't. He shouldn't offer too much, too soon.

"I'll come next week, then. Wednesday. About noon. I'll bring Elaine—Mrs. Gaskill—with me, and we can have lunch on the way back. Okay?''

"Sure.''

He wanted to believe her face was brighter, at least less dulled by despair. He smiled, hoping she'd return it. She didn't.

"Well, I guess I'd better let you get back. Dr. Bishop wants me to wait and talk with her again.''

It took a moment for the point of that to get through. Then she said "Sure" again and "Thanks" and turned away. But as she reached the door, she looked back at Marley.

"If I come to Boston, can I get my hair cut?''

BESTSELLING BOOKS FROM TOR

MORE BESTSELLERS FROM TOR

Ramsey Campbell

☐ 51652-4   DARK COMPANIONS $3.50
      51653-2   Canada $3.95

☐ 51654-0   THE DOLL WHO ATE HIS MOTHER $3.50
      51655-9   Canada $3.95

☐ 51658-3   THE FACE THAT MUST DIE $3.95
      51659-1   Canada $4.95

☐ 51650-8   INCARNATE $3.95
      51651-6   Canada $4.50

☐ 58125-3   THE NAMELESS $3.50
      58126-1   Canada $3.95

Buy them at your local bookstore or use this handy coupon:
Clip and mail this page with your order

TOR BOOKS—Reader Service Dept.
P.O. Box 690, Rockville Centre, N.Y. 11571

Please send me the book(s) I have checked above. I am enclosing
$_____ (please add $1.00 to cover postage and handling). Send
check or money order only—no cash or C.O.D.'s.

Mr./Mrs./Miss _____
Address _____
City _____ **State/Zip** _____
Please allow six weeks for delivery. Prices subject to change without
notice.

GRAHAM MASTERTON

☐   52195-1   CONDOR $3.50
      52196-X   Canada $3.95

☐   52191-9   IKON $3.95
      52192-7   Canada $4.50

☐   52193-5   THE PARIAH $3.50
      52194-3   Canada $3.95

☐   52189-7   SOLITAIRE $3.95
      52190-0   Canada $4.50

☐   48067-9   THE SPHINX $2.95

☐   48061-X   TENGU $3.50

☐   48042-3   THE WELLS OF HELL $2.95

☐   52199-4   PICTURE OF EVIL $3.95
      52200-1   Canada $4.95

Buy them at your local bookstore or use this handy coupon:
Clip and mail this page with your order

TOR BOOKS—Reader Service Dept.
P.O. Box 690, Rockville Centre, N.Y. 11571

Please send me the book(s) I have checked above. I am enclosing $_____ (please add $1.00 to cover postage and handling). Send check or money order only—no cash or C.O.D.'s.

Mr./Mrs./Miss _____

Address _____

City _____ State/Zip _____

Please allow six weeks for delivery. Prices subject to change without notice.